Ko'olau's Secret

Cover designed by Sharon K Connell
Book cover image courtesy of Pixabay 811978_640 Candace Thoth, Honolulu, USA
Chapter illustration from Clker-Free-Vector-Images - Pixabay - hibiscus-311279_640 (edited)
Scene illustration from Beverly Buckley – Pixabay - flowers-4550469_640 (edited)

Editing Services from Above the Pages

Printed in the United States of America

ISBN: 978-1-7329237-5-1

Dedication

First and foremost, this book is dedicated to my Lord Jesus Christ, without whose grace and guidance none of my books would have been written.

Secondly, I dedicate this story to the Native Hawaiian people, of whom so few are left. Mahalo for teaching me the meaning of aloha.

Acknowledgments

*Arnold C. Hauswald, retired SGM, US Army, for being the inspiration for
my story, for his service to our country, and for supporting me through the
writing in so many ways*
Steve and Gina Bradburn
Authors Fire/Rescue Facebook group, especially Ken Shoemaker
The Honolulu Fire Department official page on Facebook
Faye Hamilton, RN
Members of All Things Oʻahu on Facebook
Cops & Writers Facebook page members
Crystal Grant, my final critique/reader
ACFW, Scribes Critique Group
Gunnery Sgt. Luke and Crystal Madsen

*For all your help, technical/professional advice, comments, suggestions,
and support*

He that dwelleth in the secret place of the most High shall abide under the shadow of the Almighty. I will say of the LORD, He is my refuge and my fortress: my God; in him will I trust. Psalm 91:1, 2

Introduction

A note from the author on the Hawaiian language

For the benefit of my readers, I've given here a guide to help you avoid tripping over the Hawaiian words I used in my story. Hawaiian words were added to give you a flavor of the island. Today, approximately 0.1% of people living in Hawaiʻi speak its native tongue. But some words remain in common use.

As a part of the United States in 1978, the Hawaiʻi State Constitutional Convention made Hawaiian the state's official language (the only state in the US with a non-English official language).

Remember, while you read, each syllable will end in a vowel. Therefore, there is no "s" added to the plural form of words. The word lei, for example, is used for both the singular as well as for the plural form. The language is phonetically spoken. When you see a glottal stop (the single backward apostrophe mark called ʻokina), it means you give a slight pause, similar to when you would say "uh-oh." The little mark is actually an official consonant in the Hawaiian language.

The ʻokina is not always used in print and on the internet, but I've chosen to do so for the Hawaiian atmosphere. The ʻokina should be shown as a straight apostrophe; however, when typing my manuscript, it was difficult to use that mark, so I followed the example of Hawaiian online articles and used the backward apostrophe.

Another element in the Hawaiian language is a macron or kahako. This lengthens and adds stress to the marked vowel. Because I didn't use too many Hawaiian words, and to make things simpler for my readers, I've chosen to leave out the macrons.

The Hawaiian alphabet consists of only twelve letters. Among them are the vowels A, E, I, O, U and the consonants H, K, L, M, N, P, and W. There are also seven diphthongs: AE, AI, AO, AU, EI, EU, and OU.

Below is a simple key to pronunciation for my story.
A is pronounced "ah"
E is pronounced "eh"
I is pronounced "ee"
O is pronounced "oh"
U is pronounced "oo"

The consonants, H, K, L, M, N, and P, are pronounced the same as in English. W after i and e is pronounced v, and after u and o, like a w. At the start of a word or after an a, it is pronounced either way. The choice is yours.

Traditionally, in the Hawaiian language, the "W" is pronounced like a "V." For example, the word "Hawai'i" is pronounced "hah-vy-ee" instead of "hah-wy-ee."

I've found the language to be very easy to pronounce using the simplified key above. But as long as you enjoy my tale, you can pronounce the words any way you'd like to. I won't tell my Hawaiian friends. LOL

Please remember, the pronunciation guide is only for your enjoyment of my story and is not meant to be a definitive guide in speaking Hawaiian.

I hope this guide to the few Hawaiian words I've used in my story is of help to you in enjoying the tale. Aloha.

Koʻolau's Secret

Sharon K Connell

Chapter One

Houston, Texas

Kyleigh Flanagan slammed the envelope and document onto the coffee table. "Why, Dad?" She stormed into the kitchen and poured herself a fresh cup of black decaf from the pot she'd brewed before she opened the letter from her father.

She took a sip, lifted the single sheet of paper, and stared at it. "This is not like you at all. You never go off-grid." *Something isn't right.*

The cup and saucer made a distinct clunk when she placed them on the table. Her chair screeched as she pulled it out and then plopped into it. Her fingers flattened out the brief typed note on the table. She read it again.

Honey, I don't want you to worry, but you won't hear from me for a little while. There's something I've got to do, and I won't be able to contact you until I'm finished. But I'll contact you again as soon as I can. Dad

Kyleigh sipped her coffee. No way would her father just disappear without telling her where he went or what he was doing. She rose, drained her cup, and set it in the sink. He knew how she worried. Why would he do this? What had he gotten into?

After running water over the dishes, she grabbed her purse and dashed out the front door of her second-floor apartment. She rushed down the stairs, through the entrance, across the landscaped walkway, and into the parking lot.

Aunt Maye might know what was going on. Dad told her more details on several occasions. He must have called her. Maybe some military thing he wasn't allowed to talk about. But then he wouldn't tell Aunt Maye either.

Kyleigh jumped into her light blue Mazda and sped out of the parking lot, en route to her aunt's house in Jersey Village.

The last time Dad had been deployed, he was gone for a year, but he'd told them when he left and why. Besides, that was years ago. He planned to retire in a few months.

Half an hour later, Kyleigh pulled her car into Aunt Maye's driveway. Oh, Auntie must have bought herself a new Honda for her birthday. Auntie always did love green. "Not my favorite hue for a vehicle. But, it's not my car, either." Dad had said green was a racing color. She frowned. Could he have entered a dirt bike race? But he'd tell her that. *Hope Auntie knows what he's up to.*

As she turned off the ignition, Kyleigh tightened her forehead and brows. Great! A full-blown headache, just what she needed. She rubbed her head and neck, then exited her Mazda. Nice way to end the school year. At least it hadn't started while her kindergartners were having so much fun at the year-end party.

Kyleigh gazed at the two-story home. She half expected to see her aunt tending her flower boxes along the railings of the long front porch. Aunt Maye said she found it relaxing to water and weed, and the children she sat for during the day would have gone home by now. She wouldn't have gone out. Not on a Monday evening.

Kyleigh climbed the steps, crossed the porch, and pressed the doorbell. The six notes from "America the Beautiful" had barely finished when the door swung open. Her aunt appeared with a wide smile, her thick, dark auburn hair, the same color as Kyleigh's, piled high atop her head in a loose bun.

"Hi, sweetie. I was thinking about you. Come on in." Aunt Maye led the way through the forest green living room filled with well-worn antiques. "I can't imagine how you handle twenty or more kids all day. It's all I can do to keep up with the six I sit for, and two of them can't walk yet." She chuckled.

"I guess I don't think about it. We have a lot of fun in class, and the day flies by. Perhaps because I'm half kid myself." She tittered. "That's what you and Dad always say, anyway. Rough day today?"

"Sort of. One boy was disagreeable, and one girl, very bossy. Not a good combination."

Kyleigh couldn't hold back her questions anymore. "Auntie, do you know what's up with Dad?"

"What do you mean?" Her aunt stopped midway through the dining room, turned toward her, and brushed several strands of

Kyleigh's long, wavy hair away from her niece's face. "Hmm. Has he been bossing his grown daughter around again?"

"It's nothing like that." Kyleigh held out the letter she'd pulled from the mailbox when she got home. "Read this." Her eyes filled with tears.

Her aunt's brows rumpled. She took the paper from Kyleigh's hand and lowered herself to one of the maroon tapestry-covered dining room chairs at the table. Kyleigh sat next to her on another. Aunt Maye read the short note.

She looked up at Kyleigh. "I've no idea what this means, but I'm sure it's nothing to cause tears or worry."

"This isn't like Dad, Auntie, and you know it." A tear slipped over the edge of her bottom lid and landed on the table. She wiped it away with her hand and sniffed. "A headache started on the way over here, and this isn't helping." She rubbed her neck again.

"You always wind up with a headache when you're stressed. Let me get you a glass of lemonade. Then I'll rub your shoulders to loosen them up a little." She hurried to the kitchen. "Did you try calling your dad?" she called to Kyleigh.

"Yes. The call went straight to voicemail. That's not like him either."

"Hmm...you have a point there." Aunt Maye reentered the dining room with two ice-filled glasses of pale yellow liquid clutched in one hand. She placed a napkin from those she held in the other hand on the table in front of Kyleigh and lowered a glass onto it. "But it's not evening there yet. He may be in a meeting. Houston is five hours ahead of Hawai'i."

Kyleigh leaned forward and rested her forehead on the wooden table. Her aunt's fingers began their magic, and Kyleigh's muscles slowly relaxed. Auntie's massage always was the best remedy for one of these headaches.

After she'd massaged her niece's neck, Aunt Maye returned to her seat next to Kyleigh. "Charlie's been pretty busy ever since they assigned him to the O'ahu post. Plus, he's taken up riding those wretched trails again on those racy-type things like a skinny motorcycle. Even bought a new one." She narrowed her eyes at Kyleigh. "I assume he told you. What are they called?"

A glimmer of a smile spread on Kyleigh's lips. "Dirt bikes, Auntie."

"Dirt bikes? I thought those were the bicycles the kids rode."

"They're both called dirt bikes. Dad loves the sport. And so do I, when I can find time to engage in it. O'ahu has terrific trails up the mountains. He gets a real challenge from the brush, vegetation, and roots sticking out of the ground. He likes to have fun in his downtime. Helps him relax." Kyleigh frowned. "But why would he go off-grid like that? Most of his rides are for no more than a couple of hours. At most. Do you think the Army sent him on some secret assignment? But why? Why would they send Dad when there are so many younger guys?"

He had told her the mountains on the island held many secrets, according to the native Hawaiians. Secrets like burial caves of chiefs never located, ancient treasures stored in unfound caverns, reports by locals of hearing drums and seeing warriors and chiefs in ghostly processions marching from their burial grounds in the mountains to the sea. Kyleigh shuddered. But surely this note wouldn't have anything to do with those. "It couldn't have anything to do with the dirt bike, even if he was at a race. Why wouldn't he tell us? What's going on?"

Aunt Maye laid her hand on Kyleigh's shoulder. "Calm down, dear. You're talking a mile a minute." Auntie reached into her purse on the table, pulled the cellphone out, punched in a number, and pressed the phone to her ear. A puzzled expression replaced the quick grin she'd given Kyleigh. "My call went to voicemail too. How odd. Let me see that note again."

Dad must have a good reason not to let either his daughter or sister know where he'd gone. "I hope his commanding officer returns the call you made to him soon, Auntie." She'd already left several messages on her dad's voicemail. And his office hadn't helped. None of his coworkers admitted knowledge of his whereabouts. They referred Auntie to the commanding officer. The post was a busy place, but this busy? Besides...her Dad was a major. How busy could he be at this point in his career?

Kyleigh's aunt disconnected the call after leaving yet another message on the major's cell. Aunt Maye rubbed her forehead. This situation had probably made Auntie a little headachy as well.

Kyleigh grimaced as she continued to set the table. "Thanks for asking me to stay for dinner. Hope I didn't mess up the mashed potatoes too much. This isn't my strong suit when it comes to cooking."

"The potatoes will be fine. With your worry about your dad, I wouldn't have you spend the evening alone in your apartment. I'm sure when his commanding officer returns my call, he'll have an explanation for Charlie's note. In the meantime, let's try to be patient and enjoy the leftover pot roast from Sunday."

After they'd eaten and cleared the table, Kyleigh rinsed a plate and handed it to Aunt Maye to load in the dishwasher. "That roast was as delicious tonight as it was on Sunday, Auntie. I hope I can learn to cook as well as you do...someday."

"You're already a fine cook, dear. We'll just have to work on those potatoes...a little." She giggled.

"What? You didn't like my potato soup?" Kyleigh joined her laughter.

Aunt Maye closed the dishwasher and led the way to the living room. "Let's watch a movie." She rummaged through the DVD storage cabinet, chose a plastic case, and held it out toward Kyleigh. "This one okay with you?"

Kyleigh nodded as she eased into the corner of the dark brown leather couch and dropped her father's short letter onto the coffee table. She snatched a beige afghan from behind her and flipped it over her shoulders. Auntie sure kept the house on the cold side.

Aunt Maye started the movie and joined Kyleigh on the couch. "It's been a long time since we watched a film together. This story about the heroics of William Wallace should take our minds off...keep us busy."

Not likely. Kyleigh bit her lower lip. Not until they'd heard some news about Dad. *Why didn't he answer his phone?* And the CO still hadn't returned the call. Her neck tensed.

While the opening credits rolled, Aunt Maye lifted the note from the coffee table. Her forehead furrowed as she read it a third time. "I hate to say this. And I don't want to add more worry, but I have to be honest."

"What, Auntie?"

"This doesn't sound like your father."

Kyleigh held out her hands, palms up. "That's what I said. He doesn't do things like this, go off and not let either of us know where or what he's doing."

"But that's not what I mean. I agree it's not like him to do that. But something else is wrong. The more I read this message, the less it sounds like my brother's voice. Listen."

Aunt Maye read the note aloud. "'Honey, I don't want you to worry, but you won't hear from me for a little while. There's something I've got to do, and I won't be able to contact you until I'm finished. I'll contact you again as soon as I can. Dad'"

A straight line formed as she pinched her lips together. "Not the wording he'd have used. Your Dad doesn't use that many contractions when he writes. I've always teased him about being so formal. 'I don't,' instead of I do not. 'I've got to' isn't how he talks. There aren't any words of affection to you, except maybe for 'honey.' But he's always called you sugar. And why does he say 'contact' instead of he'll call you when he can? It doesn't sound like your dad's writing."

Kyleigh's mouth fell open. "You're right. I was so upset that he'd taken off and not told me what was going on, I didn't think about the writing." She wrinkled her brows together and clamped her front teeth onto her lower lip again.

The movie started, but Aunt Maye shut off the player and TV. "I occasionally get a typed letter from him, but do you?"

"From time to time. Most are usually hand-written on his personal letterhead. But sometimes I get one he's printed off the computer. Never this brief, though."

Aunt Maye pressed her mouth shut. "It seems strange for him to have typed such a quick note and not to just text or call to let you know." She sat on the couch and checked her cell on the end table. "Sure wish Charlie's commanding officer would call back. But then, he might not have received my message yet. It's only been an hour." She sighed and glanced at Kyleigh. "I'm sure we'll hear something soon." Her cell rang, and Aunt Maye lunged for it. "Hello?" Her aunt pressed the loudspeaker button.

The man's deep, commanding voice came through her aunt's cell. "Hello. Colonel Stevens here. I'm returning a phone call from Maye Lockhart regarding one of my officers."

"Thank you for calling back, Colonel. I'm Maye Lockhart."

Kyleigh threw the afghan off her, jumped from the couch, and joined her aunt in pacing the living room.

"Charlie...I mean, Major Flanagan is my brother. His daughter Kyleigh and I've been trying to reach him after she received a strange message, and—"

"You received a message?"

Chapter Two

E arly Saturday morning, Kyleigh packed her carry-on for her trip to Oʻahu. "Auntie, I'm so glad I was able to arrange a flight to Oʻahu so I can find out what happened to Dad." She zipped her bag. "And I don't want you to worry. I'll be fine."

Aunt Maye pulled a suitcase from the closet and handed it to Kyleigh. Her aunt puckered her lips.

Kyleigh patted her aunt's shoulder. "Thanks for coming over this morning to pick up my goldfish. I know you're going to worry anyway, but everything will be fine once I reach Oʻahu tomorrow. Dad may even have returned from wherever he went by the time I arrive at his place." She hoped.

"But dear, taking off on the spur of the moment for a place you haven't been to in over two years? Not knowing where your father is? Will your old key to his apartment even work? What if he's moved since you last visited, and he forgot to tell us? I wish I could go with you."

Kyleigh laid the suitcase on her bed and turned to her aunt. Worry lines stretched across Aunt Maye's forehead, deeper than she'd ever seen. Wrapping her arms around her aunt, Kyleigh whispered, "I know you do. But you can't leave your charges high and dry for who knows how long without someone who cares about them. You're the only caretaker they've had since they were born. And after two years, those toddlers love and depend on you almost as much as their mother. What would she do if you took off for Hawaiʻi with me and left her without someone she can trust to care for her twins?"

As she gazed into her aunt's eyes, they grew misty. "I'll be fine, Auntie. Marisa said she was happy to come along. She's like a sister to me. Our tutoring won't start until August with those three kids and their cousin."

Kyleigh went to the closet. When she came out, she laid a flowery blouse on her bed, folded it, and placed it in the suitcase. "Marisa had planned to drive to San Antonio for a couple of weeks at the end of July, but when I called last Monday and told her what happened, she was just as worried about me going alone as you are. With the money she'd save not having to pay for a motel in San Antonio, Hawaiʻi sounded like a dream vacation. She's going to help me look for Dad."

Aunt Maye pursed her lips. "I'll be praying...and worrying over both of you as much as about my brother." Her arms encircled Kyleigh.

"Come on, Auntie. Let's take a break from packing. I could use a cup of coffee. How about you?"

The two women entered Kyleigh's newly redecorated kitchen, painted mint green with a lush palm leaf wallpaper on the bottom half. Each selected her favorite blend from the pod carousel. Her aunt dropped hers into the brewer. When the machine finished its imitation of a cappuccino frother, Kyleigh started her cup.

Aunt Maye poured milk into hers. "One reason I'm envious of you going to Oʻahu and leaving me behind is their wonderful coffee. The bags you brought back last time spoiled me. Not to mention the taste of pineapple right from the island plantation." She ran her tongue over her top lip.

A giggle escaped Kyleigh. "I hadn't thought about that, but you're right. Once we locate Dad and find out what he's up to, we'll make the rest of the month a real Hawaiian vacation." She smiled so wide her cheeks hurt. But the smile didn't last. "I'll be relieved to find out what's going on. I still can't believe we haven't gotten ahold of Dad."

"Or that his commanding officer wouldn't be aware of where Charlie is and still hasn't found him. All the years my brother has served in the Army, he's never failed to show up for duty. Not without a good reason, at least."

While her aunt stirred the brew, she shook her head. "There was that time a mugger knocked him unconscious in the mall parking lot and stole his wallet. He didn't wake up in the hospital until late the next morning—oh, dear!"

"What? *What, Auntie?*"

"We should have called the hospitals. I wonder if the colonel's staff did. Of course, they did. He said they'd checked everywhere they could think of. And they have a department for that, but they've found nothing so far."

"I'm sure they did. I just don't understand. Unless...Dad's unconscious somewhere no one thought to look. He hasn't been seen for days." Kyleigh paced around the kitchen table. "I'm glad I found a flight early tomorrow morning for us. We need to start our search right away if he's still missing."

As Kyleigh finished her second trip around the table, Aunt Maye grabbed her niece's arm and drew her into the chair beside her. "The police are already doing that. When you reach your dad's apartment, call and tell them you've arrived. The colonel said he'd tell them you were coming. They'll give you an update. Then you let them work. Please don't give me cause to worry more about you and your friend because you go off on your own investigation. *Promise* me, Kyleigh."

She nodded. *I'll simply keep in touch with Auntie while we search.* What she didn't know wouldn't hurt her.

Aunt Maye stared at her niece. She knew better. There was no way she'd receive that promise from Kyleigh Flanagan. Not when the girl was determined to find her father. *Lord, please take care of her. And watch over Charlie, wherever he is.*

The women finished their coffee, and Aunt Maye took a frying pan out of the cabinet. "Let's have breakfast. I ran off some information for you about Oʻahu, where your dad's apartment is, how to get there, what would be nearby, etcetera, etcetera."

She pulled several sheets of paper with maps, pictures, and lists out of her oversized black purse and laid them on the table.

"You were a busy little bee, weren't you?" Kyleigh picked up the papers. "What's all this?"

"Like I said...information. Since you haven't been to Oʻahu in so long, I thought you might need it. When you visited your dad, you were more or less a tourist. I'm sure your dad drove you to all the attractions to show you a good time. You weren't on your own."

The thought of her only niece being so far away gave Maye a homesick sensation. She and her husband had loved Kyleigh as a daughter since she was five years old when her mother died. It didn't matter if she took a friend with her. What if something happened to her? What if she disappeared too? Maye's eyes flooded.

When she looked up from the papers, Kyleigh was biting her lip. She stopped when their eyes met.

"Auntie, you have to realize I'm grown up now. I'm an adult. Twenty-six years old. I've been on my own since I left for college. You've been a mother to me since Mom passed, and I love you as much as if you were Mom. But you have to stop treating me like I was still that teenager you raised while Dad was off in the Army."

Aunt Maye gave her a cockeyed grin. "I can't help it. You've been the only child Ellis and I ever had." She hugged her niece.

"It's too bad you and Uncle Ellis didn't have any children of your own. You were such great parents to me when I needed you the most. And if Uncle Ellis were here now, he'd tell you, 'lighten up, Maybug.' And then he'd tickle you until you cried."

Laughter filled the kitchen.

"I miss him so much. After four years, there's still a hole in my heart. Every morning, I wake up expecting to find him next to me." Her eyes took on a faraway gaze. "The love of my life, he was." She turned and smiled at Kyleigh. "Someday, that kind of love will walk into your life. Cherish every minute when you have it. It goes too fast."

Kyleigh lowered her eyes. "Auntie, I don't know if I'll ever find a love like yours. All the guys I've dated, in high school, college, or those I've worked with were all nice. They were all considerate and fun to be with once in a while, but I didn't form an attachment to any of them, except Paul. Live without one of them? Never felt I couldn't, not after the fiasco of being engaged to Paul in college and having him turn out to be unfaithful. Lucas didn't even stir up those kind of emotions after all the months of dating him and his very sweet proposal. I hated to turn him down, but the bond between us wasn't strong enough to warrant marriage. Not really. I'm relieved he handled it well and remains a friend."

A twinge of pain stabbed Maye's heart. She wanted Kyleigh to have that kind of love. The love of a father was one thing, but to be loved by one special man was quite another. She had to pray harder for her niece.

Maye slipped her hand on Kyleigh's shoulder and squeezed. "How about some of my trinity scrambled eggs for breakfast?"

"Auntie, this is my apartment. I'll make breakfast for you."

"We can do it together...unless you don't like my eggs." She pouted.

Hands on her hips, Kyleigh half-closed her right eye and grimaced. "I love your trinity scrambled eggs."

"It's settled then. I make eggs. You make the bacon. You do have green peppers, onions, and tomato—"

The doorbell rang. Both women jumped.

"Maybe we should switch to decaf, dear. We're wired enough already."

Kyleigh giggled and headed for the front door.

"Marisa. I'm not sure all of this will fit on the plane. I'm only taking a carry-on, my laptop, purse, and one suitcase."

"Silly. That's not my luggage. Since I'm staying over tonight, I'll have to drop the car back at my apartment building tomorrow morning on the way to the airport. I'll grab my bags then. Everything's packed and ready to go. This stuff," she held her hand out toward the boxes, "is for the church auction when we come back. Did you forget? Besides, I wouldn't pack boxes to go to Hawai'i. What a character you are."

Marisa dropped the last box from the hallway into the corner of the living room. "You said we could store everything here until the auction, remember?"

Kyleigh's jaw fell open. "Oh dear, I forgot all about it. People will want to drop stuff off, and I won't be here." She spun toward Aunt Maye. "What am I going to do?"

"You're going to stop worrying. I have your key. Sunday, I'll tell the pastor everyone can contact me while you're gone, and we'll make arrangements. Calm down."

"Do I smell fresh coffee?" Marisa sniffed the air. "Sure could use a cup, girl. I was in such a hurry to finish everything this morning with the auction stuff and my packing, I completely forgot to make any."

Marisa could forget coffee but never breakfast. Since high school, Marissa had been a wisp of a girl and yet ate like a linebacker for the Dallas Cowboys. Kyleigh stared at Marisa, all five feet of her elf-like frame, standing in front of the boxes. Her long, silky jet-black hair hung loosely over her shoulders. Kyleigh had always thought of herself as too large, no matter how many times people told her she had a model's figure. Why couldn't she have been petite instead of four inches shorter than her six feet tall father?

"Come on in the kitchen. Aunt Maye and I were going to start breakfast."

"Oooo...Aunt Maye's scrambled eggs, I hope."

Aunt Maye slipped her arm around Marisa's waist and pulled her to the kitchen. "I may have to adopt you, sweetie."

As Kyleigh and her aunt made breakfast, Marisa set the table. She picked up the papers with maps, pictures, and listings of stores and other businesses, then moved them to the counter. "What are these?"

"Some information I printed off for you and Kyleigh. We can go over them after we eat."

When they'd eaten their fill of the fluffy scrambled eggs laden with green peppers, onions, and chopped tomatoes and had loaded the dishwasher, the three women drifted into the living room. Aunt Maye brought up the rear with the stack of papers."

Marisa rubbed her stomach. "Aunt Maye, you can cook eggs for me any time you want to. Those are the only scrambled eggs I've ever liked." She sat up straight and pinned Kyleigh with a stare. "So, have you heard any more from Oʻahu about your dad?"

"Not a word. His CO only said Dad never showed up for duty a week ago, after he'd taken the previous week off for some personal business. Dad never told Auntie or me he had something important he had to attend to. And all we got was that strange note, which neither of us thinks was really written by him."

"This is beginning to sound like a first-class mystery story, Ky. But we'll get to the bottom of it once we land in Oʻahu. You'll see."

Chapter Three

After arriving at Bush Continental Airport the next morning, Kyleigh and Marisa checked their bags and waited for the boarding call. Kyleigh drummed her fingers on the arm of the seat. What little patience she had to begin with had left her. All she wanted to do was get to the island and find her dad. Was it a mistake to bring Marisa along? She might not be up to playing detective.

Marisa flipped through the papers Aunt Maye had printed out for them. "I still can't believe your aunt looked up all this stuff for us. This is great! Driving directions, nearby stores where we can shop, and a list of sites to visit once we find the major."

Kyleigh shook her head. She only hoped it would be soon. Marisa was a good friend, volunteering to go with her to find her dad. If only they'd find him safe at home when they arrived. Boy, would he be in for a lecture. But then they could all spend the rest of the time enjoying the island. *If only.*

"Wow! Ky, your aunt even included directions to the police station and the base. She covered everything."

"Post, Marisa. The Army calls it a post, not a base like the Navy." Kyleigh resumed drumming her fingers.

Marisa tossed her a tentative smile. "Don't worry. We'll find him. Your dad may even be at the airport to greet us since his commanding officer is sure to have told him we were coming...if he checked in." She shrugged, then showed Kyleigh the pictures of the mountains surrounding the Army post. "Those will be fun places to hike when we have time."

Mountains. Could he have? "Marisa! I just thought of something. I wonder if those mountains have been searched. Oʻahu has two ranges. The Waianae to the west and Koʻolau to the east. They run almost parallel to one another. The last time I visited, Dad took me on a bike trail on the Koʻolau range." A vision of the scenery flashed into her mind. Her mouth curled up at the corners. "Then he wanted me to see the fantastic view from the Nuʻuanu Pali Lookout. It's his favorite." She grasped her chin as she thought out loud. "But maybe...maybe, he rode his dirt bike up on Koʻolau too fast, like he does when he needs to relieve stress, and something happened to him." She lowered her hand to her side and fought back the lump in her throat. "Some of those trails on Koʻolau are difficult to negotiate. Well, none of the paths are really easy for a motorized dirt bike. They can be dangerous."

"You mean your dad rides those crazy motorized dirt bikes up a mountain at his age? Alone?"

"Yes, alone...sometimes."

Marisa's eyes grew round. "Isn't he a little too old for stuff like that?"

"Don't let my dad hear you say that. He's ridden dirt bikes forever."

"One of my boyfriends loves that hobby. Always tries to get me to join him when he goes riding. I tell him, *no way*. And these are only a bunch of small dirt hills they ride their bikes on. Drew told me he rode in Oʻahu once. He said the range is super dangerous, full of tree roots like petrified boa constrictors, crisscrossing each other, and drop-offs you aren't aware of because of all the vegetation. I sure hope your dad didn't go on those."

Kyleigh suppressed a grin. "I've ridden the trails with Dad. Yes, if you don't watch what you're doing, if you're a hot-rodder or a showoff, you can wind up hurt...or worse. Dad isn't like that. He sometimes goes a little too fast, but he's normally very careful. The worst thing that ever happened to Dad was the bike slid out from under him and dumped him on his side when he skidded around a turn. He taught me to ride. But he was adamant I use caution and drive responsibly. We had a lot of fun in past years." She chuckled. "Sometimes we had to carry the bike instead of riding because the roots were too many and too big, but the scenery and excitement made it worthwhile." She glanced up and caught Marisa's eye.

Her friend's brows wrinkled. "Are you serious?"

"Quite. What worries me is the occasional showoff who thinks he's hot stuff on the trail. They're not only a danger to themselves but to other riders as well. But if an accident had occurred, you'd think someone would have notified Aunt Maye or me to let us know, or even his CO. Dad would have had his identification on him, including his dog tags, if he'd been knocked unconscious." She rubbed her forehead. "I don't know. I can't imagine something like that would happen to Dad. But still."

A sweet female voice on the intercom announced, "United Airlines flight UA two-five-three from Houston to Honolulu is now boarding."

"That's us, Marisa." Kyleigh took a deep breath and stood. *We're on our way, Dad. Please be at the airport when we arrive.*

Kyleigh and Marisa followed the rest of the passengers down the boarding bridge to the plane. "Our seats are toward the back, Marisa. If you like, you can have the window seat. I doubt I'd pay much attention to the view outside, since my mind is filled with places to check for my dad. If he hasn't been found by the time we reach his apartment."

"Are you sure, Ky? It might take your mind off the stress of not knowing." She located their seat numbers.

A smile spread across Kyleigh's face. "I'm sure. Besides, I've been to O'ahu before. You haven't. You'll want to see it from the air as we land. I remember the amazing view of Diamondhead as we made our approach in past visits." She held out her hand for Marisa to slide in. Her friend scooted across to the window and eased into the seat. Kyleigh dropped into the aisle seat next to her. "Once we're up in the air, I'll try to take a nap. Last night was pretty much a sleepless one."

After takeoff, Marisa slipped on a pair of earphones and watched the inflight movie. Kyleigh yawned and pushed the seat back as far as it would go. *Glad no one is sitting behind me.* Her lashes sank.

At a nearby metallic sound, she jolted awake. Her eyes popped open, and her heart raced. She bolted upright in the seat. *Oh.* It was only a dream. Not a bike crash.

The dark-haired air hostess's eyes twinkled. "Would you care for a beverage?"

Marisa cocked her head. "You okay, Ky?"

"Yes, yes." She let out the breath she'd gulped in as she awoke. She was still on the plane. It was the beverage cart that made the noise. How long had she been asleep? "Water, please."

The slim girl handed her a small, cold bottle.

"Thank you."

The stewardess addressed Marisa. "And for you?"

"I'd like diet cola, please."

Diet cola. Kyleigh laughed to herself. Like Marisa needed a diet anything. "I'll never understand why you drink that stuff when you could have the real thing. You could drink a milkshake with every meal and not gain an ounce. I'm jealous." She giggled.

"A mere precaution. I have an aunt on my dad's side who's big enough to make three aunts."

The stewardess's lips twitched as she smiled and held out the diet cola to Marisa.

"Thanks." Marisa took the offered drink and napkin. "I was kidding about my aunt." The dark-haired young woman nodded, and the beverage cart rolled on to the next row of seats.

"Ky, I take it you didn't have a peaceful sleep before you woke."

"Not really. I had a bad dream. Then I heard the flight attendant's beverage cart roll next to me. I don't remember most of my dream, but right before I awoke, two dirt bikes crashed into each other. One soared into the brush on the side of the trail and down a hidden cliff. The beverage cart must have bumped my seat, and I jumped." She raised her brows. "I think I was on one bike. Not sure. But if it was my dad...do you believe dreams can reveal the truth?"

After a long drink of cola, Marisa placed her hand on Kyleigh's arm. "Do you remember the Scripture our pastor read in his sermon about a month ago? The one where Joseph interpreted the dreams of the cup-bearer and the baker in Egypt. Those dreams came true.

But surely you don't believe you'll take a tumble off a cliff in Hawaiʻi, do you? Or that your Dad has?"

Looking into the water bottle as if it were a crystal ball, Kyleigh couldn't say no. But did the dream foreshadow her fate or provide a vision of what had already happened to her father? She shuddered. "I'm not sure what to think, Marisa. I'm so worried."

Twelve hours later, the plane landed in Oʻahu. While the girls hurried to baggage pickup, Kyleigh scanned the area. She crossed the fingers on both hands. Oh, how she wanted her father to be there at the end of the corridor. No sign of him. Her heart sank as though it held rocks.

"It's only three in the afternoon here, Marisa. With the time difference, it'll be a long day for us. Come on. Let's find our bags and pick up the car I reserved. We have to get to Dad's apartment. He might be there if his CO neglected to tell him we were coming." *I hope.*

Marisa looked around the baggage area. "Some passengers from our flight are wearing a lei, others aren't. I thought they presented everyone with one when they came to the Hawaiian Islands. We weren't. Did we do something wrong?"

Kyleigh spotted her bag and grabbed it. "No. People prearrange to have a lei greeting as part of their package deal for vacation, or whoever meets them here at the airport might present them with one. But in general, you have to preorder them. See the girl over there?" She pointed out a smiling young woman with dark hair and an armful of purple and white lei. "She could be waiting for a group of people who've arranged for the 'lei greeting.' Visitors usually hold up a sign with their name on it so the greeters can find them." Kyleigh turned her friend toward several people, including children, entering the baggage area and talking among themselves. "That must be the group."

"Oh." Marisa's tone sounded disappointed.

Kyleigh smiled at her. "I'm sorry, Marisa. I didn't think to order a lei for you since it's your first time here." She should have thought of that. Kyleigh pressed her lips tightly. Dad had always had one for her when she'd landed. A twinge of unease hit her. "Too much on my mind. But I intend to present you with a lei to take home. Not quite the same, but it'll be my gift."

Marisa interlinked her arm with Kyleigh's. "That's okay, Ky. You have more important things to think of right now. But I will be thrilled to have one to show Mom and Dad." A grin stretched her lips and revealed her perfect, white teeth. "Let's get the car and go."

After they'd picked up the rental, Kyleigh drove to the off-post apartment her father kept. The half-hour drive seemed more like an hour.

For as long as she remembered, he'd always maintained a two-bedroom flat, so she'd have her own room when she came to visit. Guilt pangs consumed her. It had been a full two years since her last visit. Last year she'd opted to go with friends to Key West on vacation. This year, the plan had been to visit Washington, DC. Not one negative comment had been uttered by her Dad when she told him she wouldn't be able to visit. A tear slipped from her bottom lash.

As she pulled into the parking lot at the Makakilo Kauhale Apartments, she spotted her dad's white Mustang. "He's here!" She shut off the engine and ran for the building.

"Ky, wait for me."

Kyleigh stopped dead in her tracks at the stone steps to the apartment entrance. She turned and waited for Marisa to catch up to her. "Sorry."

They walked down the side porch to the front door, and Kyleigh rang the doorbell. Her heart raced as if she'd run all the way from the airport. No answer. She rang again and pounded on the door. "Dad!" Still no answer. *Come on, Dad. Be here.*

"I don't think he's home, Ky. He could be at work. He may not have been able to leave, even if he knew you were flying in."

Kyleigh rummaged through her purse for the key to her dad's apartment and unlocked the door. Her heart was so low it could have scraped the threshold as they entered the living room. Magazines and newspapers littered the coffee table. Dad was never the neatest person, unless he had houseguests. On the end table next to his favorite chair, a mug with dried coffee in the bottom sat on a coaster.

As Marisa picked up the cup, she scrunched her nose at the remnants. "I'd say your dad hasn't been home for a few days, at least."

Waterworks gushed from Kyleigh's eyes. "Where could he be?"

Marisa enveloped her friend and hugged her. "Take heart, Ky. I shouldn't have said that. He probably hasn't cleaned up for a day or two. You know bachelors. Why don't you call the base...er post and ask if he showed up?"

While Kyleigh looked through the papers from Aunt Maye for the phone number of her dad's commanding officer, Marisa brought in her bags. She dropped them next to the tan cloth-covered couch and hustled back out the door for Kyleigh's. When she brought the rest of the bags into the house, she tossed the car keys onto the coffee table.

"Here it is." Kyleigh picked up her cell and dialed. The colonel answered on the third ring.

"Colonel Stevens, this is Kyleigh Flanagan. Has my dad shown up yet? We arrived at his apartment, but he's not here, and yet his car is in the lot."

"No, Miss Flanagan. I'm sorry to say, we've had no word from the major. The local authorities have been informed and initiated an investigation while they look into the information your aunt gave them. Our investigative department has also instituted a search for your dad. Do you need anything?"

"No, thank you. I don't think so. Just my father." Tears threatened and then overflowed. She lowered herself to the couch.

Marisa took the cell from her hand and held it to her ear. "Colonel Stevens, this is Kyleigh's friend, Marisa. She's a bit overwhelmed right now." Marisa listened to the colonel for a minute. "I understand, sir. You're doing all you can do. Thank you. I'll let Ky know." She hung up and ran to the kitchen for paper towels. Marisa handed the sheets to Kyleigh.

When the sobs abated, Marisa put her arms around her friend. "I think you need to call the police department to find out what they know and what they're doing."

Kyleigh nodded but couldn't answer.

Marisa scanned the notes from Aunt Maye and found the number. She punched it in on Kyleigh's cell, then ran into the kitchen with the phone to her ear and grabbed a couple more paper towels. She scooted back to Kyleigh and held out the cell, laying the towels on the coffee table.

Kyleigh took the phone from Marisa, wiped her face with the towels, blew her nose, and waited for someone to answer.

A hurried female voice said, "Honolulu Police Department."

"This is Kyleigh Flanagan, Major Charles Flanagan's daughter from Houston, Texas. We arrived at my father's apartment, but he's not home. I called the post, and his CO said you've started an investigation into his disappearance. Can you tell me anything?"

Chapter Four

yleigh threw her cellphone onto the couch and paced her father's apartment. "Useless! Law enforcement is once more absolutely useless. Just like when Mom died. What good are you if you can't tell me what you've found out about my father's disappearance? Investigation, my foot." She gritted her teeth and dropped onto the sofa next to her phone. "Keep calm, they say. How am I supposed to keep calm? Stay put. What am I supposed to tell Aunt Maye?"

At the end of her tirade, Kyleigh stared at Marisa.

From a kitchen stool, Marisa stared back with her mouth open. "I've never seen you this upset about anything."

"Well, of course, I'm upset. My father's never disappeared before. Not even while in Afghanistan." Kyleigh lowered her head to her hands and braced her elbows on her knees. "Imagine, the entire time he was stationed in that hostile place, he was fine. Now he disappears. In Hawai'i of all places."

She hopped up from the couch. "I can't sit here. I've got to find him." She headed for the front door.

"But Ky, you don't know your way around." Marisa jumped off the stool and followed her to the foyer. "Maybe you should let the authorities handle the search for him?"

"*No.*" Kyleigh spun. "The colonel said he advised the police a week ago that my dad hadn't shown up for duty. *Seven days.* You'd think in that time someone would have something to go on. But did they tell me anything? *No.* I'm not really sure they've started a search for Dad."

The bags still sat in a pile in the living room. Marisa glanced at them and then toward Kyleigh. "Let's settle in first, eat dinner, and then we'll talk about where to start, okay? Please, Ky. You can't take off without a plan. Please?"

A long breath of air escaped between Kyleigh's lips. She continued to pace the room, then dropped back onto the couch. "I'm sorry. You're right. Let's put our stuff away first."

"Where should I put my things?"

Kyleigh pointed to the hallway. "You take the room I usually use. The door to the right. It has a queen-sized bed. I'll sleep in Dad's bed. I wouldn't want my tossing and turning to keep you up at night."

Marisa nodded and grabbed her bags.

Kyleigh carried hers to the master bedroom. Outside the door, she pointed again to the guestroom at the opposite end of the short hall. "Make yourself at home while you're here. Dad always keeps a cabinet full of snacks in the kitchen, to the left of the refrigerator." She stepped into the bedroom but turned. "After we put our things away, we'll have to go out to eat. Dad never keeps much normal food in the house unless I'm here. And depending on how long he's been gone, I can't guarantee what condition the food in the fridge is in." She scrunched her nose.

"Right." Marisa made a sour face. She opened the guestroom door. "I want to change before we go anywhere. Now that we're here in Hawaiʻi. I'll shed my jeans and western garb and dress more like a native. I don't mean a real Hawaiian...I just mean as if I live here."

Kyleigh laughed. "Girl, with your jet-black hair and olive skin tone, which gives you the appearance of a year-round tan, you'd pass easily for a native Hawaiian. But I understand. No sense showing off you're a *haole* with your Texas garb."

"Howlee? What's a howlee?"

"Not how-lee. H-a-o-l-e. How-lay. What the Hawaiians call visitors to the islands, even those who've been living here for years. And though you may appear somewhat native, they'll probably refer to you like that, anyway. Somehow, they can tell." She raised her brows.

"So what do they call themselves?"

"Offhand, I don't remember. Dad would know. There aren't that many pure-blood Hawaiians left. Most are only half or less true Hawaiian. But regardless, the people are heritage-minded. Guess it's what gives Hawaiʻi the charm that brings so many people back here, over and over. Did you know this is the only place in The States where you'll find a royal residence?"

"You mean an actual castle...here?" Marisa's eyes grew round.

"You remind me of Frodo Baggins in *The Lord of the Rings* when your eyes get huge." She chuckled. "No, not a castle. A palace. ʻIolani Palace in downtown Honolulu. The only royal palace in the United States. I'll take you to see it before we leave. It is quite something. But enough of the history lesson, let's freshen up."

Marisa stepped into the guestroom but leaned into the hallway. "I'll look forward to the typical tourist...*Haole*...thing before we leave. I've heard and seen so much about Hawai'i in books and magazines, on TV shows, and...well, I never thought I'd be here. But only after we find your dad." She disappeared into the room.

Kyleigh shook her head at her friend's excitement over the island's attractions. She closed the bedroom door. Exactly as she had felt as a teenager the first time Dad had her visit him here on the post. The excitement never wore off, no matter how many times she'd been here. *Oh, Dad. Where are you?*

Kyleigh washed, changed into a light blue sundress with a white hibiscus pattern, slipped into a pair of white sandals, and entered the kitchen to brew a cup of coffee. She took a seat at the tan marble kitchen island and perused the papers her aunt had printed.

Marisa emerged from the guestroom in green capris and a leafy patterned loose top. She dangled her white flip-flops from an index finger as she joined Kyleigh in the kitchen. "So, where do we go for dinner?"

"Let's head over toward Ford Island. Dad's favorite place to grab a bite to eat is near it, right on Pearl Harbor." She placed her finger on one of the maps. "The Battleship Missouri Memorial and Pearl Harbor Aviation Museum are on the island. After we find Dad, we'll make sure you see them before we go back to Houston. I promise." She finished her coffee and stood. "The Pearl Grill isn't a posh place, but Dad loves it." *Wish he were with us now.*

"Sounds good to me. My stomach acts as though I'm on a starvation diet. Do they serve authentic Hawaiian food like poi, coconut, and pineapple?"

Kyleigh lips twitched with the snicker she suppressed. "I'm sure. Although, people usually eat poi with meat, not coconut or pineapple. They'll have American food too."

Marisa grabbed her purse and followed Kyleigh out of the apartment to the covered sidewalk.

As Kyleigh locked the front door behind her, she spotted her father's dirt bike secured to the last awning post on the narrow walkway beyond the entrance. "That's odd."

"What?" Marisa spun to face her.

"When Dad phoned me a couple of weeks ago, he told me he bought a new bike. But this is the old one." She stepped to the bike and ran her hand over the wheels. "He cleaned and polished it up completely as if it was ready to be sold."

"Well, he could've changed his mind."

"Maybe." An uncomfortable sensation ran up her neck. She narrowed her eyes at the bike.

"Come on." Marisa pulled on Kyleigh's arm. "I'm getting hungrier by the second. Let's go. Did you bring the directions from your aunt?"

"Yeah." As Marisa pulled her away from the bike, Kyleigh dismissed the edgy sensation and handed Marisa the papers. "I don't need these. I can find the grill without a map. Dad and I have been there enough times that I could probably drive there in my sleep."

A minute later, Kyleigh slid behind the wheel of the silver rental car, and Marisa closed the passenger door with a thud.

As Kyleigh drove out of the parking lot, the old dirt bike niggled at her. She tried to listen to Marisa's chatter as she drove, but her mind kept going back to the bike.

Marisa paused her comments for a moment as she gazed out the side window. She glanced at Kyleigh. "I don't think you've heard a word I've said. And you haven't made a peep since we got into the car. Are you still worrying about the bike?"

"Marisa, the more I think of it, the more it bothers me that Dad's new bike wasn't at the apartment. From what he said, and because of his excitement about buying it the day he called, I doubt he changed his mind. And his Mustang was at the apartment. He took the bike somewhere. It's the only explanation that makes sense. But where did he go? Surely not on a week-long bike ride. Not without telling his CO."

"Your Dad's been missing for over a week. Right?"

"Yes. And no accident report was filed, or the police would have said so." She gnawed on her bottom lip.

Marisa patted Kyleigh's arm. "There's nothing we can do about it right now. But when we return to the apartment, we can brainstorm some places he might have gone. Tomorrow, we can go to the police department and ask what they've done to find your dad. You know what they say about squeaky wheels?"

While Kyleigh waited at a stoplight, she wrinkled her forehead and glanced at Marisa. "What do squeaky wheels have to do with anything?"

"Duh. The squeaky wheel gets the oil, girl. If we bug the police department, which case will gain attention?"

"Oooh, I see." The light changed, and Kyleigh drove on. "You're right. You're a genius, my friend."

"I know." Marisa's grin spread as wide as her cheekbones were high. A grumble came from her tummy.

"You weren't kidding. You are starving." Laughter filled the air as Kyleigh drove toward Pearl Harbor, but her mind raced back to the dirt bike and her father. Where could Dad have taken the new bike, and why hadn't he told her or Aunt Maye where he planned to go? What kept him from his duties at the post? *Lord, we need Your help.*

Chapter Five

fter they'd ordered their food at the grill, Kyleigh leaned her elbows on the table. "You're disappointed in the place, aren't you, Marisa?"

Marisa shifted her eyes from one end of the room to the other. "Well, you said it wasn't posh, but I would have thought there'd be more island decor instead of it looking like an officer's club in Korea back in the nineteen fifties." She giggled. "Where are those cute little tiki lamps and palm trees in pots next to the tables and surfboards and fishnets on the walls?"

"I'm not sure you'll find much of that here on the island. Not from what I've seen so far, anyway. And this place caters to the military. Hence the military theme. Before we leave O'ahu, I'll see if I can find you a nice tropical restaurant."

Kyleigh turned her attention out the window to the waterfront and stared at the choppy water. Pearl Harbor beyond conjured up scenes from movies she'd seen about the surprise military strike by the Imperial Japanese Navy Air Service. Being near the battle zone hit her that way each year she visited.

"Ky? What's wrong?"

She focused her misty eyes on Marisa. "Nothing. Just thinking of the area's history. All the people who died in the December attack in nineteen, forty-one. Every time I come to Pearl Harbor, it takes my breath away."

"Yeah. It's an emotional place. I'm breathless at the thought of it, and I've never been here before."

"Good evening, ladies." A tall man, who Kyleigh guessed to be in his early thirties, placed the girls' hamburgers and fries in front of them. He rested his hands on his hips. "I never get tired of visiting the Pearl Harbor Memorial." A lock of blond hair fell over his brow when he bent. He finger-combed it into place. "Your waiter got an emergency phone call and asked me to serve you. Hope you don't mind. I'm Dave, Mike's partner in crime." His denim-colored eyes locked onto Marisa's. "Are you here on vacation or part of the more elegant locals I haven't had the pleasure of meeting?"

She giggled. "We're here to—"

Under the table, Kyleigh bumped Marisa's leg with her foot.

Marisa's line of sight traveled from Dave to Kyleigh, who gave a quick shake of the head. Marisa lowered her brows but apparently understood what the tap meant. "On vacation. We're on vacation."

Dave turned toward Kyleigh. "O-kaaay." He glanced back to Marisa. "Hope this won't be the only time you drop in." He flashed her a Colgate grin.

Their original server called to Dave from a hallway on the other side of the room. Dave excused himself and made a beeline for the other man.

"What was that all about, Ky? Not that I would have mentioned our mission here, but why the big secret? This was your dad's favorite place to eat, right? Dave could have seen your father and told us something that would help."

"I don't know. I just had a strange hunch it wouldn't be wise to mention Dad's name here. Not certain why."

"Okay. You and your *hunches*." Marisa shook her head and popped a french fry into her mouth. "Let's pray before I die of hunger. These burgers and fries smell fabulous."

Kyleigh chuckled. "I can't believe you ordered a hamburger and fries after all that talk about Hawaiian food on the way here."

As Marisa bit into another fry, she shrugged. "Guess I'm not as adventurous as I thought." She smiled and bowed her head.

Before Kyleigh bent hers, she eyed Dave as he talked to Mike. They appeared to be having a disagreement. Mike's hands moved as if he were demonstrating karate chops.

On the return route to the apartment, Kyleigh maneuvered through the island's traffic. She shifted her eyes to Marisa, who held a zoom lens camera on her lap, then refocused on the view ahead. "Let me pull over so you can take a decent picture." Kyleigh inched the vehicle out of the congestion onto the shoulder.

As soon as she stopped the car, Marisa hurried out. "I don't want to miss this sunset. Thanks, Ky."

Kyleigh gazed at the gold, peach, and purple, resembling an abstract painting. So beautiful. But her heart pinched. The setting of the sun had always been sad to her. As if she'd finished a novel she'd enjoyed and didn't want it to end. "Still...breathtaking," she whispered.

The word made her recall Marisa's comment about Pearl Harbor and Dave, the talky waiter. *I've seen him before.* She was positive she had. But where? She pressed her lips together while she concentrated.

Her friend slipped into the car, and Kyleigh reentered the road.

Marisa twisted in her seat to face the back window, then turned to Kyleigh. "Is traffic always congested here? Although it's a far cry from Houston. And do they always drive so slowly?"

"Pretty much. Dad told me to relax when I come to visit if I planned to use his Mustang. No one's in much of a hurry on the island unless they have an emergency or they're a haole who's in a rush to have dinner." She eased off the gas. "This is a different culture. Dad said the locals never honk their horns. Generally, they don't drive fast, and they're courteous to one another. They call it 'driving with *aloha*.' You'll definitely be pulled over if you exceed the speed limit."

A titter escaped her friend. "I thought aloha meant hello and goodbye."

"It does, but it means much more. I'm not sure how to explain it, but aloha is like the way you treat people too."

Marisa shook her head. "Taking a trip here is like going to a different country."

"No more than someone coming from the northern states to the south. Colloquialisms, the dialect. My neighbor told me he had culture shock when he first moved from Wisconsin to Alabama. And then again when he relocated to Texas." Kyleigh laughed. "While you're here on Oʻahu, you may as well learn some Hawaiian words. If you go off without me, they'll no doubt come in handy."

"Shoot 'em to me." Marisa yanked a pen and small notepad from her purse and poised her hand, ready to write.

Kyleigh's lips rose on one side. At least this kept her mind off her missing father and from thinking about the guy at the restaurant who gave her such an uncomfortable sense of foreboding. "Okay. Number one, Mahalo. M-a-h-a-l-o."

"Mahalo...and it means?"

"Thank you."

"Good one to learn. I read somewhere that Hawaiians are very gracious people. You know, my class might do a session on Hawaiian culture next semester. What do you think? As long as I'm here, I can research."

A grin formed on Kyleigh's face. "You don't think second graders are a little young for a subject like that?"

"You've been teaching kindergarten too long. My students are smart and curious. It would make their social studies class exciting. We could even do something in art class. Have a luau." She bit her bottom lip. "Say...with all the research I'll do, I should take the trip's expenses off on my taxes for this year." Marisa giggled.

By the time they returned to the major's apartment, Marisa had filled three pages with Hawaiian topics to research. She stuffed her notepad into her purse. "I'm all set. Now to the real reason we're here. Let's wake up early tomorrow and head over to the police department to find out what they've learned about your dad's disappearance. Then we'll start our own investigation." She gave a no-nonsense nod.

Kyleigh parked the car and slid out of the seat. She glanced at her father's car. Still there. Hadn't moved an inch. She stared at the apartment windows. Dark. "Yes. Early tomorrow. Someone has to know what's going on."

Kyleigh awoke with a start. What was that noise? She checked her cell for the time. Just after midnight. She slipped out of bed and tiptoed to the bedroom door. As she cracked it open, a dim light from the kitchen glowed across the spacious living room. Was that a flashlight? Kyleigh's heart pounded. She backed up and grabbed her dad's baseball bat from the corner of the room.

She pulled the door open several inches, squeezed through the space, and peered around the wall that separated the short hall from the living room. The soft illumination in the kitchen dimmed. A prickle ran up her neck as she listened for footsteps. The room held only enough light to make out shadowy objects.

As she raised the weapon over her shoulder, she flipped the light switch on and lunged from the hallway, ready to swing at the prowler.

A scream echoed in the room. A plate flew to the ceiling. The dinnerware landed with a crash as a shiny cylinder fell to the hardwood floor and rolled toward the kitchen stools. "*Ky!* You scared me half to death. What are you doing with that bat?"

"Me? What are *you* doing traipsing around in the dark in the middle of the night?" She breathed in a gulp and stared at the pieces of yellow dish, french fries scattered in every direction, and the penlight. Kyleigh lowered the baseball bat and laid her hand over her heart, then cocked her head to one side. "Midnight snack?"

"It would have been." Marisa looked up from her bent-over position, hands on knees. Then with a sigh, she stooped to pick up pieces of shattered earthenware and a handful of fries. She threw them into the trash. "I'll clean the floor in the morning."

"I'm sorry I scared you." Kyleigh helped her scoop up the rest of the food and tossed it in the garbage. "I heard a noise. Thought you were an intruder. Guess my nerves are really on edge."

Marisa curled her arm around her friend. "It's okay. Sorry I broke the plate...and frightened you."

"I should have known you'd be up for a snack in the middle of the night. But I could have *clobbered* you." She blew a long puff of air and rubbed her forehead. "You must have a record high metabolism. I remember when we attended the church retreat last year. You were up each night in search of goodies."

"And I tried to be so quiet, so I wouldn't wake you tonight."

Kyleigh's bare feet shuffled into the living room, where she dropped into the corner of the tan cloth-covered couch. "I'm a super light sleeper. And the dream I had probably woke me."

"Mind if I have a snack? Do you want something?" Marisa scooted back to the kitchen.

"No food. My stomach is performing a hula at the moment. But if you'll run water through the brewer, I'll have tea. That should settle my nerves. Dad keeps tea and coffee in the right overhead cabinet."

Marisa poured a cup of water into the coffee maker, opened a package of chamomile, and placed the bag in a mug. She pressed the blinking button. While she returned to the refrigerator, the machine made its cappuccino noises, and billows of steam rose from the mug, filling the room with an earthy, herbal scent.

"Marisa, I dreamed the waiter from last night followed us here. I thought for sure he'd broken into the apartment."

The microwave beeped, and Marisa pulled out a blue dish of hot fries. "Good thing we ordered extra french fries before we left the restaurant." She added ketchup to her snack and stepped back to the kitchen island. "You meant the second guy who was so flirty...Dave, right? You really have it in for this guy." She lowered a dangling fry into her mouth.

"Yes. I finally remembered where I'd seen him before. It was two years ago at the same place when Dad and I had stopped there for dinner."

"He's worked there that long?"

"I guess so. After Dad and I entered The Pearl Grill and sat down, he saw Dave with some other guys at a table across the room. Dad kept his eyes on him. There weren't many customers that day. I didn't recognize the other servers tonight as being with Dave back then."

"How could you tell your dad was watching Dave and not someone else?"

"Because when he got up from his table and headed for the restroom, Dad's eyes fixed on him until he went down the hall. When I asked if something was wrong, Dad didn't say a word, just picked up the menu. And when Dave returned to his table, Dad's eyes were glued to him again. Throughout the meal, he kept glancing toward Dave."

"But he didn't tell you why?"

"Eventually, he told me that, on more than one occasion, he'd seen Dave hanging around teens whose parents were stationed on the post. And that Dave started a fight with one of the fathers."

"What else did your dad say?"

Kyleigh pressed her mouth into a straight line. "I learned a long time ago, when I ask a question, and Dad gives an answer, don't ask for further details. When he's ready to tell me, if he wants to, he will. One of his annoying quirks." She tried to smile, but her lips quivered. She tightened them again.

"So what do you think it all means, Ky? Should we go back to the restaurant and ask Dave if he's seen your father?"

Chapter Six

After a fitful night's sleep, Kyleigh took a shower and made breakfast. At least there had been eggs and frozen sausages in the fridge. With a deep sigh, she dumped a moldy bag of bread into the trash can.

"Good morning, Ky. Sorry I took so long getting dressed. Marissa came into view from the bedroom. What can I do to help?"

"Not a thing...unless you can make bread within the next few minutes." She pointed to the garbage.

Marisa peeked into the can. "Eeewww. The last time I saw a loaf that green was when my mom made some Irish Soda Bread for St. Patrick's Day. But Mom made it green on purpose." She giggled.

"We'll have to do without toast this morning. The lack of fresh bread definitely tells me Dad's been gone for over a week unless it was old before he left, and he forgot to throw it out. Not likely. He loves his bread." She opened the freezer and took out a frosted plastic sack. "What's this?" With the dishcloth, she wiped away the frost, then unzipped the bag. "Hey, we're in luck. Dad froze cinnamon rolls. From a bakery, no less. Good deal."

"Oh, yum. I love cinnamon rolls." Marisa licked her lips.

Kyleigh separated four pastries and placed them on a dish. She slipped the plate into the microwave and set it to defrost. "Marisa, crack some eggs into that frying pan for me, will ya? I can eat two scrambled eggs." Kyleigh aimed her elbow at the open burner as she turned the sizzling sausages in the pan in front of her. "Add as many as you want."

Her friend hopped off the kitchen stool and began her task. "Thanks. I hate to sit around while others work. I think it's why I became a teacher. Always something to do in the classroom, whether teaching, grading, or preparing for lessons. I can't imagine myself in any other career, can you?"

"Nope. I love kids. And it's a privilege to help and guide them along during their first experience in school. What a blessing."

"Speaking of help, since you don't want to go back to the restaurant to question Dave about your dad, will we still go to the police department this morning to check if they've found out any more about him? They might have an idea where we can search?"

"Yes, we will. But don't mention our plan to hunt for him. I've seen enough cop shows to expect they'll advise us to stay out of their investigation. In fact, they may order us to." *If there even is an investigation.* "We'll simply pump them for information and then make our plans."

"Right! Now we're thinking. Hey, watch those sausages, girl."

Kyleigh spun to the frying pan. "Yikes. Thanks. We almost had elongated meteorites, but they're just super-browned."

While Marisa set out the plates and tableware, Kyleigh finished cooking the eggs. The microwave dinged, and she took the rolls out, placing the dish on the countertop. The aroma of cinnamon filled the kitchen.

"Mmm...I'm starved." Marisa moved the pans of food onto hot pads in front of their plates. She jumped up on a stool and passed a napkin from the holder to Kyleigh. "Shall I say grace?"

"Sure."

After Marisa asked the Lord to bless the meal, she asked God to help them find the major and keep him safe.

Tears filled Kyleigh's eyes.

"...and please, Lord, ease Ky's stress. Amen."

With a lump lodged in her throat, Kyleigh could barely utter her amen. *Lord, please lead us to him. I can't stand the thought of never seeing my dad again.* Where could he be?

Marisa watched her friend's face as they rode in silence to the police department. Ky's stress level had elevated again. She needed answers. What a valiant effort she'd made not to get too upset, but to find her dad's empty apartment after the strange message he'd sent her was too much. Marisa pressed her lips together. *Then we'd run into that waiter last night, which added more fuel to her anxiety.* She'd never witnessed such high tension in Ky before. Not even when one of her kindergarten boys brought his pet snake to the school cafeteria...without its carrier. Marisa's mouth pulled to one side. But then, she'd probably be just as bad off if one of her parents were missing.

Kyleigh pulled the rental car into the public parking lot. The girls exited the vehicle and approached the building.

"You okay, Ky?"

"Sure. My father is AWOL. There's no logical reason for it. The military has nothing new to tell me. The police department didn't tell me anything when I called either. And I have another headache coming on. Why wouldn't I be okay?"

Whoa. Marisa's eyes widened. She laid her hand on Kyleigh's shoulder. "You have every right to be upset. Let's go inside. The police may have more information about your dad today."

"Remember, Marisa. After I ask for an update, don't ask any more questions. Let them do the talking. If they say something that gives us a clue where we can search, I'll try to coax more info out of them. But I don't want them to tell me to stay home and out of their way. The dumbest thing they could ever say to me is, 'Don't try to find your father.' Better yet, let me do all the talking in there. You do have a tendency to—"

"I understand. And I'll try to simply be the concerned friend who's here for moral support." *Lord, please keep hold of my tongue.* Her Italian temper could cause problems. Why couldn't she have inherited her mother's Irish temperament? Nope. That wouldn't work either. *Lord, just help me zip it.*

They ran up the short flight of steps to the front door. As Marisa reached for the handle, the door flew outward, and two very tall, well-built men rushed through, almost knocking her over and pushing her into Kyleigh.

"*Hey!*" Heat raged in Marisa's neck. "What's the rush, guys? Do you want to kill someone? Are the police chasing you, or what?" She glared at the two men.

Kyleigh held onto Marisa's arm. "They're obviously not from around here and don't know how to treat people with *Aloha.*"

The dark-haired man laughed. "Listen to the haole teach us about proper Hawaiian manners."

Marisa sharpened her glare at the Hawaiian-featured hunk with crystal blue eyes.

The man with light brown hair grabbed the other man's shoulder and pulled him away. "She's right. We were rude. I'm sorry, ladies. We were in a rush and didn't pay attention. Hope we didn't hurt you."

Kyleigh released Marisa's arm. "No. Just startled us, I guess." A glow rose in Kyleigh's cheeks.

The light-haired man reopened the door and held it while the girls entered the building. He ran a hand through his mop of wavy hair and smiled. His face reminded Marisa of a young Brad Pitt.

"Come on, man. We don't have time." The dark-haired hunk grabbed the other man's bicep and spun him around. They hurried away.

As the two men disappeared around the corner of the building, Marisa whispered, "Guess they weren't running away from the law after all." She giggled. "The cinnamon-color-eyed guy sure gave you the once-over. I think he pulled Mr. Blue Eyes away to have a better gander at you. What a nice smile."

Kyleigh gave Marisa's arm a slap. "Right." She rolled her eyes and then approached the front desk. "We're here to ask if you've found anything new about my missing father, Major Charles Flanagan."

From behind her friend, Marisa pinched her eyes shut. *Lord, please let them have some information for Ky.*

Kyleigh fumed as they left the HPD building and walked to the car. "I doubt they've even tried to find him. No one seems the least bit concerned that he's been missing for over a week. Neither his CO nor the police department. Nobody cares but us."

"Yeah. They sure didn't say much, except that a neighbor saw him ride away from the apartment complex last week. And for us to let them do their work. Do you think it means we're not to bother them again? Surely they don't think you're to sit on your thumbs and wait for them to call you."

"I don't care if it does. As you said, it's the squeaky wheel that will get the oil. I intend to keep calling to ask where they are in this investigation. Two detectives are working on the case, huh. And they'd both left the building right before we got there. Really? How convenient. What did the officer say their names were? I was already steaming hot when he told us and can't remember."

"He called one of them O'Shea and the other Swanson."

"Humph! Sounds like a daring duo. Do you suppose they have an idea where Dad is? I wish there was a way we could find those detectives, if they exist, and follow them."

"Yeah. But we wouldn't recognize them from Cain or Abel." She shrugged. "Where are *we* going to look for your dad when we aren't familiar with the island?"

Marisa took her seat on the passenger side of the rental car. Kyleigh slid behind the wheel.

Her friend's eyes narrowed. "Maybe we should start with the base—I mean post—and talk to your dad's commanding officer. Surely they'd be doing something to find him."

"You're right, Marisa. When we're back at the apartment, I'll call him. But first, let's go to the apartment and get Dad's Mustang. I found his keys in the nightstand drawer this morning. No sense in having two cars. I'll follow you to the return lot."

She pulled out of the parking lot and smoldered about the little information the desk sergeant had told her. *Let them handle it, my foot!*

Kyleigh heard a grumble from Marisa's stomach. "We'd better stop and buy some food before we go back to the apartment. Something tells me we'll have to stay for a while."

"Groceries would be wise. My stomach's registering empty again. And while you try to get somewhere with the colonel, I'll check out historical sites listed online for Oʻahu. After we locate your dad, I plan to load up on information for next year's lessons." She tilted her head forward and caught Kyleigh's attention. "We will find him, Ky. Remember, God's on our side."

Marisa was trying to make her feel better again. Kyleigh smiled. What a terrific friend. She'd given up her vacation plans to San Antonio and traveled all the way to Hawaiʻi. Just to be with her in this crisis. Kyleigh wrinkled her forehead. Marisa said she was saving money, but she wasn't. She had a cousin to stay with in San Antonio. Her vacation would have been virtually free. And she'd have been able to eat all the Mexican food she desired. "Marisa, what's the longest time you've ever gone without eating?" Kyleigh laughed to herself.

"Huh?"

"Nothing. There's the grocery store up ahead. We should have taken time to make a grocery list. Don't grab a bunch of junk food. Let's try to figure out meals for the next few days at least. Hamburgers, hot dogs, and entrees we can heat up easily in the microwave. Any other suggestions?"

"How about a steak? I noticed your dad has a grill on the porch."

"Great idea. Another Hawaiian word to jot down in your notebook. They call those porches lanais here. We can buy a couple of baking potatoes too. Sour cream. Dad has butter. Oh, and milk. Do you recall how many coffee pods were—"

A black vehicle swerved in front of them. Kyleigh slammed on the brakes.

Marisa clamped both hands onto the dashboard. "*Hey!* That's not driving with aloha for sure. Did you see the driver, Ky? It was the tall, blue-eyed guy who almost knocked us over at the police station. What a menace."

"No, I didn't see him. I was too busy trying not to hit the car next to me." Kyleigh took in a deep breath. There went her last nerve. She rubbed her forehead. "Was the other guy with him? Did you get the license plate number, make, and model?"

"Didn't notice any of that. It happened so fast. All I saw was a black *whatever* coming at us. When he swerved into our lane, he looked straight at me. What an idiot that guy is."

"At least no one got hurt. We'll probably never run into the guy again. He's sure to be stopped by the police if he keeps driving that way. I told you they're very strict about speed limits here. Remember, ease off the gas pedal if you go anywhere without me."

"Check. Mr. Blue Eyes...you'd better hope I don't run into you again."

Kyleigh grimaced. If only HPD would be as concerned about her father as they were about how people drove. *But if we bug them enough, they might be more inclined to find Dad.*

Chapter Seven

K yleigh picked up the last can of tomato sauce from the grocery bag, stowed it in the kitchen cabinet, and sat on a stool at the counter. "Well, we're stocked for about a week now. Hope it doesn't take that long to find out where my dad has disappeared to. Since I got a run-around when I called the post, I'll take a ride down there to see if I can corner the colonel. I may not get anywhere, but I'll feel better for trying."

"Right. I'll grab my purse." Marisa sprinted toward the guestroom.

"No. You stay here and do your research on what you want to see before we go home. I'll be fine." She snatched the car keys from the table in the foyer and hastened for the door. But before she turned the knob, she spun and stuck her head into the living room, where Marisa had plopped onto the couch.

"Hey, better yet. I'll leave the car for you in case you want to go somewhere while I'm gone." Kyleigh tossed the keys to Marisa. "I'll take Dad's dirt bike." She rushed into the guestroom and clutched her helmet. It had been a couple of years since wearing it. Not since her last visit with Dad. She returned to the living room.

"Ky, are you sure you'll be okay on the bike? What's written on the helmet?"

Kyleigh laughed. "I'll be fine. It says, 'Let me teach you a thing or two.' Dad bought me a new one the last time I was here and had this written on it to remind me of what he taught me about riding." She drew in a deep breath. "I should have visited more often. We had such fun riding the range that summer."

Marisa's expression had changed from amused to puzzled.

"Not that kind of range." Kyleigh shook her head. "It's what they call Koʻolau. We rode bikes all over the mountain range."

"Oh, okay. I didn't think they had ranges like Texas." Marisa giggled. "Don't worry. We'll find your dad, Ky. There must be some sort of mess up somewhere. I'm sure he'll show up. Maybe it's all a mistake at the post. He could be off on an assignment nobody told the colonel about."

After Kyleigh had wiped the moisture from her eyes and blown her nose, she took the bike lock key out of the drawer in the foyer table and moved toward the front door again. "That's unlikely. You obviously don't know anything about military life. Trust me, nothing happens his CO doesn't know about. Anyway, I'm off for the post, and then probably wherever the information the colonel might give me leads. If nothing else, I'll take a long relaxing ride to clear my mind. If you do decide to go out, take care, and have a good time exploring."

"You be careful, too, Ky. And call me if you find out anything...or get lost...or—"

"I'll be fine." Kyleigh slipped out the door and unlocked the chain that secured the dirt bike to the post. She walked the off-road vehicle down the long entrance porch and onto the street. Swinging her capri-covered leg over the seat, she mounted the bike. She engaged the starter lever and pushed down firmly, bringing the engine to life. She'd forgotten what a rush it gave her.

As Kyleigh neared Ft. Shafter and viewed the Koʻolau Mountain Range in the distance, she pictured the trails through the dense forest she and her father had taken on the mountains two years ago. She cringed at the memory of the root she'd tried to ride over that almost resulted in her flying off the dirt bike and into the vegetation, which hid a sheer drop-off. If her dad hadn't been close enough to grab her, she'd have soared over the edge of the cliff like a baby eagle and then dropped without a momma eagle to catch her. Her heartbeat zipped into overdrive. Somehow the bike had escaped damage, and she'd survived the incident with only scrapes and bruises. *Thank You for Your protection that day, Lord.*

Wait a minute. Could Dad have gone up there with his new dirt bike? He may have had an accident. "He might be up there now, somewhere no one has seen him."

Kyleigh continued east, past Ft. Shafter. She turned left to Kamehameha IV Road and sped on to Highway 63 and then 83, taking her north. The Koʻolau mountain range loomed large and ominous in front of her on the east side of the island. The top shrouded in a cloud.

Marisa finished her list of information to research and places to check out before they went back to Houston. She'd need interesting things to show the class, as well as tell them. It would be a fun social studies project. She could find small trinkets from the island to give to the boys and girls at the luau party.

She stuffed the list into her purse, grabbed the maps from Aunt Maye, and sauntered to the foyer. As she was about to open the front door, a phone rang. "That's not mine." She followed the sound toward the bedrooms.

In the master bedroom, the nightstand drawer gaped open. The strap from Kyleigh's purse hung out. "Oh, no! Ky left her bag and cell here." She lifted the phone from the drawer and answered. "Hello?"

"Marisa? What are you doing with my niece's phone? Is she okay?"

Marisa clenched her teeth. "She's gone off without it, Aunt Maye. She took her father's dirt bike to the Army post to talk to her dad's commanding officer. I guess she was in such a hurry, she forgot it."

"How long has she been gone? I just spoke to Colonel Stevens. She's not there."

"About half an hour, and according to the map you gave us, it takes at least that to get there. She should arrive any minute unless she realized she left her purse and phone here and is on the way to pick them up. Did the colonel have any news about your brother?"

"Yes, he did. This morning he found out Charlie suspected a civilian of selling illegal drugs on the post. The colonel contacted the Honolulu Police Department about it. Charlie's secretary, or staff personnel sergeant—that's what the colonel called her—has been sick with bronchitis for several days. She's the one who knew what Charlie suspected but didn't realize the major had turned up missing. From the morning reports, the colonel knew she was sick at home last week. But he had no reason to contact her while she was on medical leave. He had assigned a substitute to help out in the office." This morning, when the sergeant found out they were looking for Charlie, she got ahold of the colonel and told him the major had planned to talk to him about the suspicious activity on the post."

"So, I'm assuming the colonel didn't know anything about the drugs. I wonder why your brother didn't tell him in the first place."

"You're right. He didn't know. Colonel Stevens told me he remembered my brother asking to talk with him about a problem. The colonel said he told my brother he'd meet with him the next day, but then Charlie didn't report for duty. So, he never had a chance to tell his CO."

"Oh, dear. Ky's gonna really be worried now. We were at the police department this morning, and they had nothing new to tell us except two detectives were working the case. We didn't get to meet with them because they had just left the building. I wonder if they knew about this."

"I imagine they must since the colonel contacted the Honolulu Police Department early this morning. I'm sure the detectives were told. Well, I have to go. The mother of one of my charges is here to pick him up. Please have Kyleigh call me when she gets back. I'd like to reassure her the police know what they're doing."

"Yes, ma'am. I will. Bye." *Wow.* As if Ky's stress level wasn't high enough already. *I wonder why Aunt Maye wants to reassure her.* Almost as if Ky didn't trust the police to find her father.

A red light caught Kyleigh before she turned onto the highway that led to the mountain range. She'd better call Marisa and tell her about the altered plan. When the light changed to green, Kyleigh maneuvered the bike to the side of the road.

That's just great. She'd left her purse and phone at the apartment. Oh well. She'd be okay as long as she abided by the speed limit. No way would she waste time going back for them.

Kyleigh pulled out onto the highway and proceeded on her mission. *Lord, please keep Dad safe.* Tears fogged her eyes. One at a time, she wiped away the mist with her fingers. She had to get herself together, or she wouldn't be any good to him.

As she drove on the elevated highway that led to the mountain range, the majestic Koʻolau range ascended skyward like a heavy green curtain. Volcanoes, landslides, and erosion had carved the fluted cliff face into a breathtaking view, rising over three thousand feet at its highest point. Not as grand as the Rockies in the upper states, but just as magnificent, if anyone were to ask her opinion.

With her anxiety in full swing, Kyleigh made her way up the road to the spot where her Dad had started their trail ride a couple of years earlier. Fortunately, she'd remembered the place, although it looked like the path hadn't seen much traffic recently. There probably weren't too many people experienced enough to handle the twists and turns, bumps and dips on this stretch. Hard to believe all this unspoiled nature could exist so near to modern civilization. Half an hour or less away.

Kyleigh paused at the entrance to the route they'd taken and ran her hands across the tops of ferns on either side of her. So lush. She'd forgotten how beautiful it was up here. She wrapped her fingers around the clutch lever and throttle and started down the trail at a slow pace. Her eyes moved from side to side to make sure she didn't miss any broken twig or place that looked like someone had gone through the overgrowth. Other dirt bike engines whirred not too far away. Surely, if Dad had fallen, someone would have come across him within the past week, even on this obscure run. Unless...he'd gone over. Her stomach dropped.

At a slight clearing, Kyleigh stopped. Three narrow trails intersected the path she followed. Barely visible, hers continued on the other side. She took a deep breath to calm herself and readied to continue her search. Dad had to be here somewhere. The way would be harder from here on with all the roots sticking up above the ground. She'd better get a move on if she wanted to find her father before dark. This wasn't a safe place to wander after sundown.

She took the path she and her father had taken so many times, following the edge of the cliffs. After coming over a low hill, she descended to another small clearing and stopped to check a thick stand of ferns. No sign of disturbance here. She stretched her neck to gaze over the drop-off. The rocky edge of the range resembled a petrified waterfall with tufts of vegetation poking out. Far below appeared a dense forest. She pulled herself back with a gasp.

As she moved into the trail, the high-pitched whine of the chain from another dirt bike neared. Someone was coming. She only hoped they wouldn't ruin any evidence she might find further down the path. She'd better get into the brush on the other side.

Kyleigh inched away from the cliffside of the mountain and aimed the bike forward toward the inside of the trail. A screaming exhaust note broke through the air from the rise behind her. She turned to look.

The bike and rider sailed over the hill right at her.

Kyleigh's mouth dropped open. *"Stop!"* Too late.

Chapter Eight

With an *oomph*, Kyleigh landed on her side with her left leg wedged underneath the bike. Her head smacked the ground with a thud. She gasped for breath. The whirring of engines stopped.

"Hey. Are you okay?" a muffled masculine voice said. "I'm so sorry." A blur of blue dismounted his bike, laid it onto the path, and lifted the bike off Kyleigh.

She eased off her helmet, grabbed her head, and slowly rolled onto her knees. A whirl of green, blue, and brown made her lower her forehead to the dirt. Would she pass out? She couldn't. Not up here in the mountain. Not with a stranger and no one else around. *God, help.*

"Don't stand up yet," the male voice came a little clearer as the ringing in her ear diminished. "Do you feel any pain?"

Kyleigh peered up to the blue blur and focused. She raised her eyes to the man who stood over her. "Yes! In my neck. But I'm sure *he'll* leave in a few minutes." Ignoring his outstretched hand, she rose to her feet and pressed her eyes closed for a second. After a deep breath, she opened them again, and her vision cleared. She turned her head to glare at the careless rider who had slammed into her. "*You!*"

Brad Pitt's double stared at her. "You're one of the girls from outside the police department."

"That's right, mister. You have a problem with knocking down visitors to your island, don't you? Can't you watch where you're going? You shouldn't have driven that fast in the first place." Kyleigh brushed the dirt off her capris and shirt. "Of all the stupid things—why didn't you slow down?"

"Look. I apologized once. I admit it's my fault."

"It sure is, buster." She hauled her dad's bike up by the handle and remounted.

He rushed to her, straddled the front wheel, and latched onto the handlebar. "You can't ride off after an accident like that. You might pass out."

"Let go. Leave me alone. I'm fine, despite your attempt to run me off the cliff." Who did this guy think he was? She jerked backward to free herself from his grip.

He held fast. "Please listen to me. I said I'm in the wrong, and I'm trying to apologize. Riding up here on Ko'olau usually takes my mind off things, but it didn't work this time. I was going too fast while mulling over a problem, and when I came over the last rise and saw you, it was too late to slow down or avoid the collision. I was already airborne. But I never expected someone to be idling there in the middle of the track."

Kyleigh glowered at him and tried again to yank the bike away from his grasp. Was that a smirk on his face?

"Don't misunderstand me." The man continued to hold the handlebar. "I'm not blaming you for being there."

Kyleigh narrowed her eyes. "Some people just love to ride like no one else matters. The get-out-of-my-way-coming-through attitude. Do you drive a car like that too? Your friend does! He almost ran us off the road earlier today when we left the police station."

Her assailant dropped his head. "I was in that car. Again, I apologize. We were on our way to—well, we had to go somewhere fast. My partner felt bad about it afterward."

Her fury ebbed. This guy did sound sincere. "Will you *please* get off my bike?"

"Are you going to accept my apology?" He added a smile to the earnest appearance.

A tingle went through Kyleigh's chest. "Are you holding me for ransom?"

He sighed and swung his leg back over the wheel to free her bike. "I want to make this right." He held out his hand to her. "Can we start over?"

"You mean you want another shot at me? Maybe you'll run me over the side of the mountain this time."

As his smile faded, he reminded her of a sad puppy. A twinge of guilt hit her.

He blew a lungful of air between his lips and withdrew his hand. "Shot down again. My name is Jerard, but everyone calls me Jer. I'm sorry I didn't pay attention. I'm even sorrier that I almost—I'm sorry. *Please* forgive me."

There was that sincere expression again. *Cut the man some slack, Kyleigh.* He sure was cute. A smile tickled at the corner of her mouth while warmth rose in her neck. She focused on the bike frame.

He tilted his head to the side and gazed into her eyes. "You still haven't told me if you're hurt."

She mentally checked for pain. "No. I'm fine. I'll be sore tomorrow, but for now, I'll live. And yes, I'll accept your apology. Are *you* okay?"

He had the most alluring smile she'd ever seen. Even bigger than at the police station. Big as a Texas sunset. *Easy, girl.* She knew his name, but he was still a stranger.

"I'm fine. I've had worse spills than that on the track. These tree roots will kill you." He pointed down the trail where she was headed. A massive root protruded from the dirt at least a foot high.

"Yes. I remember from the last time I rode here. That particular one and I have a history, I believe."

"So we're good, right?" He thrust his hand at her again.

She placed her hand in his. "I guess so."

"And your name is?" He squeezed.

"Kyleigh. Kyleigh Flanagan."

His eyes popped.

She withdrew her hand and backed away. Why the reaction? Her eyes narrowed.

Jerard retreated to his bike. Could she be—? Was that why she'd been at the station? "Kyleigh, are you by any chance related to a Major Charles Flanagan?"

Her eyes rounded. "You know my dad? Where is he?" She jumped off the bike and grabbed his arm. "Tell me."

"I don't know. He told me about you when he came to see us last week."

"What do you mean? What did he say?"

Her face was a mere two inches from his. At least, it seemed like it to him. Jer put his hands on her upper arms and held her at arm's length. "Calm down, Kyleigh. Your dad came to us with suspicions of illegal activity on the post. He wanted to contact someone there but said he wasn't sure who to trust. He planned to talk to his CO, but from what the colonel said, he never did. "

"Don't tell me to calm down. Who are you? And why were you talking to Dad's CO?"

"I'm Preston O'Shea. A detective with the Honolulu Police."

"You said your name was Jerard." She glared at him.

As heat rose in his neck, he pressed his lips together. "Yeah, I did. My full name is Preston Jerard O'Shea. I only use Preston in an official capacity. Can't stand the name."

He viewed the clouds, which had grown thick with mist. "Let's shelter under those trees before we're soaked. This'll pass soon. I call this dewy, soft rain a love shower because it's like getting kissed by the cloud. But after a while, you'll be as wet as if you'd run under a faucet. Actually, I didn't come up with the name. I heard it from my father, who heard it from an Army buddy of his, who said it was the popular name for the mist back then about twenty-odd years ago. Many here on the island now call it the manoa mist. Manoa means thick or solid, so I guess that fits too. But I like my name for the misty rain better." He smiled. When had he become such a motor mouth?

Her brows pinched. "I don't care what it's called or if I get drenched. Where's *my* dad?"

Jer took her by the elbow, picked up her bike, and rolled it to her. "I'll tell you everything over there." He pointed across the brush to a large tree, resembling ferns perched on top of the many branches of a sizable old Spanish oak trunk. "The big koa over there. Come on." He took hold of his motorbike and led her across the trail.

They braced the bikes against the koa tree and leaned on the trunk.

Jer gazed into Kyleigh's eyes, which misted as much as the overhead clouds. He touched her shoulder with his fingers. "We have no idea where your dad is right now. We only found out he was missing this morning. He was supposed to meet with us today. When his CO told us he hadn't reported for duty, my partner and I decided to check a couple of places we thought he might be. We were on our way there when my partner Swanson almost hit your car. You've not heard from your father?"

"No. What's the illegal activity you mentioned?"

He hesitated before he answered. "Kyleigh, I can't discuss an ongoing investigation with you. Trust me. We'll locate your dad."

"Why should I trust you?"

"I told you, I'm a detective with the Honolulu Police Department."

"So you say."

"Here." He flipped his wallet out of his pocket and showed her his badge and identification. Whoa, buddy, she was beautiful. But annoying. He wasn't sure if he wanted to hug her...or throttle her. "Now, let's make our way to where I parked my truck. I need to ask you some more questions."

Kyleigh's anger soared again. Why were they leaving the trail? She stood still as the soft rain stopped, and Jer pulled his bike from the koa tree. "No. My dad could lie hurt out here somewhere, and all you can think to do is question me? Uh-uh. No. I'll continue my search."

She grabbed her bike and headed back to the spot where Jer had run into her.

"Wait. I'll come with you."

"Don't bother. Make your report. I don't care. I need to find my father." Now, who wasn't using aloha toward others?

Kyleigh mounted the bike and sped down the trail as fast and as far away from him as possible. She'd have to be careful going over the roots to avoid an encore performance of two years ago. There'd be no father to catch her.

Within minutes, she had arrived at another trail crossing. Jer came up right behind her. She glanced back at him and huffed. "If you *must* come, keep your distance from my bike. I don't want a repeat of what happened a little while ago. Better yet, go ahead of me." Maybe he'd break his neck on one of those exposed roots. *That was horrible, Kyleigh.*

Jer made his way around her and entered the narrow trail. Several yards further, he stopped and faced her. "Don't ride too close to the edge. The path is wider ahead, but the left side drops off to the forest far below, and the shower may have made the ground soft. We'll take it slow. Look for any damaged plants."

"Really? What do you think I was doing before you ran over me?" She did it again. *Quit, Kyleigh.*

"Enough." He turned around on the bike seat and frowned. "I just want to help. You don't have to bite my head off at everything I say."

Kyleigh's cheeks flooded with heat. He was right. She bit her lip. *At least try to be nice, even if he is annoying.*

They rode through the trail and watched for signs of anything unusual. For an hour, they searched the trail for evidence her father had been there. Jer stopped and turned off the engine. "We'll have to carry the bikes over this next section. The roots are too numerous and too high. Can you lift yours?"

"I'll do fine." She dismounted and hoisted the bike. Heavier than she'd thought. It had been too long since she was on a dirt bike.

Jer looked back at her. She'd fallen several yards behind. He lowered his bike, walked it back to her, and braced it against the head-high rock edge on the inside of the trail. "Let me have it."

He lifted the bike onto his shoulder. "No sense wearing yourself out. Increases the risk of an accident. Sit on this rock and wait until I come back. I'll walk the bikes one at a time over this rough area. You can follow me when I come back for mine."

Without waiting for her to answer, he left with her bike. Not more than several feet into the trail, he disappeared into the foliage. Kyleigh surveyed her surroundings. So quiet. She'd forgotten *how* quiet. Not even a bird chirp. Sure different from the woods in Texas. The noisy dirt bikes no doubt scare the birds away.

Leaves rustled in the breeze over her head, and an uneasy sensation gripped her. Was someone out there in the brush? Great. Now she'd developed paranoia. *Relax. Enjoy the peacefulness.*

Several minutes passed, and Jer didn't return. Should she take his bike and follow? He said to wait here. *Come on, Jer.*

Footfalls running through vegetation sounded from above and behind her. Kyleigh jumped off the rock and spun. She tried to peer past the brush at the top of the rocky wall, but it was too tall. As she backed up to the other side of the trail for a better view, she ran into a huge spider web. Kyleigh moved to the middle of the trail. Her arms flailed to rid herself of the sticky mess.

Thump! Jer landed right beside her. She inhaled a sharp breath.

"Will you stop doing that?" Was that a snicker?

"Doing what? I took a shortcut across the brush instead of the trail and had to jump down. I know this range inside and out. Lived here all my life. Did I scare you?"

She glared at him. It *was* a snicker. "I don't scare that easily." She brushed off the remnants of the web and went back to the rock.

"No. I didn't think you were the type. Let's go." He raised the bike to his shoulder and headed down the trail.

Kyleigh fell into step with him. "I take it you noticed nothing abnormal."

"Not a thing. From here on, the path is downhill with fewer roots sticking out, so it'll be an easy ride." He checked his watch. "We'd better go. It starts to get dark on the range around six-thirty this time of year, in one and a half hours. We still have to ride back to my truck, but at least the road's paved. Did you come by car?"

"No, I rode the bike."

His brows raised. "Are you staying at your dad's apartment or a hotel?"

"The apartment."

"That's a long ride on a dirt bike. I'll give you a lift back."

They reached her bike and continued down the mountain range to the road. Kyleigh's heart sank. Not one sign of any disturbed flora along the way. The rock in Kyleigh's stomach grew harder. But that could mean he's okay.

When they arrived at Jer's truck, Kyleigh asked, "Now what? I still don't know where my dad is."

"*Now*, I drive you back to your dad's, and *you* let us continue our investigation."

Wonderful. She was back to where she'd been this morning. Could she trust this man to find her father?

Chapter Nine

*J*er and Kyleigh arrived at the base of the mountain range. He glanced at her. Why had she seemed so distrustful of him? Had he said something wrong? He leaned his bike against the side of the truck. "Roll yours over here, and I'll lift it into the bed."

"This isn't necessary. I rode it here. I can ride it back to the apartment."

"You can't."

Kyleigh crossed her arms and glared. "Why not?"

"Because, when you lost your balance and fell at the bottom of the trail, your headlight broke. Plus, your fall indicates you're not steady on your feet yet from when I slammed into you." While Kyleigh examined the light, Jer pulled the bike away from her and hoisted it into the truck bed. "I'll fix it since I'm to blame for your lightheadedness."

He opened the passenger door for her. Before slipping into the seat, she inspected the interior.

Jer lifted his dirt bike into the bed, grabbed straps and tie-downs from the utility box, and secured both vehicles. He jumped to the ground and hopped into the driver's seat. "What were you looking for in here?"

"Nothing. I was impressed with how clean you keep the truck. You must not use it very much."

"I drive it everywhere. She's a classic seventy-two Jeep Gladiator, and Nellybelle deserves to be taken care of. When I graduated from college, my dad gave her to me. He's restored vintage cars and trucks all my life."

"Nellybelle?" She covered her mouth with her hand. "Where did you come up with a name like that?"

"From watching old Roy Rogers reruns with my dad." He pursed his lips. "They had a Jeep in the series. Dad dubbed her." He stuck the key in the ignition and glanced at Kyleigh. "Quit trying to stifle that laugh before you hurt yourself."

She held one hand out, palm toward him while chortling into the other. When she calmed herself, she took a deep breath. "My dad's been interested in old cars for as long as I can remember. But he's been too busy with his career in the military to work on them. This is immaculate...as if it just came off the showroom floor. And I like the name Nellybelle."

"Mahalo. She has some battle scars on the exterior, but I never had an accident with her."

Kyleigh smiled. "You probably wouldn't be able to say that if you lived in Houston."

"You mean y'all don't ride horses everywhere?" He laughed. The ice had finally melted.

"Horses?" Kyleigh chuckled. "I wouldn't take a horse on the highways in Houston or anywhere near it." She pressed her lips together.

Jer pulled onto the road, which led out of the mountainous area.

"Visiting Oʻahu is like coming to another country in some ways." Kyleigh gazed out the side window as he drove. "Beautiful."

"Have you visited our island much?"

"Not as much as I wish I had. I could've spent every summer here, spring breaks, Christmas. Many missed opportunities to be with my dad, and now—" She sighed and focused on the scenery.

Jer reached over and touched her arm. "Kyleigh. We will find your father. You'll have many years to visit the island and spend time with him."

She sniffled. "Thanks. I hope so."

He brought the truck to a stop on the side of the road and rummaged around in a box behind the driver's seat. A flashlight fell to hand and then a pack of tissues. He handed the tissues to Kyleigh. "Didn't you have a purse with you? Did you lose it on the trail?" Jer aimed the beam at the windshield, causing the light to reflect on her face.

Kyleigh turned a beautiful shade of rosy pink. "Um. I was in such a hurry to leave the apartment this morning..." She grimaced. "I left it behind. I'm in trouble, aren't I?"

Jer suppressed a laugh. How could he report her when she was so—? The laugh burst out. "I'll let you off with a warning."

"Thank you...or, mahalo."

As Jer continued his drive south toward the apartment complex, Kyleigh rested her head on the back of the seat. "I *had* planned to go to the post and see if I could get information out of Dad's CO before I decided to check on Koʻolau. So far, he's told us nothing except that my father hasn't shown up or called. I'd think by now their investigative unit would have found something. Wouldn't you?" Her brows pinched. "You said you're working on the case. Isn't there anything you can tell me?"

The Makakilo Kauhale Apartments came into view. Jer pulled into the entrance and followed Kyleigh's directions. When he parked the truck in front of her dad's apartment and turned off the engine, he twisted to face her. "Kyleigh, all I can say is your dad was suspicious about something on the post. When he dropped in to talk to us about it, he had no proof. We told him we'd take it from there. A couple of days later, I called him more than once, but they went to voicemail. And when I called the post, they said he wasn't in. Did you see his phone in the apartment?"

"No. Didn't think to look for it. I've phoned him several times since we arrived, but never heard it ring. I got voicemail each time too." She bit her lower lip.

Jer glanced at his watch. "Too late to go to the post now, but I could go with you tomorrow. We'd need to keep it under wraps that I'm a detective. You could say I'm your boyfriend." He peeked at her from the corner of his eye. That idea didn't seem to bother her.

"Okay. Guess you want to observe his reactions while he talks to me."

"That and keep an eye out for anything going on. I figure we can ride around and check things out while we're on the post."

"Check what out?"

"Not sure yet, but I'll know it when I see it."

He wasn't at all what she first thought he'd be like. Instead, he's a real gentleman. Kyleigh's neck grew warm. Pass him off as her boyfriend? *Hmmm.* She tittered to herself. But she'd known him less than a day.

A flutter rose in her stomach. Even when she'd lashed out at him, he treated her with respect. *Get a grip.* She'd be back in Houston soon. Her heart sank, and a homesick sensation overcame her. Was it because of her father...or Jer?

Kyleigh fidgeted with her hands. "What time do you think we should leave tomorrow?"

"I'll check and call you tonight if I may."

"Yes." Her heart skipped a beat. "Give me your phone, and I'll punch in the number for you. Better yet, you could come in for coffee?" She checked the parking area and saw her dad's Mustang. Good. "Marisa's back from her day of exploring."

"Coffee sounds great."

Kyleigh opened the passenger door and slid out. She waited while he drove into the lot and parked. With a grin, Jer jumped out of the cab, hoisted the major's bike from the truck bed, and jogged toward her with it.

She spun, and he followed her through the covered entry to the front door. Before Kyleigh could knock, the door flew open.

"You've had me on pins and needles all day, Ky." Marisa's eyes were like saucers. "You left without your purse, and when I called the post, no one had seen you. Where have you been?" She stared at Jer. "With him?" She stretched her neck to look around him. "Where's your hotrod friend?"

"Ahhh..." Kyleigh reached her arm around her friend's shoulder and drew her into the foyer while Jer leaned the bike against the lanai awning support. "Do you suppose we could come in before I give my explanation?"

Jer entered the apartment behind them and shut the door.

"You're worse than my aunt." Kyleigh led the way to the kitchen and took two mugs from the cabinet. "I invited Jer in for coffee."

Marisa glanced at him, then back to Kyleigh with a quirked eyebrow. "*Jer?*"

A smile stretched across his face. He held out his hand to Marisa. "Jer O'Shea."

"You're one of the detectives on the case."

"Guilty as charged."

She took his hand. "That means Swanson is your hotshot partner, right?"

"Guilty again." Jer snickered.

"Do you have a cup, Marisa?"

"Yes." She hustled to the living room.

Kyleigh brewed the first cup. "When I left here, I started for the post and then had a notion to check the bike trails Dad frequented. Thought something might have happened to him on the mountain range. I couldn't call to tell you because I left my purse and phone here."

Marisa returned to the kitchen island with her mug and hopped onto the stool next to Jer. She lowered her brows. "You two were up there all this time? And why didn't you come back first to tell me?"

"By the time I realized I didn't have my purse, I was almost to the mountain. I wasn't about to drive all the way back."

"And you?" She turned to Jer. "You didn't answer me. Where's your maniac partner who almost ran us off the road?"

Kyleigh muttered to herself, "Jer did a pretty good job of almost running me off the road too."

Marisa shifted her stare. "What did you say, Ky?"

"Nothing. I'll tell you later. Right now, coffee." Kyleigh handed the first cup to Jer and slid a creamer, sugar bowl, and a spoon next to it. She started Marisa's brew. "I haven't eaten since breakfast. Jer, would you like to stay for dinner?"

His smile widened. "I don't want to put you to any trouble." He turned to Marisa. "To answer your question, Bryce isn't with me.

We tend to find our own amusements after work. We left at noon today. I picked up my bike and ventured to Koʻolau. That's where I ran into Kyleigh...literally." He chuckled.

Kyleigh peeked at Jer. He had shown concern for her up there. "Yes. He almost ran me off the mountain. But, as I said, I'll tell you everything later. Have you eaten dinner, Marisa? Dinner's no problem, Jer. We have to eat anyway."

As she pinned Kyleigh with a stare, Marisa planted her hands on her hips. "You've got a lot of explaining to do, lady. I've been too nervous and worried about you to eat. Haven't even had lunch."

"Oh, dear! You really were upset. I'm sorry, Marisa. I'll make it up to you." She handed her the steaming cup of coffee and started her own. "So, let's have three of those steaks we bought this morning. Jer, there's a grill on the lanai. Would you mind firing it up? And while you do that, I'll enter my number into your phone."

He laid the cell on the counter and saluted her. "I'm a pro with a grill." Jer headed for the sliding glass doors at the back of the living room.

While he prepared the bar-b-que, Kyleigh gave Marisa a rundown of all that had happened on Koʻolau.

"I'm sorry you didn't find your dad, Ky. Ooo...almost forgot. Aunt Maye called after you left and said the colonel found out the major was investigating something and had talked to the police about it. I think we need to go back to HPD and demand answers."

"Dad *did* contact them. He talked to him." She pointed to Jer just as he lit the grill. A whoosh of flames shot out. "He and his partner, whom I assume you're still angry at, are investigating. Jer and I are going to the post tomorrow morning. The colonel may know more about what's going on than he told Aunt Maye or Jer. I'd better call her. Here." She handed the package of steaks and the bottle of seasoning to Marisa.

Aunt Maye must be beside herself with worry.

As Jer stepped back into the apartment, Kyleigh hung up her cell with a reserved smile. "Was that word about your dad?"

She shook her head. "No. My aunt. She's worried about Dad. He and his sister are close. She's been like a mom to me since my mother died. Aunt Maye feels helpless being stuck back in Houston and not able to do anything but pray."

Jer nodded. "Fire's going. It should be hot enough in about fifteen minutes. The best thing she can do is pray." He could understand now why Kyleigh was so resolute about finding her dad. Only one parent. And with her aunt worried too—.

"Thanks. I told her." Kyleigh leaned on the third stool at the kitchen island. "Marisa, would you set the table while I make a salad? Jer, you sit and relax. Wouldn't want you to *bump* into one of us and cause an *accident*." She chortled.

"Hilarious. But I'd like to help. I don't mind working for my dinner."

"We've got this. You already paid your dues with the grill."

Jer laughed and hopped onto the stool. "Have you two been friends long?"

Kyleigh glanced at Marisa, who grinned like a Cheshire cat. In unison, they said, "Since we were in high school." Kyleigh added, "And these days, we teach at the same school."

As Marisa placed plates and utensils on the dining table a few feet away from the kitchen island, she said, "Ky has the fun job. She teaches kindergartners. I have it rough. Second graders." She laughed. "But I love them."

"Boy. Wish I had had teachers as pretty as you two when I was in school." Especially one who had strawberry-colored streaks in her long, wavy hair. He winked at Kyleigh and turned to Marisa. "Hope you're easier on those kids when they mess up than you have been on my partner and me for our carelessness this morning." His mouth formed an exaggerated pout.

Kyleigh shook her head. *Drama king.* As Marisa waltzed by with an armful of condiments, Kyleigh elbowed her.

"Hey! I almost dropped the bottle of steak sauce." She looked from Kyleigh to Jer. "I was never mad at you. You weren't driving the car that your *partner* almost hit us with. Scared me to death."

"I apologize for Bryce's driving. As I explained to Kyleigh, we had gotten a phone call and needed to check out something right away. But I gave Bryce a tongue lashing." Jer raised his brows at her. "He's an okay guy. Somewhat flippant now and then, but he means nothing by it. To change the subject...judging by your last name, I take it you're Italian."

"I am. Something wrong with that?" Marisa placed the condiments on the table, turned toward Jer, and folded her arms across her abdomen.

"Not a thing." Italian. That explained her ire. What a little tiger. "I was just wondering how Irish and Latin temperaments became such close friends."

Kyleigh flashed him a narrow-eyed stare. "Marisa's also half Irish, but how did you know *I'm* Irish?"

"Never met a Flanagan who wasn't. I've met some feisty Irishmen in my profession." None as gorgeous as this one, though.

"Right. Speaking of your profession. What have you heard of the trouble at Ft. Shafter?"

"Nice try, *Miss Flanagan*, but I told you I can't discuss an ongoing case."

Kyleigh frowned at him.

He bit his lip to hide a grin. Adorable. Even when she didn't smile. Would she still be able to smile after their trip to the post tomorrow morning? Would the colonel give them any information that would lead them to Kyleigh's father?

Chapter Ten

The following morning, Kyleigh awoke to the aroma of bacon. *Ha.* Guess Marisa got hungry and couldn't wait. She peeked at the clock on her dad's nightstand. "Wow. Eight o'clock already." She shouldn't have stayed up so late talking to Jer last night. But she hadn't met a man who wasn't full of himself in such a long time, until now. He might prove dependable after all.

Kyleigh swung her legs out from under the sheet and planted her feet on the floor. After a quick shower, she dressed, made her bed, and then strolled into the kitchen.

Marisa sat at the island with eggs and bacon in front of her, a large bowl of yogurt and fruit to the side. "Sorry, Ky. I just couldn't wait any longer. My stomach felt like I'd forgotten how to swallow." She slid a forkful of scrambled eggs into her mouth and smiled.

"I understand. You do have to eat often, don't you?"

Marisa nodded as she chewed and washed her food down with a gulp of coffee. "Yes. Never can go for long without getting hungry. I've been this way since I was a little kid. Mom said I was as bad as my brothers when they were teens. I could have eaten one of those high-protein candy bars we bought, but the bacon had my name on it. What are your plans with Jer this morning?" She bounced her brows up and down. "Last night, I left you two involved in a *cozy* chat out on the lanai. I needed my beauty sleep."

Kyleigh laughed. "Hey, this is a vacation for you. You eat when you want to. You don't need to wait for me. Jer is taking me to Ft. Shafter this morning to talk to the colonel." Her phone jingled from the bedroom. "That'll be Jer."

She ran and snatched the cell. "Jer?" The line went dead. She checked the screen. Must have been a wrong number.

She jogged back to the kitchen and poured herself a bowl of cornflakes, splashed milk on top, and sprinkled the cereal with sugar. At the counter, she slid onto the stool next to Marisa, who finished her yogurt.

"So you're hoping to get more information about your dad from his commanding officer? Is your new boyfriend on his way?"

"Marisa, he's not my boyfriend." Kyleigh narrowed her eyes at her friend. "I only met him yesterday. He's the detective searching for my dad, remember?" She spooned cereal into her mouth.

"Yeah. But he carried on like he was your boyfriend last night, sure 'nuff. Didn't you notice the way he kept his eyes on you? And his expression said it all. He's got it bad for you, girl."

Kyleigh almost choked on the cereal, swallowed, and dropped her jaw. "*Marisa.* You've jumped to a conclusion, as usual. He couldn't possibly be that interested in me after one day, any more than I could be interested in him." Or could she?

"I'm sorry, but he *did* appear to be in love when he gazed at you. Wish someone would fall in love with me while we're here in paradise." Her hand flew up to her mouth. "That sounded pathetic, didn't it? Guess I watch too much TV. All those quickie romances. That doesn't really happen. But Jer acted like he was smitten, as they say in those historical novels you read. Smitten like a kitten." She laughed.

Kyleigh chuckled. She took a sip of coffee and finished her breakfast. "I'm anxious to talk to Colonel Stevens and find out if he knows more than he's told us so far."

Her cell jingled again. The picture she'd taken of Jer last night popped onto the screen. "That's Jer now." She lifted the cell from the counter. "Hi."

"Good morning. I'm on my way to pick you up. Will you be ready?"

Jer pulled the truck into a parking space at the apartment complex and hopped out. He strode toward Major Flanagan's front door, but Kyleigh rushed out before he got halfway there.

No waiting for this lady. "Alrighty then. Let's go." He led her to the truck.

After he got behind the wheel, he turned to her. "Hope you won't act as anxious when you talk to the colonel. Most of those guys don't like to be interrogated. You'll have to remain calm and collected, even though your insides are running wild. Which is understandable. And I won't say anything since your dad said...well, I'll just be quiet."

"There you go again. The more you won't say about what's happening or happened, the more I worry about Dad."

Jer's lips pulled to the left, and he nodded. He faced the windshield, turned the key to start the engine, and headed for the street. "Remember, I'm your boyfriend if anyone asks." That rolled off the tip of his tongue easily. Not a bad thought. He peeked at her. A glimmer of a smile sat on her lips. *Nice.* "Were you able to sleep enough last night? I shouldn't have stayed so late."

"I slept well. Did you?"

"*Very* well. Dreamed of a lovely cowgirl." He glanced at her for a second and then focused on the traffic. That smile had to mean something. "Hope you enjoyed our chat last night as much as I did. I learned a lot about Texas. And the company was the best I've had in a long time."

Again, he glanced at her. Her face glowed. The smile had grown, so she must have enjoyed it too. Silence took over the cab for a minute before she responded.

"Thank you. Since I first got that letter from Dad, I've not had a moment of relaxation. Or, I should say, the supposed letter from Dad." She took a deep breath and leaned back against the headrest. "I always appreciate a chance to watch the sunset from the lanai. And our conversation was enjoyable."

"Kyleigh, I'm sorry to change the subject, but did you bring the letter with you? I should have asked when you first told me you'd brought it to Oʻahu."

"Drat! It never occurred to me to show it to you. I have it in my carry-on."

"When we return from the post, I'll take the letter and have it checked at work. We might be able to tell if it came from your father or not. And if it didn't come from him, who did write it?

Fingerprints are no doubt out of the question by now because of all the hands it may have passed through, but we could get lucky and find something."

At Ft. Shafter, Kyleigh and Jer waited outside Colonel Stevens' office. Kyleigh watched as Jer rose and strode to the wall-to-wall windows across the room. With his cheek almost pressed to the window, he gazed down to the street. She studied his profile. Such a serious look. His eyes narrowed. He seemed more than interested in something outside.

The clean-shaven personnel assistant in his crisp uniform rose from his desk. "Miss Flanagan, the colonel will see you now." He opened the colonel's office door.

Jer turned from the window and followed her to the door.

As they entered, the colonel hung up the phone and stood. "Miss Flanagan, it's a pleasure to meet you, although I wish it were under better circumstances." While shaking her hand, he directed his attention to Jer.

"Colonel, this is...my boyfriend, Jer. He didn't want me to come alone...because of the stress I've been under."

"Of course." The colonel stretched out his hand to shake Jer's. "Please have a seat." Her father's CO reseated himself and trained his eyes on her. "What can I do for you?"

"Sir, my aunt relayed to us what you told her. What the sergeant working with dad knew, that is. But I was wondering if you remembered anything else about the day, or days before Dad turned up missing. Anything at all?"

Jer placed his hand on Kyleigh's back. She lowered herself to a chair in front of the colonel's desk. Jer sat in the other beside her. She rested her arm on the armrest, and he gently laid his hand on her wrist. He gave her a quick smile that told her she was doing fine.

"Miss Flanagan, I've been trying to think of anything your father said to me that would tell us what or who he suspected here on the base, but I can't. I had personal matters going on that week, which kept my mind occupied. If there was anything I could tell you, I would."

She glanced at Jer. He stared at the colonel as if trying to read his thoughts.

The colonel continued. "I've alerted our criminal investigative department that the major is missing and told them what little we know of his suspicions here on post. They're doing everything they can to locate him. As they have news, I will relay it to you and the Honolulu Police. I promise you, if I think of anything—anything at all—that might help, I'll call you."

Kyleigh studied the colonel's eyes. They exuded concern for her father.

"Your dad is one of my best officers. I've been hoping he'd change his mind and not retire. But I understand his wanting to move home to Houston and spend more time with you and his sister." The colonel's mouth formed a half-smile. "When we went to lunch a couple of weeks ago, he told me how much he's missed both of you. He said he's been gone too much of your life and didn't want to miss any more of it. He's a good man. I'm sure we'll find him soon, and he'll give us a reasonable explanation why we haven't heard from him." He gave her a confident nod. "You hang onto that hope, young lady."

His forehead wrinkled, though the corner of his lips had turned upward into a full smile. She pressed her lips tight and allowed her eyes to wander around the office. A well-worn Bible lay on the credenza. She met the colonel's eyes. Yes, he was telling the truth. "I'm hanging onto prayer for his safety, sir. God knows where he is. I have faith."

The colonel deepened his smile. "Let's hang onto that and keep praying."

Kyleigh rose. "Thank you for speaking to me, Colonel."

Jer shook hands with the colonel again and followed her out of his office.

When they left the building and headed for Jer's truck, she stopped and faced him. "Well? What do you think?"

"I think the colonel told the truth. He showed sincere concern for an officer under his command."

"Yes. I believe him. Um, you showed an inordinate interest in something out the window. What were you watching before we went into Colonel Stevens's office?"

"You don't miss a thing, do you?" He chuckled. "You'd make a pretty good detective."

Jer continued walking toward his truck. "I'd better get you back to the apartment. I have to be at work in a couple of hours."

Kyleigh hurried to keep up with him. He opened the passenger door, and she slid into the cab. "You won't tell me, will you?"

When he got in on the driver's side, he faced her. "What do you want me to tell you?" He snickered. "Kyleigh...you know I can't—"

"You can't discuss an ongoing investigation."

"Exactly." He started the engine and drove toward the exit.

"Then you did see something to do with this case."

He blew air between his lips. She wouldn't give up the search for her dad no matter what he said. How could he keep an eye on her and still work on the case? Maybe Marisa could help. From the way she had answered the door yesterday, she was as concerned about her friend as he was.

After the thirty-minute ride, Jer parked the truck at the apartment complex and escorted Kyleigh to the front door. "May I call you later?"

"Yes." Her head dropped forward a bit, and she glanced away. Rosy pink flooded her cheeks.

So now she was shy? He liked that. "You won't go off on your own to search for your dad, will you? I'm worried that you might...wind up lost...or have an accident...or wander where you shouldn't. Promise me you won't."

She met his eyes. "I promise I won't wander or get lost."

"But you *didn't* say you won't look for the major."

She dropped her gaze to her feet. "What am I supposed to do?" Her eyes riveted his. "Nothing?"

"You're supposed to stay safe and let us handle this. If something happened to you, how do you think your dad would feel?"

Her eyes locked onto his. Tears welled. "If you'll agree to tell me the moment you find anything, I'll agree to not go out tonight and wait for your call."

Would she? "Deal. As soon as we find something, I'll call you. And I'll call when I have a break and can talk, regardless."

Kyleigh opened the front door and stepped inside.

Jer inched closer to the door. He peered through the foyer and the archway at the end. Marisa sat cross-legged on the couch. "Would you mind if I used your restroom before I go?"

She let him in and pointed to the hallway.

In the bathroom, Jer took out a notebook and pencil from his rear pocket. He scratched out a note, tore it from the pad, and put the pencil and pad back. After he washed his hands, he stepped from the hallway into the main living space. Kyleigh wasn't in the room. "Marisa, where did she go?" He slipped the note to Marisa.

She read it, nodded, and pointed to the lanai. "On her *new* favorite spot to be," Marisa lowered her voice to a whisper. "Since last night." She giggled.

He grinned. Kyleigh must be in the hidden corner. As he joined her on the balcony-like porch, she turned. "I'm off to work. Remember your promise."

She smiled and walked him to the front door.

From behind Kyleigh, Jer glanced at Marisa and shrugged. With a nod, she pointed to her eye and then to Kyleigh. Guess that would mean she'd keep tabs on her friend. *I hope so.*

Chapter Eleven

Jer and his partner left the police station bound for Bryce's car in the back lot. This was the lead they'd hoped to find. Jer clamped his jaw tight. They had the major to thank for steering them in the right direction, and now he was missing. It all had to tie in with the illegal drugs at Ft. Shafter. "Come on, Swanson. Let's move it."

As they neared the car, Jer's mind was more than thirty minutes away at the major's apartment complex. That Kyleigh sure was something. He snickered to himself. She had tried her best to wheedle information out of him regarding what they knew about her father's disappearance. He could understand. But he couldn't give her info he didn't have...yet. And she had no idea their investigation involved more than a missing major. How he hated to disappoint her, but hopefully, she'd forgive him when they tied up everything. This tip might lead them to the major... eventually.

Would Kyleigh want him around after they found her dad? He had longed for a relationship with a woman like her. A Christian, smart, funny, lovely, and she enjoyed riding. What more could he ask for?

Bryce slapped Jer's bicep. "Hey. You didn't hear a word I said."

"Sorry. What did you say?"

Detective Swanson hopped behind the wheel and waited to answer until Jer got in on the passenger side. Bryce stuck the key in the ignition and faced Jer. "You met someone, didn't you?"

"Huh?"

"I haven't seen you smile that big since you bought your new dirt bike. Let's have it, man. No secrets between partners. Who is she? Where'd you meet her, and what's she like? Would I like her?"

"You? Are there any attractive, single females you don't like? Let's go."

"Not until you tell me her name and when I can meet her, so I can steal her away from you." He laughed. "Any woman that can put a smile like that on your face has got to be something special."

"You've already met her and her friend. You almost knocked them over yesterday."

"Ha! You mean that cute haole from outside the station? The one with the silky black hair, silvery-gray eyes, and scorching hot temper?"

"No. The other one. Major Flanagan's daughter, Kyleigh. She was the taller of the two. Deep blue eyes and light reddish streaks through her hair."

"The major's daughter? Wow! What a coincidence. Where did you run into her?"

"When I left work yesterday and headed up to Koʻolau for a ride. I didn't simply *run* into her. I almost knocked her off the range. At least off her bike."

Detective Swanson tried to contain his laughter, but it spilled out. "And the cute little one was furious when I only tapped her with the door. What a pair. What did the major's daughter say?"

"You don't want to know. Her temper flared. Don't you think we should go?"

"Oh. Yeah." Bryce started the engine. "But you have to tell me what she said. How mad did she get? I understand those Irish girls have terrible tempers."

Bryce pulled out of the lot and headed toward Pearl Harbor. "So tell me."

"She asked if I had a problem with visitors to the island. Then she accused me of speeding on the trail and basically running her over on purpose. I think that about sums it up. I remember her using the word *stupid*. And she wouldn't let me apologize. Called me *buster* too." He laughed. "Now that I think about it, I would have been amused had I not been so worried I'd injured her."

"Was she hurt?" Bryce's expression turned serious as he drove.

"She said she had a few scrapes but nothing bleeding. And this morning, she didn't seem any worse the wear for it."

Bryce pulled the car over to the curb and gawked at Jer. "This *morning?*"

"Don't look at me that way. I dropped her off at her father's apartment last night. She invited me to eat dinner with her and her friend. Early this morning, I went with her to Ft. Shafter to talk to the major's CO. Now let's go."

One of Swanson's brows lifted. "Did you kiss her?"

"*No!* Are you kidding? I just met her." Jer shook his head and closed his eyes. But he would have liked to. What would it have felt like to hold her in his arms?

"Perfect. I'd hate to take her away from you if you've already gotten that far with her."

Jer's mouth dropped open. "Don't you have enough women dangling on that stringer of yours? Hands off Kyleigh, Swanson."

"Oooo...I think I touched a nerve." He pulled back onto the road and continued to their destination. "How do you know I have a stringer of women? We never spend time together outside of work. What was the major's daughter doing on Koʻolau, anyway? Don't tell me she loves dirt bikes. Or was she searching for the warrior ghosts that haunt the Pali? Koʻolau Range is the wrong place. She should have been on the windward cliffs above route sixty-one."

"Yep. She's a rider. An experienced one at that. And, no, she wasn't ghost hunting. She probably hasn't heard those stories about ancient warriors forced over the cliff above the highway tunnels. What a grisly event." He grimaced.

"Anyway, she was up on Koʻolau, combing the place for evidence her father had been there. She thought he might have had an accident, and no one had found him yet. She said the range is his favorite place to ride. Not the main trails, but less frequented ones. Like I usually take." Small world.

"After work, I took a ride on Koʻolau. As I rode, I mulled over the next step in our case. I wasn't aware I'd picked up speed right before the paths intersected. When I rounded a bend and topped a small hill, there she was, stopped in the middle of the trail. Her bike was idling, so I didn't hear the engine sound ahead of me, only those farther away. I ran into her." He winced.

Bryce guffawed. "Literally. She may have preferred the ghosts." He continued to laugh.

"Right. Bryce, I could have really hurt her." Jer's heart thumped like a rabbit pounding his hind foot on a hollow log. "She had every right to be hopping mad at me."

"Okay, so how did you go from the display of her Irish temper to sharing dinner with her that evening?"

"I'm not sure. Somewhere in the initial moments of anger, she gave me her name, and I realized she was Major Flanagan's daughter. I identified myself, she told me why she was on Ko'olau, and we had a short...*discussion* about her leaving the case to us. But she was determined to find him, so I joined her. Somewhere along the range, her temper cooled. By the time we'd gone through the trail without uncovering anything, she agreed to let me drive her and her dad's bike back to the apartment." Jer smirked at Bryce. He didn't need to know everything. "I met Marisa at the major's apartment. You know, 'the cute little one?' " He gave his partner a lopsided grin.

"*Hmmm*...would I like her...if she's not still holding a grudge because of the door incident?"

"You're a lamebrain, Bryce. If we didn't work so well together, I'd ask for a new partner. One with some sense." Jer chuckled. "Now, let's get to the grill."

About twenty minutes later, Bryce parked the car in The Pearl Grill's lot. When they walked through the entrance, he gazed at the military decor. His jaw tightened. Would he never be over losing his father in Kuwait? Fourteen years. Seemed like yesterday.

After choosing a table in the center of the room, Bryce ordered kalua pork with rice and salad for lunch. Jer chose a chicken sandwich. While they waited for their food, Bryce watched the waiter named Dave Whitehall at a table full of young men across the room. Was he aware they had him under surveillance? "Jer, check out the huge wad of bills he's flashing around."

Jer nodded, then spoke under his breath. "Better keep more of a nonchalant appearance. Don't stare at him."

"He's too busy showing off that cash to notice me. Bet I can guess where it came from."

Their server placed their food in front of them, and Jer bowed his head.

"Hey, O'Shea. Do you have to pray over everything? You've drawn attention to us."

Jer didn't move for a few seconds. He raised his head and smiled at Bryce. "Yes. I do. About everything. After being my partner for two years, you should be used to it. Don't you give thanks for the food you eat?"

A niggle skittered up Bryce's neck. "Nope." He speared a chunk of pork with his fork and popped it into his mouth.

"I thanked God for this food and asked Him to bless it to my body. You should try it sometime. Maybe you wouldn't get sick to your stomach as much while eating all that raw fish you devour. And while I was talking to the Lord, I asked him to help us crack this case and find Major Flanagan."

Bryce stuck a forkful of rice in his mouth, chewed, and swallowed. "I believe in God. But I don't talk to Him like you do. Like a phone call to your best friend. I save my praying for church... which is where I think it belongs."

"What would your mom say? Since she got saved last year, she's been taking her relationship with the Lord seriously. You've been coming to church even longer than she has."

"So?"

"So. Did you ask the Lord to save you at the camp meeting last year, or not?"

"*Jer.* Let's drop it. We have work to do here. Let's concentrate on the suspect." This was why they didn't spend time together away from the job. He'd accepted that his ancestors' worship of animals and trees was all off. Wasn't that enough? Yet, when his mom went to the altar to pray a year ago, she'd come back happy. She'd been different ever since. Until then, she'd been depressed.

Bryce peeked at Jer as he ate his lunch. Enough of these unwelcome thoughts. Time to focus on the waiter, as he'd told Jer.

Bryce ate half the plateful of pork and rice while he kept a surreptitious eye on Whitehall, who still talked and laughed with the men at the table across the room. The waiter turned and entered a corridor at the far side of the room.

"That hall," Bryce nudged Jer's arm with his hand, "must lead to the kitchen."

Jer nodded and took another bite of his sandwich.

While they waited for Dave to show himself again, the military paraphernalia on the walls recaptured Bryce's attention. His mind returned to his mother and her sadness after his dad's death, which had left her broken. Involvement with the church had filled the void left in his mom's life. But religion wasn't for him.

She needed a crutch like the church and God. *Not him.* He was doing fine on his own. He *liked* his life the way it was. No way would he turn into a Bible thumper like Jer. An uneasy sensation wriggled itself into Bryce's heart as if a hole had opened that yearned to be filled.

As Jer observed the table across the room, Bryce studied him. Jer never argued when asked to stop talking about God. Bryce took a bite of salad, but his appetite had left him. How long would it be before his partner brought up the subject again? He always did. *Why does he feel the need to convert me?*

Whitehall returned to the table and laid an envelope in front of one man. He laughed at something another said and then strode to the door.

Jer finished his sandwich, swallowed the rest of his lemonade, and wiped his mouth on a napkin. As he rose from the table, he slapped Bryce on the shoulder. "Pay for lunch, buddy. I'll follow him." Jer had reached the entrance before Bryce could respond.

"Sure, *buddy*. Anything you say, *buddy*." How did this always happen? He needed to be faster on his feet. Bryce found the server and handed him the bill together with enough cash to cover it and the tip. "Great pork."

Bryce rushed out of the grill to find Jer.

"Hey, Dave." Jer trotted up to the waiter as he unlocked his silver Toyota Tundra. "Nice ride."

Whitehall turned to face him. "Do I know you?"

"No. I overheard your friends at the table in there say your name." Jer pointed his thumb toward the entrance.

"What do you want?" He opened the driver's door and leaned on the frame. His eyes ping-ponged from one side of the parking lot to the other before landing back on Jer. He took a pack of cigarettes out of his pocket, pulled one out, lit it, and returned the pack to the pocket.

Jer rested against the trunk of the car next to Whitehall's. "Didn't I see you at Ft. Shafter this morning? My girlfriend and I were visiting there when I saw you with a group of teenagers on the sidewalk."

"Yeah, so, what of it?" Whitehall blew out a long puff of smoke and sucked in another from the cigarette.

"Just curious. I've seen you there a couple of times."

"What business is it of yours what I was doing there?" He jumped into the pickup and slammed the door shut. The engine came to life, and Whitehall drove off.

Hmmm. "Why so hostile over a simple question, buddy?" Jer whispered. "Too nervous."

As Whitehall's truck raced from the parking lot and turned down the street, Bryce jogged up to Jer. "What did I miss?"

"A distressed waiter. A little too agitated when I asked about seeing him at Ft. Shafter this morning." Jer faced Bryce and raised his brows. "If you ask me, I hit a nerve."

Chapter Twelve

By the end of the afternoon, Jer had gained the information he needed on The Pearl Grill's waiter, Dave Whitehall. He turned to Bryce, who sat at the desk next to his. "The guy has a full-time job as a plumber's apprentice." Jer bit his bottom lip and narrowed his eyes as he leaned back in his office chair. "I'd say, even with those two jobs, that brand new Tundra he drives is a lot of truck for the pocketbook. Major Flanagan had to have been on to something."

Bryce nodded and picked up the file he'd been reading. "I'll say. I priced one of those babies."

"And when I approached Whitehall to ask what he was doing at the Army post, the quick glance he took around the grill's parking lot was as suspicious as a cat with feathers sticking out of its mouth. We need to keep an eye on him without arousing his suspicion. But how?"

Swanson threw the file onto Jer's desk. "You won't believe this. Dave Whitehall is the son of a convicted drug dealer in California. Apparently, *Daddy* shipped sonny boy off to Hawaiʻi and had his name changed, so he wouldn't be involved in Dad's mess. But...since his dad is in for a long stretch of time, I guess junior decided to follow in the family business and opened his own branch on Oʻahu."

Jer picked up the folder and perused the pages. "Well, we have to prove it first." He dropped the folder onto his desk and stood. "I'm starved. Ate lunch too fast while we surveilled this guy. I've got an idea."

"Your ideas usually encompass me getting shot at. But shoot." Bryce laughed.

Jer glared at his partner as he wadded a piece of scratch paper and threw it at him. "A comedian you are not. Keep your day job. You said you wanted to meet Kyleigh and Marisa, *properly*, that is. How about we take them to dinner? If the girls are willing, we'll go back to the grill and see if we can pick up more info on Whitehall's activities."

Bryce's eyes lit up like sparklers on the Fourth of July. "Yeah. Brilliant idea. The little dark-haired spitfire was really something."

"Don't even think of adding this girl to your list of conquests. From what Kyleigh told me about Marisa, she's a Christian. A nice young lady. Not one of your dangling fish."

"Jer, where did you get the impression I'm a player? I thought you've been kidding me all this time."

"The gossip mill, buddy. The dispatcher you dated last year has spread the news. And named names. Didn't you know?"

Bryce's jaw dropped. "What did she say?"

For the next fifteen minutes, Jer repeated Jessica's tale about how Bryce had come on to her and her best friend. "She said you took advantage of them. And it had happened to other girls she knew."

"Why the little vindictive—"

"You mean it's not true? None of it?"

"*No.* Her friend, Brittany, and I went out off and on for several months. I thought we had a pleasant relationship going, but nothing serious, although I never dated anyone else until I met a friend of hers at a party." He slapped his hand on his desk. "Jessica and I hit it off, so I asked her out. There was never an understanding between Brittany and me that we were exclusive. It never came up. She assumed it."

"So, you dated her friend, and Brittany found out."

"Yep. She started calling me all the time. At first, it didn't bother me, but then it was like an obsession of hers to talk to me morning, noon, and night. She kept it up for about a week. When I asked her to stop, she said she would, but the calls continued." Bryce threw a pencil into the holder so hard it popped back out. He retrieved it and placed it back in the cup. "Finally, I'd had enough. She called one night and demanded I take her to a movie. I said I already had a date."

"She guessed with whom, I suppose."

"She didn't have to. Her *friend* boasted I made a date with her for dinner on Waikiki Beach. Brittany insisted I break the date with Jessica, which I did, but only because I didn't want to be in the middle of the feud they'd started. They both wound up mad at me. End of any dates with either of them." Bryce shook his head. "When I threatened to report Brittany to her super for harassment, she finally stopped the calls."

Jer chuckled. "Yep. Guess our dispatcher is sore at you."

"An understatement, for sure." Bryce pursed his lips. "The woman has some explaining to do. I enjoy a casual date with a girl, but that's it. This Marisa sounds like the type of girl I'd like to go out with...as long as she doesn't bite my head off again." He snickered.

"Okay, Romeo. I'll give Kyleigh a call and ask if they'll agree to dinner on us."

Kyleigh grabbed her cell. When Jer's face appeared on the screen, she smiled. If only he weren't with law enforcement. She really liked him, but how could she even consider a relationship with a detective? Before she pressed the button to connect, she gazed one more time at his picture. But he was so handsome. And a gentleman too. "Hi, Jer."

"Hi. Told you I'd call. I'm about to leave work now. Bryce and I wondered...if you haven't eaten yet, would you and Marisa join us for dinner?" He paused. "Too late, isn't it?"

"Actually, no. We spent the afternoon at the infamous Dole pineapple plantation and only arrived here a couple of hours ago. When we got back, I couldn't move. After a while, we both admitted to being too exhausted to cook and talked about where we should go to eat. Wonderful timing."

"Great! Not that you're so tired, but that you haven't eaten yet. Your friend isn't still mad at Bryce for the incident at the police department, is she?"

Kyleigh laughed. "She hasn't mentioned it for a while." She wouldn't spoil a dinner invitation by telling him Marisa's earlier comment about Bryce's rudeness. "And if he's willing to make it up to her with a meal, I'm sure she'll forget the entire thing."

"It's a date then. Tell her she'll find he's not a rude person. Yesterday, he was just having an off day. He's a nice guy. Loves to tease, but a nice guy. Hang on for a second."

Hmmm. Jer had played his friend up pretty hard. He'd *better* be nice. It was bad enough they were with the police department. What was she doing? Now she'd involved Marisa with them. Her heartbeat sped up. She ought to back out of this date.

Jer answered someone's muffled question on the other end of the line and laughed.

But if she told Jer she'd changed her mind, how would she learn anything about her father? She had to keep in contact with him.

"Kyleigh, we can be at the apartment in about forty-five minutes. Is that all right with you? I need to stop at my place first and change my shirt. Bryce wants to clean up too."

"That'll be fine. You're not planning on anything fancy, are you? I'd prefer casual. It takes too much energy to dress up."

"Casual it is." A chuckle came through the line. "See you in about forty-five minutes."

"We'll be ready." Kyleigh dropped her phone into her purse and joined Marisa on the lanai. "Jer just called with an invitation to dinner. For both of us."

"Both of us?" Marisa glanced up from her ice-packed glass of cola. "Didn't he want to take you to dinner alone, and you talked him into taking me too? Hmm? How are you going to develop this relationship in the short time we'll be here if you don't spend time alone with him, Ky?"

"First of all, I'm not trying to develop a relationship with him. He's a detective. I have no desire to attach myself to anyone in law enforcement. And second, his partner Bryce is going too."

"The smart-alecky partner? Count me out." She rose from the chair and went inside.

Kyleigh followed her to the kitchen. "Marisa. Please. We haven't had dinner, we're too tired to cook, and frankly, I'd rather be driven to dinner tonight than do the driving or have you do it. When he asked, I kind of told Jer you were over the incident at HPD."

Kyleigh took a seat at the breakfast bar. Marisa narrowed her eyes.

"Come on, Marisa. Please?" Kyleigh folded her hands as if in prayer and brought them to her face, touching her lips.

Marisa placed both fists on her hips. "I'll go...but that detective better be on his best behavior." She huffed. "You owe me, girl." With a giggle, she dropped her arms to her sides. "Why wouldn't you want to attract someone like Jer? From the little I've seen of him, he's a wonderful guy. And he's, *without a doubt,* cute. What do you have against cops?"

"I'll tell you the long story some other time. Jer and Bryce will be here in less than an hour, so I can't go into it now. I have to freshen up a bit and change my clothes. Jer said the place we're going to is casual, but I feel kind of grungy from the walk around the plantation. I need to clean up." She waltzed toward the bedroom, peeking over her shoulder at Marisa.

Her friend finished her drink, set her glass in the sink, and ran water in it. She turned to Kyleigh. "Me too. Not that I'm freshening up for the smart-alecky dude."

Kyleigh closed the bedroom door and grinned. "Oh, no?" Jer wasn't the only guy Marisa thought was cute. This should make for an interesting evening.

Bryce leaned on the hood of his new Toyota Prius while he waited in the parking lot outside Major Flanagan's apartment. A fingerprint on the windshield caught his attention. Cleaned less than half an hour ago and already smudged. He popped the hatch and grabbed a shop towel. As he wiped away the print, he scanned the windows of the misty green vehicle for other marks.

Fortunately, Jer had asked him to drive tonight, which would keep his mind occupied with traffic instead of the petite beauty he'd offended the other day. He blew out a long slow breath.

Girls on a stringer. Yeah. If anyone found out how nervous he was around beautiful women, he'd never live it down. Brittany had approached *him first* for a date. And Jessica had done the same thing. He should have known they were trouble from the beginning.

Jer and the two women emerged from the covered walkway. Bryce sprinted around the front of the car and opened the rear passenger door for his partner and Kyleigh to sit in the backseat. He held out his hand to Kyleigh. "Hi. I'm Bryce. Because of my rudeness at our first meeting, we didn't exchange names. I'm honestly sorry." He winced.

She placed her hand in his. "You're forgiven. A pleasure to meet you, Bryce." Kyleigh slipped into the seat.

Well, she was sociable but had no smile. Wonder what bothered her if it wasn't his attitude at the station. Her friend squeezed between the car and Jer before he could slide in next to Kyleigh.

Bryce smiled at her. "I hope you've forgiven me too, for—"

"No problem." Marisa gave him a side-glance as she joined Kyleigh in the back.

Bryce blinked at Jer, then shrugged. This would be a strange evening.

Jer whispered, "Give it time, buddy. The night is young." He hopped in on the front passenger side.

As Bryce drove onto the road that led to Pearl Harbor, he glanced at the raven-haired beauty in the rearview mirror. "We haven't met formally. I'm Bryce Swanson. Thank you for joining us for dinner tonight."

For an agonizingly long moment, Marisa stared at him in the mirror. "I'm Marisa. Marisa Romano. An Italian haole from Texas." She continued to stare, but then a sparkle shone in her eyes, and she giggled.

Bryce pulled in a deep breath and relaxed. "You have a wicked sense of humor. I like it." He laughed and looked over to Jer. "Did you tell the girls where we're headed?"

"I did. And I told them why we chose the place too. Turns out Kyleigh has seen Dave Whitehall before. She said her father wasn't pleased to see him a couple of years ago when they ate dinner at the grill."

Kyleigh leaned forward. "Which reminds me, what information have you gained on my dad's disappearance since this morning?"

Jer closed his eyes. His head fell back against the headrest.

Bryce frowned at him. Just how much about the case had his partner told her?

Chapter Thirteen

*J*er shifted in the passenger seat to face the back. Kyleigh'd be disappointed when he told her they still hadn't a clue to where her father went. "It's only been hours since the last time I told you we'd found nothing new on your dad. And I can't discuss the case. So how about for tonight, no questions?" He suspected she had every intention of continuing to ask until they found her dad. Wouldn't he if it was his father?

Her eyes narrowed as she stared out the windshield. She pressed her lips into a straight line. He didn't blame her for being upset, but why such an angry demeanor? Kyleigh slumped back in the seat and folded her arms across her abdomen.

For several minutes of the ride, relative silence filled the vehicle's interior, except for whispers between Kyleigh and Marisa as they drove past the Pearl Harbor Wildlife Refuge. Gloom reigned as they encountered minor traffic near the Pearl Country Club with its lush green terrain and stately trees on the slopes of the Ko'olau mountain range.

He needed to do something to break the coldness which had invaded the air. Jer turned to face the girls. "Did you enjoy the pineapple plantation today?" Marisa's eyes widened with excitement. "Judging by your expression, Marisa, I'd say yes."

"You'd better believe it. I assumed only England grew mazes of this magnitude. I heard it may be the world's largest, and I think they're right. Whew! Who would have thought we'd have so much fun getting lost?" She giggled. "Acres of paths and so many different kinds of plants that make up the maze. No wonder we were so bushed when we got back to the apartment."

Bryce grinned.

Jer studied Bryce's face as Marisa rambled on about the plantation. With their laid-back personalities, these two would hit it off just fine. Bryce may have found the girl he'd longed for.

"And you, Kyleigh? What was your favorite thing about the place?" Jer smiled at her. As if the black thundercloud that hung over her had eased past Ko'olau, her scowl disappeared.

She straightened in the seat, then glanced in turn at Marisa, Bryce, and Jer. "I liked the gardens. I've never seen some of those plants before. Unique." She leaned back and gazed out the side window as they shot by the shores of Pearl Harbor.

"That's all you liked?" *Come on, Kyleigh. Snap out of it.* "Did you see all eight gardens? Which did you like the most?" What girl didn't like to talk about gardens? "What about the waterfall and koi?"

She gave him a sideways glance. "Yes, they were nice."

Marisa grabbed her forearm. "And what about the train ride? Wish I could bring my second graders here."

Kyleigh smiled at her friend. "They'd love it, wouldn't they? What about my kindergartners?" A smile spread across her face. "Can you imagine them with the fish? I'd have my hands full, keeping them out of the pond. Better to take postcards back for each of them instead." She laughed.

Mahalo, Marisa. Jer smiled at her.

As Bryce adjusted the rearview mirror, the beam in his eyes shown like a light bulb. "So you're a teacher, too, Marisa? Do you work at the same school as Kyleigh?"

"Yes, it seems we've done everything together ever since high school. Went to the same college, took the same classes...since we both wanted to be teachers. We applied for jobs at the same places. Never imagined for a minute we'd teach in the same district, let alone the same school. But that's what happened." As her face took on a serious mien, she glanced at Kyleigh. "The only difference is...I teach difficult subjects to second graders while Ky plays with kindergartners all day." She grinned.

Kyleigh slapped her arm and rolled her eyes. "If you only knew, Marisa. If you only knew how peaceful your class is compared to mine." They both chortled.

Jer could almost hear the wheels turn in Bryce's brain. No doubt saying to himself, *a girl after my own heart.* Well, if Bryce and Marisa hit it off, he'd be happy. Jer sneaked a peek at Kyleigh. He'd be even happier if Kyleigh allowed him to develop a relationship with her. But every time he'd gotten close, something happened to irritate her. It showed in her eyes. Except for last night on the lanai when they had talked as though they'd known each other for months. What had he done to anger her today?

Bryce pulled the car into The Pearl Grill's parking lot, shut off the engine, and twisted to address Marisa. "I wish the teachers had been as pretty as you two when I'd been in school." His eyes devoured Marisa.

Jer laughed. "Precisely what I said yesterday...almost word for word." Bryce's gaze didn't leave Marisa. A slight glow came to his tanned skin. "Hey, Bryce, do you remember Mrs. MacGraf and her yard-long index finger in fifth grade?"

As Bryce's head fell onto the headrest, he groaned. "Don't remind me." He straightened in the seat. "Let's not spoil the evening." He turned back to Marisa. "Hope you girls are hungry because this place has great food. At least that's what the guys at the station boast. Jer and I usually eat at the joint next door, but we stopped here earlier—anyway, let's go in and have dinner."

"Relax, Bryce. I filled the girls in on why we chose this place. They're okay with it." At least Kyleigh had been before they left the apartment. Had she changed her mind? If only he could figure out what was eating at her. Every time he'd assured her they'd find her dad, she'd accepted it. It had to be something more than his disappearance.

Why hadn't they found out more about her father? He wasn't at the top of their concerns. That was why. Finding a drug pusher was much more important. After they solved the case, a story of a drug bust always made better headlines than finding a lost major. Kyleigh ignored Jer's offered hand as she stepped out of the back seat of Bryce's car.

Not the hurt puppy face again. She'd been unfair. After all, she'd only known Jer for two days. Bryce for less. And just because the police back home had dropped the ball in her mother's case didn't mean Jer and Bryce would. She had no idea how hard Jer was working to find her father. Better cut him some slack, as Dad would have said.

They rounded the vehicle to join Bryce and Marisa.

As the foursome strolled toward the entrance, Marisa and Bryce walked several feet in front of Jer and Kyleigh. Jer turned to her. His warm brown eyes captured hers. The corners of her mouth lifted. She traced her eyebrow with her fingertip as heat rose from her neck into her cheeks. The sparkle returned to his eyes.

When Jer touched her elbow, a light electrical charge zinged through her arm. "Earlier, you told me you ran into this Dave character on Sunday when you and Marisa ate here. I didn't have a chance to ask before we left the apartment if he was with anyone else."

"Not that I noticed...other than the grill's staff. Another waiter took our order, but when the food came, Dave delivered it and proceeded to flirt with us. He said the other server got a call he had to take care of. There isn't going to be any trouble tonight, is there? I don't want Marisa to get involved with anything more than to help me find my father. And I'd like her part in the search for Dad minimal. I allowed her to join me here on Oʻahu more for moral support. Not to help me play detective."

He nodded. "And I hope you'll let us do the detective work. You don't know the island as we do, and it could be dangerous for you to ask questions of the wrong people. I don't want you or Marisa to get hurt."

"I don't want my father hurt either." Her volume rose as they walked. "He may already be hurt. Or worse." Tears threatened, but she blinked them back.

Jer stopped and slid his fingers around her elbow. "Kyleigh, I promise you we're doing everything we can to find your father. Please let us do our job."

Could she trust him? She wanted to. Would he be any different from those officers who assured her they'd find the man who attacked her mother? And didn't.

Inside the grill, Jer and Kyleigh caught up to Bryce and Marisa.

Jer glanced around the huge room. "A lot of people decided to eat late tonight." But no sign of Whitehall. What would be the best way to approach this? Maybe he should talk to the manager. Bad idea. They have no idea whether the manager was in league with the waiter or not. Even if he wasn't, he might say something to Whitehall about a guy asking questions. Best if no one here was aware of their suspicions about the coworker.

Kyleigh and Marisa left to visit the restroom before they sat down.

"Bryce, we didn't discuss what ruse we'll use to ask questions about Whitehall. Did you have something in mind?"

"No. Didn't you work all this out at the station? Fine time to ask me about it, man." He quirked his mouth into a lopsided smile. "You came up with this plan for dinner as an excuse to take Kyleigh out. I guess that means I'd better figure out what we're to do."

"Hey," Jer raised his index finger like an exclamation mark, "I've got it. When I saw him earlier today and asked him about being at Ft. Shafter, he became defensive and drove away before I finished talking to him. I could say we came back to ask him if he also worked on the base. We wondered how many civilian jobs there were. He might have an inside with someone who'd find jobs for us. We may gain his phone number or address. What do you think?"

"Good idea, as long as the person or persons we speak to didn't watch us drive up in my new Prius."

"Hmm. Even if they did, you bought the car before we were laid off. You had no idea you'd be without a steady income. How does that sound?"

"And we're having dinner out with our girlfriends because we have so much money saved up?"

Jer pressed his lips together. "No, credit cards, buddy. Like everyone else, we're living off credit cards. Besides, if Whitehall gets wind of our predicament and our suspicions are correct, he may offer us an entirely different proposition. We'd learn more information...if you know what I mean."

Bryce nodded and smiled. "A place in his operation. Genius. Pure genius. I take back all the nasty things I said about you." He chuckled. "Here come the ladies."

Chapter Fourteen

Kyleigh scrutinized the menu. She always had such a hard time deciding what she wanted. "Do either of you gentlemen have a recommendation?"

Bryce's bright blue eyes sparkled from the wooden tiki light in the center of the table. "Do you like fish? Or what do you have a taste for?"

"Fish sounds good to me." She laid the menu on the table.

"Then I'd recommend the Furikake Ahi." He pointed to the choice on his menu. "My favorite."

She opened hers again and focused on the description. "Oh, yes. Tuna with the special Japanese seasoning with seaweed. I remember, though I haven't eaten it in a long time."

Marisa stared at her as if she had two heads. "*Seaweed?*"

Kyleigh stifled a laugh and nodded. "The flavor is wonderful. You should try it."

After perusing the choices again, Marisa wrinkled her nose and closed her menu. "Still no Italian food? I thought it was just a lunch thing." She giggled. "The rice sounds delicious, but I don't want a burger again."

Bryce showed her the pasta section and grinned. "Anything for our tourist haoles."

"I deserved that after my crack on the way over." She giggled again and glanced at Kyleigh. "How'd I miss this when we were here before? Took my new Hawaiian *friend* to steer me in the right direction." She elbowed his arm. "I guess I'll try the Seafood Alfredo. Although I've never eaten a mussel in my life. What do they taste like?"

"Gee, don't know." Bryce's eyebrows shot upward. "To me, they've always tasted the same as the food they're cooked with. Like any other fish in a sauce, I suppose."

"So not *fishy?* Strong fish, I mean."

"I've never noticed it. What about you, Jer?"

He shrugged.

She turned to Kyleigh. "Kyleigh, you've had mussels, right?"

"Yes, I've had them. As Bryce said, they must have a mild flavor that picks up whatever they're cooked in."

"Great. That settles it then. Seafood Alfredo. Sorry guys, I'm not adventurous, especially when it comes to food."

As Bryce grinned at Marisa, his eyes glowed even more. Kyleigh smiled. She'd almost bet he'd been hit in the heart with not one but a dozen of Cupid's arrows. This should be interesting. The gleam in Marisa's eyes as she conversed with Bryce couldn't be brighter. *Very interesting.* Marisa had never dated one man for more than a few months...and she had *never* looked at any of them *that* way. Hope the poor guy doesn't wind up hurt. He seemed decent enough, aside from his being a detective.

She met Jer's gaze. He was nice too. She could fall for—*get the thought out of your head, Kyleigh Flanagan. He's a cop. He lives on this island. You live in Houston.* Besides, he'd only asked them out to dinner so the guys would appear to be on a date. They simply had wanted to gain more information on Dave. That was all.

When Kyleigh's eyes met his, a tingle shot through Jer. He returned his attention to the menu. Before she left the island, he'd take her on a proper date with only the two of them. Would she go out with him if he didn't find a clue soon to where her father had gone? The more time passed, the more he feared something serious had happened to the major.

A waiter stepped to the table and took their orders.

Jer handed him the menus. "So, what all have you girls visited since you arrived on Oʻahu? We could give you some suggestions before you have to leave. And whenever I'm off, I'd be happy to take you anywhere you'd like to go."

He leaned back in the chair and studied a congregation of three male Hawaiian waiters, chatting with the male haole who took their orders and one blond waitress near the kitchen. This would be the time to approach them.

Bryce took out his business card and passed it to Marisa. "That goes for me too. Here's my card. My mom gave me these for Christmas last year. First time I've given one out." He laughed. "She said I had to sell myself if I was ever to make her a grandmother." His jaw fell open, eyes rounded, and his tanned face darkened as if he'd laid out in the sun too long. "I didn't mean—I'm sorry. That didn't come out the way I intended."

Marisa giggled. "Don't worry about it, Bryce. My mother says similar things to me all the time."

Marisa read the writing aloud. "Bryce...Kalani...Swanson. Your middle name is Hawaiian, your last name is Scandinavian. Swedish, I believe. I hadn't paid attention to your last name before now. Your features are definitely more Hawaiian than Swedish, except for your blue eyes."

Jer chuckled. "He's a hapa."

"A what?" She whipped her head around to Jer.

Bryce answered for him. "Hapa is the term used around here for someone like me. Half and half, or part Hawaiian and part something else."

Her mouth formed a perfect circle. "And how does Bryce fit into this? Where did your first name come from?"

"Buddy, while you explain your moniker to the girls," Jer nodded toward the group at the back of the room, "I'm going to strike up a conversation with the staff over there. Let's hope someone will talk to me." He rose from the table and strode to the four waiters and one waitress.

"Is there a problem, sir?" the blond waitress asked.

"Not a problem. But I was wondering if any of you can help me. My buddy and I were here for lunch today. The food was so good, we brought our girlfriends back tonight. The guy who served us was at Ft. Shafter yesterday, and I wanted to ask him something. I thought he might hook us up with someone there for a job, but he left before I had a chance. Our company laid us off. Would it be possible for me to get in touch with him? I overheard someone call him Dave before he left."

All five of their gazes darted back and forth from one to the other. The girl pursed her lips. "We can't give out personal information, but if you come back tomorrow, he's working the lunch shift."

Nuts. This idea was a bust. Jer surveyed their faces. The short waiter who had taken their orders shifted his weight from one foot to the other as if uneasy. Bet he could tell them what Whitehall was into. Might be in on it himself. "I understand. Mahalo."

Jer rejoined his group at the table. When he caught Bryce's eye, he gave him a shake of the head.

Bryce kept talking. "Dad was in the Navy, stationed at Pearl Harbor when he met Mom. She said she couldn't resist the haole with his big blue eyes. They married a year later. When I came along, Mom decided I needed to have at least one Hawaiian name, Kalani."

Jer seated himself but kept tuned in on the short waiter.

"What does the name mean?" Marisa's eyes latched onto Bryce's.

Jer peeked at Bryce, whose complexion darkened again. Poor guy. Where had this shyness come from? Bet the guys at the station never saw this side of him. Bryce had them all fooled.

Bryce slumped back in the chair and pinched his lips together. "It means of the heavens or chieftain. Not sure which she had in mind. You see, my mom is a native. *Pure* native. She's all about tradition, so she must have thought my dad was *really* something for her to marry a non-Hawaiian."

Kyleigh leaned in and lowered her brows. "Why do you say '*must have thought*,' Bryce?"

"He died overseas when I was young." Bryce stiffened in his seat. "Is it okay if we change the subject? I don't want to spoil the evening with sad reminders...if you don't mind."

"Not at all, Bryce." Kyleigh's eyes filled with sadness. "I'm sorry I brought it up. Marisa, do you remember the little boy in your class last year that had a Spanish last name, but his first name was François?"

Bryce turned to Jer and spoke softly while the girls chitchatted. "What's the verdict?"

"As expected, they wouldn't give any info about an employee, but I have a feeling—" The short waiter came across the room, carrying a tray full of food. "Here comes our dinner. Bryce's recommendations are now to be tested."

The server placed each plate in front of the appropriate diner without a word. When he came to Jer, he lowered the dish and leaned closer. "If you want a contact for Dave, I'll meet you behind the building when you leave."

An uncomfortable sensation snaked up the back of Bryce's neck as Jer paid for their meal. The two of them followed Marisa and Kyleigh into the parking lot. "Jer, let's take the girls to the car before we search for the waiter. There's no one else out here."

"Right. But you stay with them. It won't take two of us to talk to him, and if he spots both of us, he might spook. Something tells me he has more to say than just where I can contact Whitehall. The guy was too edgy when I first approached the group of them inside. I'll have a look around."

Bryce grabbed his elbow. "Be careful. I have one of those intuitive hunches coming on. The kind that makes me *real* nervous."

Jer waved him off and headed around the side of the building.

Bryce joined the girls at the car and opened the rear passenger door for Marisa.

"Would you mind if I sat in front with you?"

What a smile! Sweetest thing he'd ever seen. "Be my guest. And Jer might be pleased with the idea, too, when he's finished his chat with the waiter." He grinned and leaned closer to open the front door. The scent of fresh strawberries floated in the air as she flicked her hair off her shoulder.

Marisa slid in, and Bryce shut the door. Kyleigh slipped into the rear seat with a huge smile.

Before he got in on the driver's side, he scanned the parking lot. No sign of Jer. *I don't like this.* He should drive closer to the water's edge.

The engine revved, and Bryce checked out the rear window before shifting into reverse.

Kyleigh's expression mirrored the uneasiness in his stomach. "Bryce, where did Jer go?"

"He's meeting a waiter outside. The guy said he'd give him Dave's contact information. Jer said it didn't take two of us to talk to him, and he wanted me to stay with you girls." *No point in telling her what else he said.* "Thought I'd find a place closer to the water to park, so he won't have to walk as far." The prickling sensation in his neck worsened.

As he prepared to back out of the parking spot, movement across the lot at the edge of the water caught his eye. *That's not Jer.* Bryce shifted to reverse, tires screeched to a stop, and he pulled forward. He drove toward the north side of the grill and came to an abrupt halt at the bushes which lined the back of the lot. Nothing there. Beyond, Pearl Harbor silently glistened in the moonlight.

"I'm not sure where they were to meet. Maybe they went back inside." He could hope.

Marisa twisted to face him. "You never told us where your first name came from. Bryce is neither Hawaiian nor Swedish, is it?"

At least one of them was calm. "Mom decided it was unique." He smiled and feigned a chuckle. "She named me after an author of a book she had read. Hated the book but loved the name, so I'm stuck with it."

"I think it's a nice name." Marisa's chin dipped.

"Thanks." He dragged his attention to the harbor, rolled down the window, and surveyed the water's edge. Where was Jer? Bryce's heart rate increased. It wasn't like his partner to—"I think I saw Jer in the shadows over there." Bryce pointed toward the water. "He's beckoning to me." He glanced at Marisa, then Kyleigh. "Would you two mind if I left you in the car for a minute?" *Hopefully, only a minute.*

"Why don't we go with you?" Marisa smiled.

"No. You don't want to go near the water at night. Rats. By the harbor." That should deter them. "Better for you girls to wait here."

"Thank you, Bryce. Not my favorite critters." Kyleigh gave him a nod.

"Since it's pitch dark at this end of the lot, I'll lock the doors. Safety first." He hopped out of the car, pressed the lock button on his key fob, and jogged to the water's edge, following it behind the building to a short pier with a small speed boat tied to it. The boat bobbed in the water even though there were scarcely any waves at the shoreline. Was that an arm draped over the far side of the boat?

As he neared, the arm slipped out of sight. A soft splash sounded. Bryce bolted for the dock and climbed into the boat. Someone sank out of sight into the water.

Kyleigh fidgeted in the back seat of Bryce's car. What had happened to them? First Jer, and now Bryce. Something was wrong. "Marisa, unlock the back door. I'm going after the guys. You stay here."

"Oh, no, you don't. You're not leaving me alone here in the dark. Where you go, I go, Ky." Marisa pressed the door lock, rushed out the passenger side, and closed the door as Kyleigh hopped out. "Should we lock it?"

"What if we had to jump back in the car right away? We couldn't unlock it again. I think it'll be okay. We won't be gone long." She hoped. "I want to find out where Jer and Bryce went. Stay close to me."

"Oh, like you're going to protect me?"

"*Exactly* like that! With Dad in the military and gone so much from home, he made sure I knew how to protect myself. And others."

"Well, then. Let's go, Wonder Woman." Marisa sidled up to her friend. "Sure is dark here. And eerie."

As they reached the water's edge behind the grill, a wraithlike figure crouched on the pier next to a boat. Kyleigh seized Marisa's arm and pointed. "Is that Bryce over there?"

"I think it is. What's he doing? Someone's lying on the dock." Marisa raced toward the pier with Kyleigh right behind her.

Sirens broke through the air as the girls reached him. Kyleigh dropped to her knees on the wooden jetty beside Jer's prone body. "Jer?" Tears flooded her eyes. Bryce knelt on the other side of his partner. She gripped Bryce's arm. "What happened? What can I do?"

He laid his hand on hers. "Jer was in the water when I got here. I managed to pull him out and did what I could. Now that the paramedics are here, let's move out of their way." He helped her to her feet as the EMTs thundered onto the dock.

She stared at Marisa, whose hand covered her mouth.

Chapter Fifteen

Kyleigh moved as if in a fog while the paramedics slid the gurney with an unconscious Jer into the ambulance. Bryce led her and Marisa back to his car.

As they reached the car, Kyleigh hesitated. Never before had she felt so helpless. Had Bryce gotten enough water out of Jer's lungs? He had to recover. Her father lost, and now Jer...possibly near death. *Why are You testing me this way, Lord?*

Kyleigh broke away from them. "I need to go with Jer."

Before Bryce could stop her, she ran to the ambulance and hopped into the back. As they drove away from Pearl Harbor, siren blaring, her pulse sped to an all-time high. *Lord, please protect Jer.* What kind of a fiend would do this to him? Thank God Bryce had pulled Jer from the water, but how long had he been under? Bryce hadn't said. It wasn't that long since they'd left the grill. Was it the waiter who did this? Did he have her dad too? Or had he already— *No! Stop such defeated thinking. Get your head on straight.*"

Dizziness assaulted her for a moment. She lowered her head into her hands.

The paramedic attending to Jer glanced at her. "Are you all right, miss? We'll be at the ER in a few minutes."

Kyleigh raised her head and focused on Jer as her ears rang like an old-fashioned telephone in a movie, and sparkles danced in her peripheral vision. She rested her head back into her hands. "Yes. I'm okay. I guess the stress...too much. Dizzy, that's all." She lifted her head again. "Will he make it?"

The driver called to her, "He's got the best taking care of him back there. Don't you worry. And we're headed for more of the best on O'ahu."

For Kyleigh, the trip took forever. She wrung her hands until the ambulance pulled into the emergency drive at The Queen's Medical Center. As she exited the vehicle, Jer was hustled through the ER doors. She watched as the paramedics wheeled him past the waiting room and down a hallway beyond double doors that flapped shut behind them.

The ambulance driver led Kyleigh to a crowded waiting room. "Miss, are you sure you're all right? You're pale. Do you need a drink of water or something? Maybe we should have someone look at you."

"No. Really. I'm fine. It was just the—"

Marisa, her eyes wide, ran to Kyleigh before the door from the parking lot slid completely open. "Are you okay, Ky? You're as white as fresh milk, girl."

The sliding door opened again, and Bryce strode in. As he reached her, Kyleigh burst into tears. "I don't know how Jer is. No one has said anything to me. They took him through those doors." She pointed to the set of double doors.

Bryce took her in his arms and patted her back. "Take it easy, Kyleigh. Jer's one strong guy. He's been through a lot more than getting his lungs waterlogged by Pearl Harbor, and I'm pretty sure I got most, if not all, of it out of him."

She gazed up at his blue eyes. "Why haven't they told me anything? No one's said a word since I got here. I have no idea if he's alive or—" Kyleigh buried her face in his shoulder.

Bryce grasped her by the upper arms and backed her away. "It's been no more than a few minutes. It seems forever when you're waiting, but we have to give them time." He lifted her chin with his index finger. "Besides, Jer had better recover. He owes me for lunch today." Bryce raised his brows. A silly grin formed on his face.

Kyleigh stared at Bryce. "What?"

Marisa shook her head and hugged Kyleigh. "Ignore him, Ky. I think it was a feeble attempt to make you smile." She let go of her friend, pulled a tissue from her purse, and wiped tears from Kyleigh's face. "You really care about Jer, don't you? God's not going to let a great guy like him drop into your life and then yank him out again. Jer will hold up. You wait and see." She dug into her purse for the rest of the pack of tissues and handed it to Kyleigh. "Hang onto this." Marisa pulled Kyleigh down to a seat.

After blowing her nose, Kyleigh let her head fall against Marisa's shoulder. "I'm useless. I can't help anyone. My dad, Jer..."

Bryce sat on the other side of her. "Kyleigh, we will find your dad. Jer promised, and I do too. And we'll catch who did this to Jer as well. I have a hunch...as Jer was spitting out the fish water, he kept trying to talk. All I got out of him before he passed out was the sound of 'da.'" Bryce's cell rang. He pulled it out of its belt clip and checked the screen. "Excuse me."

He rose from the seat and walked away from Kyleigh and Marisa until he disappeared beyond the entrance.

Kyleigh stared at the blackness outside the doors. She couldn't take much more. *I can't stand not knowing where Dad is.* And the man she'd been drawn to since she first saw him lay unconscious or— More tears streamed down her face. She didn't care if he was with the police department. She hadn't had a chance to tell him she...she what? Had she fallen in love with Jer this soon? Not possible. But if he died...a piece of her would die too. She was certain.

Bryce sprinted back into the waiting room. Sure hated to leave them right now. "Girls, I have to take off, but you'll be safe here until I get back. Something came up at The Pearl Grill. Marissa, what's your cell number? I can call you if I'm delayed."

As she gave it to him, Bryce punched the buttons on his phone.

"What if we get news about Jer? Do you want us to call you? I'll need your number." Her cell rang. She snatched it from her purse and answered.

When she said hello, Bryce chuckled to himself. "Hi. Wanted to make sure I got it right. And now you have mine." He snapped a picture of her with the phone, placed the cell in its holder, and touched Marisa's cheek with his fingers. "Okay, little haole, take care of Kyleigh. I think Jer needs her."

"I will. And you be careful, you big Swede." Marisa took a picture of him.

He winked at her, turned, and hustled out the doors.

Bryce raced across the lot and jumped into the driver's seat. Before he drove away, he assigned Marisa's picture to her number.

What a doll. Never met anyone like her. He secured the cell, started the engine, and sped onto the road in the direction of the grill. He hated to leave the girls there, but they'd be safe with so many people around.

Why hadn't he seen the other body in the water when he pulled Jer out? But the officers didn't say they'd found him in the harbor, only behind the building.

Was it the guy who'd brought their food to the table tonight that they'd found? The one who wanted to talk to Jer? If so, he might have had information to divulge that somebody didn't want to be revealed. Jer could have witnessed the murder, which would explain the attack on him

Bryce called the station and was connected with his supervisor. "Sir, we'd better send an officer to Queen's Hospital, under the circumstances. O'Shea's in an exam room, and the girls who were with us tonight are sitting in the waiting room." Bryce explained there was a possibility the killer might try to finish the job.

"Good thinking, Swanson. I'll get someone over there right away."

When Bryce arrived at The Pearl Grill, blue, red, and white lights from police and emergency vehicles flashed in the air. The usual amount of spectators crowded as close to the cordoned-off perimeter as they were allowed. Bryce pushed his way through the onlookers, past the officer keeping the people at bay, and rushed toward the building. He'd never understand why people hung around gawking when a murder had taken place. They had to find out what was going on and couldn't wait to hear about it on the news. He hated to call them vultures, but it was what they reminded him of.

As Bryce reached the medical examiner, squatting in front of a body lying in the bushes at the back entrance, the older man rose. "I'm finished with my initial assessment of the body." He faced

Bryce. "Can't tell you a lot yet, but the victim appears to have been strangled. I found ligature marks on the victim's throat." The man left the scene while his assistant zipped the body bag.

Bryce's mind whirled with questions as he watched the body placed on a gurney and hauled to the waiting vehicle for transport to the morgue. He'd caught a glimpse of the dead man's face. It was the waiter, all right. The same one Jer was supposed to meet here. Bryce spun and eyed the spectators still pushing at the boundary of the crime scene. No sign of Whitehall in the crowd.

Once the medical examiner's team left with the body, the group of onlookers thinned.

Bryce roamed the dock area to see if he could find anything suspicious. Only cigarette butts scattered around. Could be from anyone. He gazed out over the harbor and listened to the waves lapping at the shore. Almost as if they were laughing at him because he and Jer had gotten nowhere with this case. And now Jer was out of commission. Bryce pressed his lips together and narrowed his eyes.

After checking in with his superior again, Bryce headed back to the hospital. Could Kyleigh's father have met with the same fate? If Whitehall had gotten wind of Major Flanagan's suspicions, he might have wanted to silence him. Was someone else at Ft. Shafter involved?

An hour later, Kyleigh paced the waiting room. She wasn't the only one with a troubled heart. The sight of so many people who no doubt experienced the same frustration she felt brought more tears. Would they never come out and tell her how Jer was? Or whoever the others in the ER were there for? *Lord, please let Jer recover. Help these other hurting people. And please let us find out where Dad is.*

She glanced at Marisa, who wore a worried expression, brows drawn together and a lock of hair twisted around her fingers. She'd never seen her friend so concerned. *Marisa hasn't taken her eyes off me for a second.* At least not since the moment she and Bryce arrived in the ER. Kyleigh sighed. Some vacation this was for Marisa.

As Kyleigh parked herself next to her friend, Bryce strode into the waiting room, nodded to a police officer stationed at the entrance to the exam rooms, and approached the girls. "Any word on Jer?"

Both shook their heads. Kyleigh's eyes burned. "I haven't been in an ER for a very long time. Is this lengthy wait normal?"

He smiled at her. "You need to try to relax. The staff here is the best on the island, and, as I said before, Jer's a tough dude. He's a fighter. If I could tell you about some of the cases we've been on where he's saved my bacon, your heads would swim. He'll be all right."

Bryce went to the admitting desk and spoke with a nurse. When he returned, he dragged a chair in front of Marisa and Kyleigh and sat facing them. "Jer's conscious. I'm going back to talk to him now. Stay here in the ER, not outside." He stepped away from them.

"Why?"

He turned to face Marisa.

She cocked her head. "Not that I planned to leave, but why?"

Bryce chewed his bottom lip.

Kyleigh's stomach churned. "What happened at the grill, Bryce? Was someone else found? My dad?"

Bryce spun and took Kyleigh's hands in his. "No. It wasn't your dad, but I can't talk about it right now. Let me get in there and see Jer. Kyleigh, I know I keep saying it, but I'm sure we'll find your dad, and he'll be fine. Keep thinking that." He turned toward the back rooms again and called over his shoulder. "As soon as I've talked to Jer, I'll be back. Just stay here."

Chapter Sixteen

B ryce strode through the double doors into the waiting room. He found Marisa dozing in the corner. As he lowered to the chair next to her, he glanced at his watch. One in the morning. She was exhausted. Kyleigh, too, no doubt. He scanned the room for her. Where had she gone?

A few people still waited to be seen, but Kyleigh was nowhere in sight. He nudged Marisa's arm. "Marisa, where's Kyleigh?"

Her eyelids opened, and she smiled. "Hi." She rubbed the sleep from her eyes and sat up straight.

"Hi, little haole. Where's Kyleigh?"

Marisa surveyed the room and shrugged. "She was here a while ago. I guess I fell asleep."

Bryce approached the police officer in the chair near the entrance. "What happened to Miss Flanagan?"

"I overheard her say she needed coffee. The admitting nurse said she'd find a machine in the hallway. She headed down there." The officer pointed to a set of double doors across the room. "She should be back any minute. But since you're here, I'll look for her."

"No. I'll go." Why didn't she stay put? *Women!* The uncomfortable, prickly sensation return to Bryce's neck. He hurried to Marisa, who had dozed off again, head propped in the corner. He touched her shoulder, and she jumped.

"I'm sorry, Marisa." He crouched in front of her. "Didn't mean to startle you. Kyleigh's gone in pursuit of a coffee machine. I'll find her. Don't *you* go anywhere!"

"I'm not sure I could if I tried. I can barely see straight." She blinked several times and let her head drop back to the wall.

Bryce smiled at her. Poor kid.

Marisa murmured something unintelligible, then her breathing slipped into a rhythmic pattern. His fingers touched her cheek. She was adorable. A strand of wispy black hair fell across her face, and her nose wiggled. Bryce tucked the hair behind her ear, rose, and made a beeline for the hallway.

As he turned the corner at the end of the hall, Kyleigh almost ran into him, two Styrofoam cups in her hands. Her eyes widened as she lifted the cups into the air and sucked in a breath. "Is Jer okay?"

"He'll be fine. Let me take those before you douse yourself with hot coffee." He seized the cups.

"Thank you. I nearly soaked you in the brew. Sorry. I should have watched where I was going. Too much on my mind. You're sure Jer's all right?"

"Yes. Just spoke to him."

He led her through the hall toward the ER waiting room. "Let's get back to Marisa. She's out like a light, so she'll need this coffee to walk to the car when we leave."

"That's why I found some. The Coke machine in the waiting room is out of almost everything with caffeine. So what happened with Jer? You're sure he's going to be okay?"

Bryce snickered to himself. Jer had her under his spell. "Yes."

They entered the waiting room and sat next to Marisa. She stirred but didn't awaken. Bryce put one cup on the table in front of them and handed Kyleigh the other. "They've x-rayed Jer's chest and given him the all-clear. He's alert, breathing well, and oriented. They said he can go home and follow up with the doctor in a day or two. He'll be off duty until released by the doc. But he's as cantankerous as ever, so he'll be good as new in no time." Bryce laughed. "I'm kidding about the cantankerous part." He took the cup of hot coffee from her shaking hands. "You can relax now."

She let out a breath and smiled. "Thanks."

"Aʻole pilikia...ah..." He chuckled at the puzzled expression on her face. "That means you're welcome. Let me drive you and Marisa home. I'll come back for Jer." He nodded toward the sleeping beauty. "She's zonked."

"I'd rather wait for Jer if you don't mind."

"But Marisa can't be comfortable in that position." He stretched to peer around Kyleigh. Marisa wore a peaceful mien. What a beauty.

"Are you kidding? This girl can sleep anywhere. During our high school days, we attended teen camp together every summer, and later as adults to the camp meetings from church. Nothing ever kept her awake. She's slept on rocky ground, in drafty cabins with coyotes howling at night, slumped on the end of a lumpy couch. Trust me, she's fine. Will it be much longer before they release him?"

"No. Before I left the exam room, they said he could go home in another hour. Half of that's gone now. I'll check on him again, but don't wander off!"

She laid her hand on his forearm and handed him Marisa's cup. "You may need this more than she does. Hope you like it black. They were out of cream."

He sniffed the brew. "The way I like it. Strong and black. Mahalo." He took a gulp. "Hopefully, Jer's ready to leave this place."

Kyleigh bit her lower lip as Bryce disappeared through the double doors to the examining rooms. She gazed at Marisa and smiled. What a nightmare vacation she'd given her friend. But...she'd met such a sweet guy here. Too bad they lived so far apart.

Jer's face entered Kyleigh's thoughts. *Really* too bad. How could a girl expect to have a romantic relationship with thousands of miles between them?

She sipped her coffee, placed the cup on the magazine table, and bowed her head. *Lord, thank You for protecting Jer. Thank You for leading Bryce to him right away, for the paramedics who arrived so quickly, for the hospital staff—* Her father's face floated into her mind. Would God protect her father too...wherever he was? Except for Aunt Maye, he was the only family she had. How would she tell her aunt they still hadn't found her father? *Please, Lord, let us find Dad, and let him be unharmed.*

Tears fell to her lap. She dropped her face to her hands, elbows propped on her knees.

Marisa's arm stretched around Kyleigh's shoulders. "Let it out, hon. You've been tighter than a Charlie horse for days."

As Kyleigh let the sobs flow, Marisa hugged her.

Several minutes later, Bryce and Jer emerged from the back of the examination area. Kyleigh wiped her eyes and nose with tissues. A wave of relief washed over her.

Hanging onto Bryce's arm, Jer lowered himself to the seat next to hers. "Are you all right, Kyleigh?"

Her heart melted at the sound of concern in his voice. "Me? You're the one who almost drowned, remember? I've never prayed so hard in my life. You scared us all to death."

His brows rose. "Sorry about that. It wasn't intentional and not a part of my plans for dinner tonight." He smiled.

The knots in her stomach loosened. "It was such a scare. What happened to you?"

Bryce sat down on the other side of him. "I haven't told them."

Jer nodded and turned back to Kyleigh. "All I remember is walking on the sidewalk next to The Pearl Grill. The waiter who said he'd meet me stood near the back door. As I stepped into the shadows, someone hit me on the head. The next thing I knew, I was under water. I struggled to the surface and managed to grab onto a boat. The last thing I remember was swinging my arm over the edge. At least until I woke up here in the ER."

Bryce laid his hand on Jer's shoulder. "Yeah. When I jumped into the boat, you were already going under. I grabbed your arms. After I pulled you onto the dock and pumped most of the water out of you, you woke up, but I guess you don't remember that. You were only awake long enough to utter one syllable. 'Da.' I mentioned it to you back there." Bryce pointed to the examining area behind the swinging doors.

"Yes, I remember. But they whisked me off for a final check before we could talk. I need to tell you...but not now." Jer tipped his head toward Kyleigh.

She stood. "I guess that means police business you can't tell me. I hate that phrase. Shouldn't we take you home? You need to rest and..." Her eyes roved over his chest and legs. "Where did you get those clothes?"

Jer glanced down at the loose-fitting, dark blue apparel. "One of the male nurses had an extra set of scrubs in his locker and loaned them to me, so I didn't have to wear a hospital gown." He held up a plastic bag. "Feels like part of the harbor is still in these. Even my skin was drenched. We've been in the ER so often, we're on a first-name basis with the staff. And fortunately, Dane is around my size."

Bryce rose. "I'll say you were drenched. More like a drowned mongoose." He gave Jer a toothy grin. "But yeah, man, time to get you home. Let's go."

Jer stood up slowly and clutched the back of his head.

Kyleigh grabbed his arm. "You should sit still a little longer."

"Outside of a whopper of a headache and a goose egg that'll hurt for quite a while, I'm fine. Not the first one I've had. Probably won't be the last either."

Should she offer to stay with him tonight? He shouldn't be alone with a concussion. "You can't stay by yourself tonight. What if you pass out?"

As they made their way to the sliding exit doors, Jer slipped his arm around her shoulders. "Bryce will stay with me."

Goosebumps ran up her arms from the warmth of his nearness. Of course, Bryce would be there for him. Her neck grew warm, and heat flooded her face.

Jer squeezed her. "Mahalo, for the concern. Nice to know you care about me."

She peeked at him. "Marisa and I would have been happy to have you stay at the apartment if you need...I mean...there are two of us there...but Bryce has everything under control." She must sound like an idiot.

They left the ER waiting room and crossed the parking lot to Bryce's car. He opened the back passenger door for Jer to slide in and then helped Marisa into the front seat. Bryce led Kyleigh to the other side of the car, and she slid in next to Jer.

Before Bryce got in behind the wheel, Kyleigh looked out the back window and caught movement near the edge of the parking lot. A man stood near a truck in front of the bushes on the other side of the street. Sure resembled that blond server at the restaurant.

"Bryce, do you see that guy standing over there in the parking lot? Is that the waiter named Dave? What do you suppose he's doing here?"

Bryce started the engine. "I saw him. Not sure it was him, though. The light from the parking lot isn't that good." But it had to have been him. Only one reason Whitehall would be around. To make sure Jer was a goner after he was dragged from the harbor. He must have hid near the restaurant and watched. When the paramedics left with Jer, Whitehall must've followed. Good thing an officer was stationed in the hospital.

As Bryce pulled out of the parking lot, he monitored the waiter's truck through the rear window. Whitehall jumped in his truck and followed at a distance as they left the hospital grounds.

Jer's head fell back onto the seat, and Kyleigh grabbed his shoulder. "Jer, are you okay?"

He opened his eyes and rolled his head toward her. "Yeah." He chuckled. "But dead tired. At least not dead, though."

Bryce focused back on the truck tailing them.

Kyleigh's stress sounded in her voice. "You're not very funny."

Bryce laughed. "I told you, Kyleigh. He's been through worse."

She sighed. "You could have been killed, Jer. Doesn't life mean anything to you two?"

Bryce raised his brows and glanced at Marisa. She stared at him.

Jer sat erect. "Yes, it does. The safety of people's lives is why we joined the police department in the first place. But, Kyleigh, a sense of humor can help you get through a lot of bad times. Psalm one-twenty-six, verse two says, 'Then was our mouth filled with laughter, and our tongue with singing: then said they among the heathen, The Lord hath done great things for them.' Don't you see? God saved me despite what the perp had in mind. Isn't that something to be happy about?"

Bryce trained his eyes on the road. He loved this guy like a brother, but why did everything have to turn into a sermon with him?

Marisa twisted in her seat. "The man knows his Scripture."

Jer rested his head back on the seat. "I have to. I teach the teen Sunday school class at my church. They're always trying to trip me up. Those kids would never let me live it down if they stumped me." He snickered.

"And, Kyleigh, this incident won't interfere with our search for your Dad. I don't want you to worry. One verse comes to mind that might help you right now. Proverbs fifteen three. 'The eyes of the Lord are in every place, beholding the evil and the good.' Is your dad a Christian?"

"Yes. He's the one who led me to the Lord when I was a kid. He always has a ready answer from the Bible when I come to him with a problem."

Bryce clamped his jaw tight. Not another one.

Jer rubbed his forehead. "Then stick this verse in your head, and promise me you'll keep it there. Psalm ninety-one, one and two. 'He that dwelleth in the secret place of the most High shall abide under the shadow of the Almighty. I will say of the Lord, He is my refuge and my fortress: my God; in him will I trust.'"

"You put me to shame, Jer." Kyleigh lowered her gaze to her folded hands in her lap. "I haven't picked up my Bible once since we left Houston. I've prayed. Talked to God. But I haven't let Him talk to me through His Word. Thank you."

Bryce peeked at Marisa. She smiled. But it had to be because Kyleigh and Jer were hitting it off big time. It didn't mean she was a Bible thumper too. Hopefully, she believed the same as he did about religion.

As they neared the complex where Kyleigh and Marisa were staying in the major's apartment, Bryce kept watch behind them. Whitehall's truck had been there most of the way to the apartment, but no sign of it now. Maybe it wasn't him after all.

Chapter Seventeen

*A*fter retrieving the newspaper from the walkway at dawn a few hours later, Marisa stretched out on the couch and perused the articles. So many things to do on the island, but would she have the stamina to visit any of these places today? After the late-night trauma, why had she awoken so early? Five in the morning and she couldn't force her eyes shut again. The catnaps she took in the waiting room last night must've given her enough sleep. Or...maybe her inner alarm had refused to accept this as a vacation. She shook her head.

She shouldn't be looking at tourist attractions. Ky sure wouldn't want to go. Not while she was so worried about Jer and her father. And even though Bryce had the day off, he'd have to take care of his partner, at least for today. If her best friend couldn't go with her, she'd rather stay and help take care of Jer too.

The door to the master bedroom opened with a tiny squeak, and Ky stepped out. She tiptoed to the foyer.

Marisa glanced at the kitchen clock. Nine. "*Ky.* Where are you going this early?"

Ky jumped and spun. "You scared the daylights out of me."

Marisa giggled. "I thought for sure you'd sleep until noon after what you've been through. Off to see *Mr. Right?*"

"Very funny, Miss-laugh-it-up. I'll never live down my concern for Jer, will I?" She grinned. "But I do believe you're correct. He is Mr. Right." Ky sashayed to the couch. "What about you, Miss *Haole?* Methinks, you've got it bad for his partner. Can't say I blame you. If I hadn't gotten to know Jer first, Bryce's smile would have reeled me in too."

Marisa's neck warmed. She darted to the kitchen and filled a glass full of ice water. "Aren't they the charmers, though? I think I'm in love, Ky. Really. For the first time in my life." With her glass in hand, she hopped onto a stool and swallowed a mouthful. "So you *are* going to visit Jer this morning. Did he give you his address? Or was he going to Bryce's place? I suppose I could call him for you."

Ky waltzed up to the island and sat on another stool. "No. Don't bother. Ummm...Marisa, please don't get your hopes set on Bryce. We'll be gone soon. At least we will when we find my dad. We won't be here for more than two weeks...I hope. Long-distance relationships are not easy, and someone usually ends up with a broken heart. I'd hate for it to happen to you."

"Look, Ky. Just because that fool you fell for in college turned into such a...*jerk*...doesn't mean all men are like that. He hurt you, but he wasn't the guy for you in the first place. Bryce and Jer are

Christians. Paul wasn't. He proved it with his action after he transferred to NYU and had a fling with every girl he sweet-talked."

"How did you find out he was...ah...dating other girls? I never said anything."

Marisa took another drink of water, jumped off the stool, and poured the half-glassful into the sink. "Drew? My old boyfriend. Don't you remember? He introduced Paul to you. When Drew visited him in New York, before Paul broke it off with you, Drew found out the seedy truth. He's the one who told Paul he had to break off your engagement, or he'd tell you what was going on."

"And Drew told you." Ky dropped her forehead to her folded arms on the island's counter. "I had no idea you were aware of why we called off the wedding. When Paul made light of how he...was so *popular* with all the girls at school, it devastated me. He said he couldn't imagine himself tied down to a country girl like me after he had seen what New York had to offer."

She rocked her forehead back and forth on her arms, then lifted her face to Marisa. "All the people I had to contact and return gifts to. It was so embarrassing. But, I wasn't thinking of Paul when I said not to plan on a romantic relationship with Bryce. Is he a Christian? He's a close friend of Jer's, but it doesn't mean he's saved. Has Bryce given you any indication he is? I caught a glimpse of his narrowed eyes while Jer was quoting Scripture. He looked none too happy."

Marisa gnawed on her lip. A wave of uncertainty filled her. "No, he hasn't said. I guess I assumed."

"Please don't set yourself up for that kind of hurt. His relationship with God and the distance between Houston and Hawai'i are two negative factors to consider. When we leave, who knows if he'll retain the attraction he's shown for you."

Ky headed for the foyer again. "I have to go."

"Sooo...where are you going? And how about some breakfast first?"

"No. Not hungry. I'm...taking my dad's bike for a ride to...relax."

"But—"

The door clicked shut behind Ky.

Oh, boy. Marisa sighed. Should she try to reach Jer? She hadn't needed to call him before when he'd asked her. After what happened to him last night, he shouldn't go off chasing after Ky. *Lord, what should I do, follow her?*

Marisa paced the living room. She dropped to her knees at the couch. "Lord, I could really use some help here." She fell silent for a moment, waiting for an answer. "Yes, thank you. I can follow her in the car once I hear the chain from the bike drop. I'll give her a minute to roll the bike to the street." She jumped up, grabbed her purse, pulled out the extra car key, and hurried to the front door.

Wait a sec. She still hadn't heard the chain rattle. Marisa opened the door a crack and peeked toward the back end of the walkway. The chain still secured the dirt bike to the awning support. She sprinted to the parking lot. "The Mustang's not there." *Oh, Ky.* Where had she gone now?

Jer stepped out of Bryce's bedroom and stared at the couch. He couldn't have asked for a better friend than Swanson. "You didn't have to sleep on the sofa last night, buddy. This would have suited me just fine."

Bryce turned off the stove and faced him. "Hey, you needed a good night's rest. Besides, I've slept on the couch before. It's comfortable. That's why I suggested my place instead of yours. Your couch is terrible." He laughed.

His partner had piled the sheet and lightweight blanket he used on the arm of the makeshift bed. Jer picked them up and folded them. He tossed the linens back on the sofa and gingerly walked to the bamboo table in the dining area of Bryce's loft apartment. "Coffee smells great." He eased onto a matching chair.

After handing Jer a cup, Bryce set a plate of scrambled eggs and toast in front of him. "From the racket you made in the bathroom, I knew you were no longer asleep. Figured you might be hungry. Now eat." He turned back for his food and coffee, then straddled a chair on the other side of the table.

"Thanks. Had a little leftover dizziness while I washed up. I tried to steady myself by grabbing the counter and bumped into the glass pineapple freshener thing. The pineapple knocked over your toothbrush holder. Fortunately, nothing broke."

Bryce laughed again. "No problem. My mom likes to come over and decorate for me. She's hoping I'll find a nice girl who might visit."

"And you may well have done that." Jer smiled. Hopefully, both of them were saved. He needed to press Bryce on that issue and soon.

Jer eyed the clock on the microwave. Nine-thirty. He'd slept well through the night. And Bryce was right, he was hungry. "What? No Spam, rice, or Portuguese sausage? I thought you always ate your eggs with at least rice and one of the meats."

"I eat *all* of it on Sundays when I go to Mom's for breakfast before church. But at home, I usually skip the meal for the option of sleeping a little longer. Had nothing but eggs and bread to whip up this morning. Sorry." He laughed. "Don't let those eggs get cold. Here's the ketchup."

"You didn't have to cook for me either."

Bryce pointed his fork at Jer. "You needed to sleep, man, and now you need to eat. Last night was quite an ordeal." Bryce's cell rang. "I gave Marisa my phone number, but I'll bet it's Kyleigh checking on you." He snickered. "She sure was worried about you last night, no matter what I said to her." He snatched his cell from the counter. "Nope. Marisa. Hi, little haole."

Jer grinned to himself. Would Kyleigh still be worried about him? As he polished off the eggs and toast, his partner paced the large room from one side to the other.

Bryce's voice tensed. "You're kidding...I'll be there in about fifteen to twenty-five minutes, depending on traffic. Wait for me." He stepped to the kitchen counter. "Yeah. I guess we'll have to, but don't worry about her. Everything will be fine. Bye."

Like a wave of water from last night's near-drowning, coldness rose in Jer's arms. His stomach tightened. "What was that about? Is Kyleigh all right?" He snatched his dish and dropped it in the sink. "What do we have to do and why?"

Bryce grimaced, then formed a half-smile. "Not we. Just me. Kyleigh went out this morning...in the car...ah, to do some souvenir shopping...before Marisa got up. Ah, Kyleigh left a note. Marisa was planning to visit the Pearl Harbor Memorial today, and she can't go without transportation. I've got the day off, so if you feel you can manage here without me and don't mind being alone...I'll drive her. You need the rest anyway, hang out, watch TV, or—"

"You're a lousy liar, Swanson." Jer stared at his partner. "What's going on?"

Bryce sighed. "Kyleigh did take off with the car. But she told Marisa she was going to ride the bike to relax and rushed out the door. Marisa wasn't sure what to do since you gave her your cell number yesterday morning together with a note saying to call you if Kyleigh left the apartment." He sucked in a deep breath. "But she was afraid to phone you now because of last night. So she called me. Kyleigh's purse is gone, but she's not answering her cell."

"So she took the major's Mustang instead of the bike?"

"Yeah. Marisa said the bike's still locked up on the porch, but the car's gone."

And Kyleigh didn't answer her phone. A chill rose in Jer's neck. "You had an officer stationed at the ER last night because of the dead waiter." He narrowed his eyes. "You said you thought the killer would try to finish the job at the hospital."

An image floated into Jer's mind. "I remember. After the hit to my head, before I was dumped into the harbor, I came to. Someone stood over me on the dock. When he turned, the light at the end of the pier revealed his face. It was Whitehall. After that, I passed out until I was in the water, choking. He was probably the one who killed the waiter."

Jer grabbed his still soggy wallet and keys from the coffee table, then reached for his waterlogged cell on the kitchen table. "Blast!" He dropped the phone. "Kyleigh could be in big trouble. Whitehall may know she's Major Flanagan's daughter. If so, he might think she has information too. Let's go."

Bryce stepped between his wobbly partner and the door. "Jer, you can't. You're in no condition. You stay here, and I'll go." Bryce strode across the living room, opened the desk drawer, and pulled out another cellphone. "Here. When I lost my phone a few weeks ago, I picked up this burner. The number's stored on my mobile, so I'll keep you updated as we go. You rest as the doctor ordered."

Jer's head, heart, and everywhere else fought the idea of not going after Kyleigh. But Bryce was right. He'd stay put and let Bryce handle it. Jer pressed his eyes closed. If he lost consciousness while they were trying to help her, he'd jeopardize her safety and possibly theirs. But how could he sit around and wait? His eyes popped open.

"You'll tell me what you find out? So I don't go nuts wondering what's happening?"

Bryce nodded. "I promise, man. You'd better plug in the charger for that phone. You'll find it in the drawer." He pointed to the desk before he ran out the door.

Bryce brought the Prius to a stop in front of Major Flanagan's apartment. Marisa must really be worried about Kyleigh to not have waited for him inside. She hopped off the stone wall next to the walkway and rushed to the car. He pushed open the passenger door for her from inside. "Come on. We'll head to the restaurant and check if she decided to do her own surveillance on Whitehall."

Marisa slipped in, and Bryce took off. "This is just like Ky to sneak off on her own. That girl is fearless. Not sure if she plans to investigate for Jer's or her dad's sake...or both. She didn't say too much to me when we got back from the ER. Of course, I was so tired, I don't remember any conversation...or going to bed."

Bryce slid his hand over hers on the console and squeezed. "Don't worry, we'll find her." He returned his to the steering wheel. "Jer said she's been tied up in knots since he met her. He warned her to leave the investigation to us."

"You guys don't know Ky as I do. She acts like she's the one serving in the Army instead of her father. Fear is not in her vocabulary."

The Prius sped through the streets until they arrived at the restaurant. Bryce parked in the lot but kept the engine running. "Car's not here. Any ideas?"

Marisa burst into tears. "I've no idea where she's gone. She wouldn't take a car up to the bike trail. Would she?"

Chapter Eighteen

*J*er paced Bryce's apartment, holding onto pieces of furniture in his wobbly state. He had to get this dizziness under control.

He glanced at the microwave clock for the tenth time. Forty-five minutes since Bryce left to pick up Marisa. Jer lowered himself to the couch. He'd go crazy if he didn't hear from them soon. The burner phone rang, and he snatched it from the coffee table. "Yeah!" Was that Marisa crying in the background? "What happened? Is Kyleigh hurt?"

Bryce's voice broke through the line tenser than Jer had ever heard. "Nothing's happened to Kyleigh that we know of. Marisa's just upset. We tried the restaurant in case Kyleigh came here to confront Whitehall, but she's not here. Do you have any idea where she might have gone? Has she said anything to you to give us a clue?"

Jer fell back against the couch, and his noggin's goose egg thumped the wall. "*Oww.*" Pain radiated from the base of his neck to the top of his head. He massaged his lower scalp. "Give me a sec." All he could think of were comments Kyleigh had made in distress as she worried about him. And those about finding her father.

"Hey, what if she's on Koʻolau? That's where she was when I first found her looking for her dad. But without a bike, how would she search the trails for him. Unless she decided to walk the path." Jer clenched his teeth.

"Hold on, man." Jer could hear Bryce as he comforted Kyleigh's friend. "Try not to worry, Marisa. We'll find Kyleigh." But his voice lacked confidence. "Jer just mentioned Kyleigh walking the bike trail on the mountain range. Do you think she'd do it?"

"You may be on to something, Jer. Marisa said Kyleigh would. And Kyleigh might have decided to check the road on the way up to where her dad rode to see if—I have no idea what she expected to see from a car. But we'll run up there. I'll call in a while. If you have any more ideas, phone me."

The connection ended. Jer rubbed his temples as he dropped the cell on the table. "What have you done, Kyleigh?" Whitehall's smug expression as he stood on the pier behind The Pearl Grill flashed into his mind. "Yes. It was definitely his face I saw." Whitehall could have waited for Kyleigh outside the apartment this morning and nabbed her when she walked out.

Jer picked up the cell and tottered to the bathroom with his feet spread wide apart for stability, supporting himself from one piece of furniture to the next. This dizziness had better clear up fast. He reached the bathroom and laid the phone on a stack of folded towels on a shelf over a clothes hamper. In the medicine cabinet, he found a bottle of aspirin and downed two. *Better call a cab and get to my apartment.*

Half an hour later, Jer plodded into his home, took another couple of aspirins, splashed cold water on his face, and hobbled to his truck as quickly as his still shaky legs allowed.

Kyleigh kept her tears at bay. Where should she look for her father? Driving in circles in Honolulu had gotten her nowhere. She could run out to Pearl Harbor and search around the restaurant. Check if there were any clues the police hadn't discovered to suggest her dad had been there. He couldn't have simply disappeared.

After driving the short distance to The Pearl Grill, Kyleigh examined the crime scene for what seemed like hours. Nothing but the yellow tape the police had used to mark off the area. What was she doing? What had she expected to find? Kyleigh dropped to a bench that faced the harbor. She was no detective. Perhaps Jer was right. The investigation was better left up to them. But her heart told her otherwise.

Traffic noise from the road and a sound like a seagull with a sore throat caught Kyleigh's attention. A beautiful white bird with a jet-black beak flew out of a tree near the restaurant parking lot to the rear of the building. Guess that was a sign she'd best move along too.

Kyleigh trudged back to the car, slipped in, and prayed. "Lord, what do I do now?" She didn't deserve an answer. "Please forgive me for failing to take time with Your Word this morning. And after being so embarrassed by what Jer said as they drove away from the

ER too." The held-back tears finally flooded her eyes and dropped into her lap. "I'm at a loss, Heavenly Father. Help."

As she mopped her face with the hem of her cotton blouse, Kyleigh ended her prayer and gazed out over the water to the Pearl Harbor Memorial. "The Army post!" Of course. She'd talk to Colonel Stevens and find out if they had any new leads. "Thank You, Lord."

An hour later, Kyleigh exited the colonel's office with a heavy heart. Fine. *Let the Criminal Investigation Department do all the investigating they wanted.* If they hadn't found her father by now, what use were they? They weren't any different from the civilian sector. She couldn't trust them any more than the investigators who promised years ago to arrest the murderer who shot her mother in the bank robbery...and didn't. They'd done absolutely nothing. The killer got away.

Kyleigh slid into the Mustang's driver seat, slammed the door shut, and pounded her fists on the steering wheel. Her eyes blurred with renewed waterworks, but she shook it off. It was time to make good on her promise to track down her father. She'd take charge of the investigation while CID and HPD twiddled their thumbs. She should have gone straight to the mountain range in the first place.

Kyleigh started the engine and pulled away from the curb. "At least the colonel had given her aunt some peace of mind when he called her this morning, telling her the investigative team was out looking for her brother." Kyleigh bit her lip. She should call Aunt Maye, too, but the last thing she needed was to know what had happened in the police investigation yesterday.

After she entered the Makakilo Kauhale complex and parked the car, Kyleigh sat and stared at the walkway to her father's apartment. Should she tell Marisa she returned Dad's Mustang or take the bike before her friend saw her? Marisa would no doubt give her what-for for taking off like she had this morning.

"Well...time to face the Italian's wrath." Kyleigh hurried to the entrance, turned the key, and swung the front door open. "Marisa, I'm back." Hmmm...no answer, and everything was dark and still. *Where is that girl?* Kyleigh flipped on the light switch. The bathroom door stood open. Darting to the hall, she found the guestroom and master bedroom doors ajar. "Marisa's not here."

Kyleigh cocked her head. Bryce wouldn't have taken Marisa anywhere, not while he was taking care of Jer. She'd best not call Bryce. If he didn't know where she'd gone, it might upset him under the current circumstances. Everyone's nerves had been stretched to the limit yesterday. Jer's phone was out of commission, but she wouldn't bother him anyway. Not in his condition. He'd gone through enough already. Maybe Marisa took a walk. The apartment grounds were beautiful, with the trickling manmade waterfalls, koi ponds, and gardens of purple lantana, white and pink plumeria, and hibiscus everywhere. *And oh, the fragrance.* Had to be where she went.

After Kyleigh dropped the car keys on the kitchen counter, she grabbed an apple from the refrigerator and hopped onto a stool. "When Marisa got back, she'd think I'd decided on the bike ride I told her I'd take before leaving for Honolulu." Strange, Marisa hadn't called and reamed her out for taking the car by now. Oh, well. *The girl's thoughts were on more pleasant things, I'm sure, like Bryce Swanson.* Kyleigh chortled.

While she finished the apple, her mind wandered to Jer. Would he still be woozy today? Last night was a real eye-opener, finding out he was a devoted Christian. Not many people quoted verses as he had without looking them up first. She pressed her lips together, then smiled. Exactly the kind of man any woman would want in her life. If only they didn't live so far apart. A sigh escaped her. He taught Sunday school as well.

She recalled his smile as he teased her those few times last night between waves of dizziness. Kyleigh rested her elbows on the kitchen island, and heat flowed into her cheeks. How could she deny her attraction to Jer now? Marisa would never let her forget it.

Kyleigh glanced at the wall clock. Almost one. Better go before Marisa showed up and tried to stop her. She threw the apple core in the garbage and stepped into the master bedroom to change into sneakers. A picture of her with her father taken on her last trip to O'ahu sat on the dresser. She sighed again. *Dad, where are you? Lord, help me find him.*

With or without Jer and Bryce, she'd find her father no matter what. *That's a promise.* Jer likely wouldn't be able to work on the case for another few days. Would Bryce continue to search? He'd have more interest in finding out who almost killed his partner. The disappearance of Major Flanagan would take a back seat for sure. It was understandable. Jer was more than a partner to Bryce. He'd said so himself. They were as close as brothers.

Hopefully, she'd find her dad before Jer was released for work. *Time to start.*

Kyleigh tied her laces and left the apartment. She unlocked the bike and pushed it into the street. Marisa, Jer, and Bryce would all be mad at her for leaving, especially with the still broken headlight, but she had to go to the Ko'olau mountain range. She had to.

After kick-starting the engine, Kyleigh donned her helmet. *This will especially upset Jer after I promised to let them handle the situation.* But as long as she was careful, she'd be safe.

As she watched out the passenger window for any sign of Kyleigh, Marisa's cellphone rang. *Please let it be Ky.* Marisa pulled it out of her bag without checking the screen and answered, "Hello?"

Kyleigh's aunt responded in a panic-stricken voice. "Marisa, Kyleigh's not answering her phone again. Did she go off without it a second time? Praise God I had *your* number."

"Aunt Maye. I'm not sure why Ky's doesn't answer. She took her dad's car somewhere early this morning." Marisa gritted her teeth. Evasiveness wasn't something she practiced, and she hated to be this way. But what else could she do? How was she going to explain to Ky's aunt? There was no way. If she told Aunt Maye the truth, the poor lady might have a heart attack. Marisa glanced at Bryce and shrugged.

He nodded as though he'd read her thoughts.

Marisa pressed the cell's loudspeaker button while Aunt Maye continued to voice her frustration with her niece. "I've called her three times, and each time it goes to voicemail. What am I going to do with that girl?"

"Ah...I'm not sure. You know Ky. She has a mind of her own." Boy, wasn't *that* the truth? If not before, it was now. "Hasn't she checked in with you?"

"No. And Colonel Stevens called this morning to tell me CID...that's the Army's Criminal Investigation Division...has taken over the case of my brother's disappearance. So far, they don't have any news, but I believe they'll get to the bottom of it. Please, have Kyleigh call me when she returns from *wherever.*"

"I will." Marisa bit her lip. "I promise."

"Are you okay, dear? You sound like you've been crying."

Bryce placed his hand on Marisa's arm and squeezed.

"Oh, no." Marisa took in a quick breath. "I had a mild allergic reaction. You know, all the flowers here and everything."

"Well, you take care."

"I will, ma'am. You too. Bye." She disconnected the call and stuffed her cell in her purse.

Bryce patted her shoulder. "You handled the call well. No sense upsetting Kyleigh's aunt over something she can't do anything about."

Marisa covered her mouth with her hand as she fought an onslaught of more tears. "Bryce, what will Ky's aunt do if Ky doesn't come back? First her brother, and now her niece."

Bryce pulled the car to the side of a dead-end street and killed the engine. "Not sure how to answer that one." He surveyed the area. "Not another car in sight. This is as close to the mountain as Kyleigh could have driven if she was checking the bike trail Jer usually rode. He's brought me up here twice, trying to get me interested in this crazy dirt bike riding on Koʻolau. Not my idea of fun." He turned to Marisa. "You didn't see the Mustang on the way up either, did you?"

"No," Marisa squeaked out.

He lifted her chin. "You all right?"

She nodded and sniffled.

"Kyleigh may have gone up another way to find a trail." He started the engine, and they continued their trek up Koʻolau.

Marisa wiped her tears as she scoured the sides of the roads Bryce drove through as they ventured further into the range. Ky had to be here...somewhere. Where else would she have gone? *Oh, Ky. What will I tell your aunt if something's happened to you? God, please keep her safe.*

Chapter Nineteen

ave Whitehall watched Kyleigh from the bushes along the parking lot at the major's apartment complex. Two days, he'd followed her. Ever since she visited The Pearl Grill for lunch with that cute dark-haired doll. After the strange way Kyleigh acted toward him, she'd made him nervous. As if she knew what he'd done. The name on her credit card gave her away. Flanagan. "Major Flanagan's daughter," he whispered. He'd seen her with her dad a couple of years ago. Even back then, the spiff-and-polish military jerk made trouble. Dave gritted his teeth. But not anymore.

He narrowed his eyes and glared at Kyleigh's back as she pulled away on the dirt bike. Would he have to get rid of her too? Dave raced to his truck and sped off after her.

She'd snooped around quite a bit in the past two days. And then there were those two pesky cops she and her friend got so chummy with. Just how much had her father or HPD told her? And where was she going now on the dirt bike? He had to follow her until he was sure she wasn't a threat.

He'd gotten away with killing the other two, his coworker and the major, but this would make three bodies. How long could his luck hold out? But it was worth the risk for the money he made on the drug operation he'd set up here on the island. No one was going to mess up his plans.

Her father snooped around once too often. And Mike should have stuck to being a waiter instead of a lousy snitch. What a cowardly weasel. Thought he'd be scot-free if he ratted, did he? Never should have trusted him.

"Careful she doesn't notice you." He pulled in behind the car in back of her but kept his eye on her helmet.

Kyleigh turned onto the road that led to the bike trail. Must be planning to ride up Ko'olau. *I wonder.* Was she searching for her father? She'd be better off combing the bottom of the mountain range. He cackled.

If he had to get rid of her, that would be the best place to do it. Right where her dad met his end. He tightened his jaw. Stupid female. If she was headed for those trails, she must think herself invulnerable going off alone. *Well, you've got a surprise coming. This ain't Texas, baby.*

Kyleigh rode into the Ko'olau mountain range and turned onto the bike trail. The grandeur of this place had always impressed her.

There was nowhere else quite as beautiful and mysterious that she'd visited. But if her dad had died here, she'd never return.

Her eyes drifted left and right as she inched along the path. She took her time to check anything unusual. At the crossing of trails, she headed down the same narrow track she'd ridden the last time she came up the range to find her father. "No wonder Dad loved to ride this seldom-used stretch," she whispered. As if she'd stepped back in time to the beginning of the world. It wouldn't surprise her if a pterodactyl flew past in the open spaces between the jagged ridges of Ko'olau. If there'd ever been such things as pterodactyls.

When she reached the spot where she and Jer had rested after he joined her that day in her search, Kyleigh shut off the engine. Had it only been two days ago she'd met Jer? Seemed like they'd known each other for months. He hadn't called to talk to her yet today, so it must mean he'd taken the doctor's advice and was resting.

The sound of another dirt bike some distance away resounded through the brush. Something she couldn't identify shuffled through the heavy overgrowth closer to the trail. Maybe one of those wild pigs Dad warned her about when she last visited him. She gulped. *Hope it stays away.* Dad said they could be really nasty. The noise stopped.

She pushed the dirt bike along the trail, stopping every now and then to examine the brush where something appeared to have trampled the growth. If it took all afternoon, she'd inspect every inch of this trail until she found something ...anything. If there *were* any clues. But there *had* to be. She just had to find her father.

A glance at her wristwatch told her an hour had gone by. She sighed. Her legs had turned to rubber from the many times she'd crouched to inspect suspicious spots. Not to mention having pushed the bike up the rises in the trail and held it back on the dips.

She came to a wall of dirt that rose above her on the right side of the trail and laughed to herself. *This was where Jer jumped down and scared the life out of me.* Such a smart aleck. She leaned the bike against the dirt wall.

More rustling from above caught her attention. Something moved closer. But what?

A chill ran up her neck. Again the noise went away. She breathed a sigh of relief.

Kyleigh sat on a rock and held her head in her hands. *Lord, will I ever learn what's happened to Dad?* When she raised her head, a glow like a sliver of silver on the cliffside of the trail beamed into her eye. Rays of the sun peeking through the clouds filtered through the trees behind her on the high side of the trail. They must have reflected off a small object in the weeds.

She rose from her perch, hurried across to the cliff, and pushed aside the vegetation. *Dog tags.*

Kyleigh brushed the dirt away from the embossed lettering. *Flanagan Charles P...Dad's!*

She slid the tags inside her capri pocket and leaned over the edge. For as far as she could see, plants grew out of fissures in the rocky face on the side of the mountain. Her stomach did somersaults.

As she pulled herself back to the trail, her hand brushed a thick patch of ferns. Something hard and black fell into the next bunch of ferns. She held onto a sapling and reached for the object farther out over the drop-off. A wallet.

After struggling back up to the path, she opened the soggy leather. Her breath hitched. "Dad's post access card. How—what?" Her heartbeat went into super-drive and hammered in her ears. "I need help."

Kyleigh wrangled her purse from behind her back and lifted the long strap over her neck and shoulder. Where was her cell? She searched every square inch of the bag. "Oh no. Great!" She'd never taken it out of the nightstand drawer when she got up this morning. How could she be so dumb? That was twice she'd gone off without it. No wonder she hadn't received a call. If Jer or Marisa had tried, they'd probably think she was ignoring them on purpose. If Marisa had tried to call her, her friend wouldn't have heard the phone with the drawer and bedroom door closed.

Those two would give her such a tongue lashing. Kyleigh frowned. She'd been in too much of a hurry to get out the door without Marisa seeing her. And it hadn't worked anyway.

Kyleigh returned to the rock and sat down again, staring at the wallet. Now she'd have to backtrack and hope to find someone up here at this time of the day who had a cellphone on them.

A moment later, she rose, stuffed the wallet into her purse, and yanked the dirt bike away from the wall. She spun the bike around toward the trail from where she'd come. The noise in the brush above sounded closer yet. She'd better hurry and leave this area.

God, help me find someone with a phone.

Dave crouched in the brush on the ledge above Kyleigh, trying to catch his breath. Good thing Flanagan's daughter had driven at a slow pace and walked the trail. He thought he'd been in pretty decent shape until this jaunt through the overgrowth. He should have taken advantage of her hanging over the cliff a moment ago, but whoever was on that other bike might have heard her if she fought back. Being an Army brat, chances were she'd be able to take care of herself.

He'd wait for her to mount the bike and then attack. Yes, that was a much better idea.

What had she found in those ferns anyway? Ironic. This was the exact spot where he'd shoved her old man and his bike off the range to meet the forest below.

Before Kyleigh straddled the bike, she brought a dark object out of her purse and gazed at it. Dave stretched and peered over the brush as far and as quietly as he could to catch a glimpse of what she held in her hand. A wallet. Had to be the major's. It must have popped out of his pocket before he sailed out into nothingness.

Stupid mistake, Whitehall. Once the old man had fallen out of sight, it would have been smart to look for any evidence someone might find to show the major had been here. Nothing to do now but rid himself of the daughter too.

Kyleigh swung her leg over the bike and settled onto the seat. As she lifted her leg to kick-start the engine, Dave burst from his hiding place and jumped to the path below.

Kyleigh's eyes popped. "What are you—"

Body hunched over, Dave rammed her in the side like a Billy goat. Kyleigh screamed, toppled off the bike, and rolled to the edge of the cliff. She jumped to her feet to face him. Her eyes widened, and her arms flailed as she lost her balance, toppling backward. Her scream was short-lived.

Dave grunted as he lifted up the bike she'd ridden and rolled it to the outside of the dirt bike trail. With a grin, he pushed it as hard as he could through the ferns until the bike sailed past the rocky ledge. He latched onto a tree to keep from falling himself. "Join your counterpart below." As he held a branch of the sturdy trunk, he peered over the ferns and plants. Nothing but more brush. No one would be any the wiser.

Below, metal crashed into stone and clattered farther downward until, seconds later, silence reigned. He smacked his hands together and smirked. "Well done, Whitehall. Another problem handled."

If only his father could see him now. How efficiently he'd taken care of business. His old man would rue the day he sent his only son away from home. "Not smart enough, am I? Yet, Dad, you're the one locked up, not me."

Now to figure out what he should do about his one failure. The detective.

Chapter Twenty

hough they'd driven along each road leading closer to the mountain throughout the entire Koʻolau range, Bryce and Marisa found no sign of Kyleigh or her father's car. Bryce pulled over, stopped, and turned off the engine. "This is getting us nowhere. I've no idea where to go next." The only thing left to do was walk all the trails unless they rented bikes, but it would be too dangerous for Marisa. Too many to check by themselves anyway, and she'd never make it. Not with that delicate frame of hers, even though he was sure she'd try.

Marisa sighed and shook her head. "Not being familiar with the island, I'm at a loss. Ky shouldn't have left like that. I am so angry at you right now, Ky." Her eyes grew misty.

Bryce cupped his hand on her shoulder. "Easy, little haole." He let go of Marisa and rubbed the back of his neck. Would Kyleigh have driven further south to the Pali? Jer had never mentioned riding around it. If Kyleigh's dad had ridden his bike in that area, would she have known about it? But then, maybe she'd simply gone somewhere to clear her head. The Pali was a terrific place to relax and think if she wanted to be alone. Plenty of places to hike and ponder.

"Marisa, we might be looking at this all wrong. Kyleigh may have taken the car to do some sightseeing and relax. She's been stressed since you both arrived here on the island. You said so yourself."

"I don't know...I guess...but," Marisa pulled and twisted a lock of her silky black hair with the fingers of her right hand, "if so, why didn't she tell me where she was going?"

Bryce took Marisa's left hand in his and ran his thumb over her soft skin. A giddy sensation filled his chest. He wanted to kiss her in the worst way. Better slow down, man. She was worried about her friend, so that was the priority right now. "Because she didn't feel very sociable? If she had told you, wouldn't you have wanted to go with her? Perhaps she couldn't find the words to explain why she needed to be alone."

Marisa grimaced as she nodded.

"I have an idea." He pulled away from where he'd parked and drove back down the road from where they'd come. "She might've decided to visit the Pali."

"What's the Pali?"

"Nuʻuanu Pali. It's a popular tourist attraction here. A significant Hawaiian battle in the late seventeen hundreds took place on those cliffs. And from the lookout, you can see all the way across the town of Kailua to Kaneohe Bay. We're not far from it."

Marisa sucked in her bottom lip. "It sounds familiar. Let's go. What happened up there, anyway?"

Bryce drove the car out of the small road and to the highway. "The conflict was called the Battle of Nuʻuanu. Kamehameha the First wanted to unite the Hawaiian Islands, so he sent his troops to force Oʻahu warriors up the Koʻolau mountain range and backed them against the Nuʻuanu Pali, a sheer cliff that drops thousands of feet into the valley. They had nowhere to go and either jumped or were pushed over the cliff. They all died on the jagged rocks below."

"Oh, yes. I remember Ky mentioning it after we'd arrived here. I think she said it was one of her father's favorite places." Marisa dropped the lock of hair she'd been twisting and grabbed Bryce's wrist with her hand. "She could've gone to this place. But I doubt it was to be alone with her thoughts. She probably went there to search for her dad."

Half an hour later, Bryce parked the Prius in the lot at the Nuʻuanu Pali. "Well, no sign of the Mustang or Kyleigh. Let's go to the lookout and check, just in case." Bryce took Marisa's hand and squeezed. "We don't want to leave any stones unturned."

They hurried to the cement walkway and followed it out to the edge of the cliff. Several people milled around taking pictures of the panoramic view, cameras aimed at the trees far below, the town in the distance, the bay beyond, and old volcanic craters.

"Ky's not here, Bryce. Unless she's become as transparent as glass."

Bryce flinched at her words. The only invisible beings here would be the ghosts of those warriors. It would be best for him to say nothing about the legends to Marisa. She was worried enough. "May as well take a moment to enjoy the sight while we're here. Then we'll try to figure out where else to look for Kyleigh. Remind me to call Jer when we get back to the car."

Marisa nodded. "The scene is amazing." She followed Bryce to the wall overlooking the massive forest area below. "The houses in that town look so small from up here. What did you say the name of it was?"

"Kailua. It is an impressive view. Although the history of the Pali is gruesome. Of those warriors I told you about, at least twelve were women. When they built the highway through this mountain, they found the skulls of the warriors. Sad that it took so many lives for King Kamehameha to win the struggle that finally united O'ahu under his rule."

Marisa's hands rested on the concrete as she viewed a historical plaque about the battle. The picture told the story of the horrific death toll. Bryce wrapped his arm around her shoulders. She flinched.

He pulled his arm away. "Are you okay?"

She smiled. "Sorry. I was thinking about all those natives who died here so long ago. You surprised me, that's all."

"You jumped as if you'd seen one of their ghosts. Many Hawaiians still believe the warriors haunt the Pali." Oops. He wasn't going to tell her about that.

A gust blew Marisa's hair into her eyes. "Sure is blustery here."

He breathed a sigh of relief. Glad she hadn't made any connection to Kyleigh's disappearance. First the major, and now his daughter. "It's always windy here." He pointed to a teenager who leaned back into the wind with his arms stretched out and was held there.

Marisa laughed. "He'd better hope the breeze doesn't die suddenly. He'll be flat on his behind."

Bryce chuckled. "Some on the island say they hear the voices of the dead in those winds." He'd done it again. As he shut his eyes, he pressed his lips together.

"The atmosphere is spooky enough up here without your adding to it, Bryce." She elbowed him in the ribs.

He grinned. "No more ghost stories. But I'll tell you some of my favorites another time. I grew up with these legends." He cocked his head and smiled. So glad her spirit lightened.

Their eyes locked. Wow, she was beautiful, even with her hair flying around in twenty directions. He reached out and touched her cheek. That rosy glow wasn't from the wind. He dropped his hand and stuck it in his pocket. *Stop embarrassing her. You'll drive her away.*

A group of teens ran past them. Marisa returned her gaze to the bay and clouds hanging over it, pressed her lips together, and smiled. As they took in the scenery, Bryce slipped his arm around her shoulders again.

After a few minutes of silence, Marisa turned to him. "Bryce, let's go to the major's apartment. Maybe Ky's back and didn't go anywhere but to the store. If I'm upset, I go shopping."

"Wouldn't she have called you when you weren't there?"

"Not really. Remember, I was supposed to be at Pearl Harbor Memorial today. She might think I found other transportation. Do you suppose she's gone to see Jer?"

"No. We'd have heard from him if she had...but I'll call him anyway and check." Bryce punched the number for the prepaid phone he'd given Jer. "No answer. Must be in the bathroom. He wouldn't be taking a nap with Kyleigh missing since he was upset that she'd left the apartment. I'll call again in the car. For now, your idea is the sensible thing to do. Let's head back to the major's place."

Marisa shivered from the wind as they walked to Bryce's car with his arm around her waist. He pulled her close to his side. Kyleigh's words from the morning echoed in her mind. *"Please don't get your hopes set on Bryce. We'll be gone soon."* Marisa's heart sank. She couldn't help herself. How could she not hope for a relationship with the nicest guy she'd met in a long time? Her pulse quickened as he squeezed her even closer.

Bryce opened the passenger door and held her hand as she slipped in. When he smiled, a tingle ran up her neck.

He hopped in on the driver's side. "I'll try Jer again." The cell rang, but Jer still didn't answer. Bryce puckered his lips and frowned. "He might have gone outside on the lanai and left the phone inside, but that would be strange when he's so worried about Kyleigh."

After he'd slipped the cell into its holder on his belt, Bryce pulled out of the parking space and drove back down the road.

As they wound their way to the highway, Marisa leaned her head against the headrest and gazed out the window. *You told me to be careful, Ky, but I can't help falling for Bryce.* It just had to work out. It wouldn't be like it was with Ky and Paul.

She kept her eyes focused on the side of the road in case Ky had stopped somewhere. An hour passed with no sign of the car.

Bryce pulled into the apartment complex and parked his Prius in the lot. He tried the burner phone number again. "He still doesn't answer."

"Hey!" Marisa sat rigid in the seat. "The car's where it was before Ky took it. She's here!"

Marisa opened the car door and hurried toward the walkway.

Bryce caught up to her. "After you check in with Kyleigh, I need to go by my loft and find out why Jer hasn't answered my calls."

Marisa darted to the entrance with Bryce close behind.

As she unlocked the door, Bryce grabbed her shoulder and turned her to the back of the covered sidewalk. "Marisa. The bike's gone."

She entered the apartment and dashed to the bedrooms. "Ky!" Marisa turned to face Bryce in the foyer as tears welled in her eyes.

He whipped out the phone and called Jer again. Still no answer. Why? "We'd better drive to my loft right away. Kyleigh might be with Jer."

Jer slid into the driver's seat of his truck. He revved the engine and took off faster than the last time a gang of cutthroats had chased him. "Lord, thanks for clearing my head up. I have to make it to the range and find Kyleigh. You've got to help me find her. She could be in danger. Why didn't she listen to me?" Great! Now he was talking to himself. This girl had caused him to lose his mind and his heart. Jer's pulse pounded like a trip hammer. His stomach churned.

He should call Bryce and let him know where he was going, but then Bryce would try to talk him out of it. Strange, he hadn't called yet.

Half an hour later, Jer pulled the truck into the parking area he used when he kicked off his treks on the trails. Should've thought to throw the bike in the back. He wasn't thinking at all anymore, but he'd better start. Now he'd have to run the trail.

He took off at a slow jog. Better not move any faster with his head throbbing worse than before. But he had to keep going, no matter what. Kyleigh needed him. He was sure of it. And he needed her. Wow. He'd met her only two days ago, and yet it was like they'd known each other for so long. Of course, traumatic situations pulled people closer.

Jer reached the dirt path he and Kyleigh had taken the first time they'd been on the trail after he'd almost knocked her over the edge. A sharp pain wrenched his gut at the thought. As he scanned the track and vegetation for signs of anything to tell him Kyleigh had been on this trail, he furrowed his brows. Nothing but tire tread marks.

A crumpled, light-colored object off in the brush caught his eye. He picked up the crushed cigarette pack. The same brand Whitehall smoked. He remembered Dave taking it out of his pocket the day in the parking lot at the restaurant. Jer's jaw tightened. His hands curled into fists.

A little further on the path, Jer found more tire marks. And footprints. He sprinted along the track, trying to ignore the increased pain at the back of his head.

Chapter Twenty-One

As the sounds of thrashing and crashing drifted upward from below, Dave grinned with satisfaction and peered over the edge of the cliff. He'd have to hang around for a while to make sure Flanagan's daughter didn't climb back up by some quirky miracle.

The metallic noises came to an abrupt stop. A faint cry for help, a yelp, and then a groan drifted upward from far below. Music to his ears. But he hadn't enjoyed this as much as when her father took flight for a sudden end at the bottom. Served that tough old bird right. All he had to do was sneak up on the old man, knock him to the ground, and roll him over the edge. He wasn't so tough anymore.

Silence reigned on the mountain range. The cacophony of distant motocross bikes faded away as well. Dave smirked. She must've landed as hard as the bike. He'd wait a little longer to make certain she was a goner.

As Dave gazed out through the branches at the edge of the precipice, a cloud skirted by. Peaceful place. Even more so now that the meddlesome major and his daughter wouldn't bother him in the future. He'd have to come up here when he needed time to think.

A snap rose to his ears. What was that? She had to be dead. But even if she'd somehow survived the fall, she wouldn't survive for long. Their bodies or what was left of them would never be found. He gloated. He doubted if anyone in their right mind ever went through the ravine on this side of the mountain. Not with all the centipedes, scorpions, and spiders that inhabited the thick overgrowth. Not to mention the wild hogs. *I wouldn't want to be down there, injured in this jungle.*

Dave kicked at the dirt as he made his way to the other side of the trail. He'd wait here.

As he was about to lean against the dirt wall from where he'd jumped to attack Kyleigh, he jerked himself to an upright position. No. He should stay out of sight. Someone might come along and wonder why he was out here. Without a bike, he'd have a lot of explaining to do. And he'd better cover up the tracks he and Kyleigh made during their encounter.

He yanked a handful of loose brush from the ground and swept away the tire tracks and footprints.

Dave headed for a cluster of trunks and plants on the cliffside of the bike path but tripped over one of the pervasive tree roots sticking up from the dirt. He toppled closer to the edge but caught a sapling. A blast of expletives filled the air as he wriggled his way into the thick greenery and trees. That was close. He'd almost joined his victims.

Great. From this perfect vantage point, he could observe the place where she fell, but no one would see him from the trail. He eased himself onto another huge root and waited. A burst of laughter erupted from him. He covered a yawn and leaned back on a group of saplings to relax.

After tumbling from the top of the cliff, Kyleigh rolled over large clumps of brush on the side of the sheer yet sloping mountain. She grabbed at stems sticking out from the rock and managed to catch herself. Kyleigh clung tightly to the dense section of brush with her head buried in the leaves. The small branches broke away, and she slid further down until she seized another clump of vegetation.

As she hung there, Dave's outburst of laughter floated down to her. She gazed up to see how far she'd fallen, but projections of roots, branches, leaves, and rock prevented a view of the top. Thank God she'd snagged the protruding shoots as she dropped. Her head ached from the jar she'd received when he slammed into her.

That *rat* of a waiter from The Pearl Grill, Dave. Why had he attacked her? Was he the one who hit Jer? The expression on his face when he jumped down next to her was pure evil with his teeth bared. His eyes held venom as if he'd been changed into the devil himself.

And then to throw the dirt bike after her. The thing almost hit her when it tumbled past. No doubt he'd gotten rid of the evidence in case another rider came along and wondered where the owner was. Dave couldn't risk someone searching for her.

She closed her eyes and strained her ears to hear while trying to find a foothold. He stopped laughing. Maybe he'd left. Her foot found a piece of rock to rest on. Should she try climbing back up to the trail? No. Not a good idea. He'd wait to see if she was alive. *Just hang on.*

A few more minutes of silence passed. Kyleigh cautiously let go of the root system with one hand to check for her dad's dog tags in her pocket. *Yes.* Her hand flew back to the snarled outgrowth. They were there, but what had happened to his wallet? Must have flown out of her hands when Dave hit her. Had the weasel found it, or was the wallet lying at the bottom of the ridge? If the wallet fell back into the ferns at the top, perhaps someone else would come along and notice it. But if they did, would they meet the same fate as she and her father? Tears flooded Kyleigh's eyes. Had her dad been pushed to his death? The rock under her foot broke away, and she swayed from the clump once more.

A heavy branch stuck out from the face of the rock. She reached for it but missed, almost losing her death grip hold on the tangled brush.

Out of breath, Kyleigh hugged the thick, twisted clump for several minutes before trying to reach the limb again. *Got it.* The limb cracked and dropped lower. She hung from the broken branch and the root system she'd still held on to as if she were part of a trapeze act at the circus. Her weak, sweaty hands slid on the smooth surface of the barkless branch. *Think fast, Kyleigh.*

In the snarled wood and vegetation sticking out of the side of the rock face below her, she located new footholds. Little by little, she entangled her fingers and feet in bunches of stems, going from clump to clump, and inched her way down the escarpment.

How far down did she have to go before she met the bottom? Would the plentiful outcropping of brush from the mountain go all the way down? What if they ended and—*stop it, Kyleigh.* Not the thing to think about under the current situation. *Keep going. God will provide your need.*

Using the skills she'd learned in her rock-climbing course back home, Kyleigh eased herself down the drop-off. She was so thankful her dad had agreed with her instead of Aunt Maye about taking the lessons. Auntie had argued against rock climbing as not a suitable sport for a young lady. What would her aunt say if she saw her hanging off the side of this mountain? *Poor Aunt Maye.* If she knew what was going on right now, she'd have a—*don't think about that either. You'd best concentrate on what you're doing.*

After what seemed an eternity, Kyleigh peered down and saw two crumpled dirt bikes not too far from each other, lying in the brush next to a wooded area. Hers and...Dad's? The nearby trees were so thick. Could she walk through them? Was it safe?

Her feet finally reached the foot of the mountain, where vegetation rose to her shoulders. What would she come across in this wilderness? Outside of wild hogs, her father had never mentioned any dangerous animals on Oʻahu. Not on the land anyway. But then, she'd never asked.

Kyleigh took in a deep breath and leaned on the side of the escarpment. Rest. She needed to rest before she started searching for a path out of here. If there were any. Her head fell back against the mountain, and she closed her eyes.

When she opened her eyes again, Kyleigh's jaw dropped as she surveyed the area surrounding her. Flowers dotted the green undergrowth and brown tree trunks everywhere as if a painter had taken his brush and fanned the bristles with a finger to spray a rainbow of color into the landscape. Trees dripped with vines. How had she missed this from the higher view? Too stressed.

She pushed off the rock wall. A second ridge rose about twenty feet away. Another rocky ascent with scraggy plants ascended from the forest. Coming down the side of the cliff had been one thing, but there was no way she could go back up, not with her novice skills and in her battered condition. But how far would she have to walk or wrestle through this impenetrable copse before she happened on civilization? "Lord, if any hikers are out here, please lead me to them." Was this a test from God too?

Kyleigh bent over, hands on her sore knees, and attempted to calm her breathing. She collapsed on the ground beneath the overgrowth, rested her back against the rock, and drew in a deep breath. Every part of her body ached or stung with pain. Hopefully, hikers would be the only things walking around she'd meet. And hopefully, she'd run into one of them soon.

As she sat in what resembled a prehistoric or unearthly world, the tales her father had told her when she'd visited him over the years here on Oʻahu weren't so farfetched. Nor were the movies with prehistoric beasts she'd watched, which were filmed on this island. Was it possible she'd find out the native warrior ghost legend was true...or the dinosaurs? *Quit! You know they're not real.*

The world around her became silent. Kyleigh softly clapped her hands to make sure she hadn't lost her hearing. Strange place. Not even a breeze in this ravine.

Several minutes later, Kyleigh rose, threw her shoulders back, and faced the woods ahead of her. At least she didn't have to make a choice on which way to go with these two ridges coming together to her left like a dead-end canyon. "What are you waiting for?" *Start moving.* It would be dark soon. She wouldn't want to be stuck out here after night fell.

Stumbling through the brush, she came across her father's new dirt bike. Totaled. She searched the area, holding her breath and hoping she wouldn't find his body. Nothing. Kyleigh breathed a sigh of relief. At least he wasn't here. Could Dad have survived the same way she had? If so, where had he gone? Her heart raced at the thought of finding him alive. "God, please show me where he is."

Kyleigh twisted her wristwatch around. She sighed. No telling how late it was. The digital watch had struck the rock face and stopped. The last time she looked, when she found her dad's wallet, it showed five-thirty. Felt like hours ago.

She gazed up at the sky before entering the thicket. The sun had gone behind the ridge, but how far down had it gone? She'd been a little too busy to notice while trying to save herself from hurtling to the bottom of the mountain.

What Jer had called love-shower clouds floated by. *Love showers.* What a lovely thing to call them. Like being kissed by the mist. Would she ever experience another? Jer's smiling face materialized in her mind. "Oh, Jer. I'm so sorry I didn't listen to you." Tears blurred her eyes.

Kyleigh wiped her face with a sleeve and entered the woods. Light streamed through the treetops to make a dappled pattern on the ferns and other plants growing under the canopy. If she weren't so scared, this would be beautiful.

If only she'd brought her cell with her today. How was it she'd become so reliant on the little machine and yet kept forgetting to take it with her? If she survived this ordeal, her aunt and Marisa would kill her.

No more than a few yards into the wooded area, Kyleigh ran across what appeared to be a well-used footpath through the brush. Could this be one of the hiking trails? Dad had said there were many on Koʻolau. She followed the path through the overgrowth.

Chapter Twenty-Two

Jer forced himself to jog as he kept watch on either side of the bike trail. The constant jarring and movement back and forth increased the pain to the back of his head, where the goose egg felt like it had grown to the size of a softball. He'd never tracked anyone so slowly in his life.

Jer tripped, fell to his knees, and cradled his head in his hands for a moment, hoping the throbs would decrease. A few minutes later, he rose and pressed on.

After cresting a rise in the trail, he slipped on a patch of mud and slid to the dirt. Better walk for a while. He'd be no good to Kyleigh if he passed out. With labored breath, Jer reached up to a small tree trunk on the side of the path and dragged himself to his feet. If it weren't for the misty rain of the love showers, he'd be sweating bullets.

Jer began a careful descent down the other side of the slippery rise. The sun had started to fade into early twilight. He'd better find something soon.

Around the next bend, Jer stopped again. He leaned against a rock on the higher side of the trail, away from the cliff, and drew in a deep breath. His eyes focused on a spot of black in a clump of ferns across the path from him. He pushed himself off the rock, crossed the trail, latched onto another sapling for support as he crouched, and picked up the object. A wallet. He opened the billfold, and his eyes widened. *The major's.*

Dave awoke with a start. He'd dozed off while he waited to make sure the major's daughter wouldn't reappear. Guess he was in worse shape than he thought. He leaned forward and peered over the side of the cliff. No sound. He stood and inspected the foliage between him and where Kyleigh had dropped off the side of the range. No flattened plants. No one had crawled through the overgrowth from the edge of the drop-off. She wasn't coming back.

A man hidden from view rose from his hunched position near the spot Kyleigh had gone over the cliff. Leaf-laden vines that hung from trees surrounding Dave obscured his vision. He rubbed his stubbled chin. Had this guy witnessed what happened to Kyleigh? Dave gritted his teeth. Couldn't have, or he'd have reported it. Then again, maybe he already had. But if he had, and seen who pushed her, he wouldn't drape himself over the edge of the precipice. He'd have either gotten away from here as fast as he could or tried to stop the act. More than likely, the dolt would have run. No, he must have arrived after the fact. Dave grinned. His presence was still unknown to the chump. Not yet.

Dave pushed leaves out of the way just enough to gain a better view of the interloper. Ahhh...the detective from The Pearl Grill last night. The snoopy cop who should've died in the harbor but only wound up in the ER. So what was he doing here on the range? The man turned his back to Dave. Wasn't it convenient that he ventured up here, though? And all alone too. Dave snickered to himself. *I won't have to find him now.* He'd not get away this time.

The detective examined the ground, and as he did, he backed closer to Dave. After a couple more steps, the cop wobbled, leaned on a tree, and held his head.

Dave huddled as close to a huge fern as he could without making it move, the new bane of his existence only ten feet away. Good thing this overgrown location was here for him to wait and hide him from anyone on the trail. He hadn't wanted the girl to spot him if she managed to survive and climb her way back up. Now he'd use the advantage for another reason. Surprise attack. The cop appeared none too steady on his feet, which ought to make this easy.

With caution, he rolled himself to his knees from the sitting position and placed his right foot on the ground. His fingers balanced him on the dirt as if he waited for the gun to fire in a forty-yard dash, then kicked off from the tree he'd reclined on. Dave rammed the detective in the back with enough force to propel the guy off the cliff. But the investigator snatched a sturdy limb and swung around the tree, landing him back on the trail.

The two men grappled and pitched from side to side. Dave clenched the detective's throat. The cop's fist smashed into the side of Dave's head at the temple, but he held onto the cop's neck despite the onset of shadows around him.

After Jer rolled Whitehall over on his stomach, he untied the laces of the perp's sneakers. It was a miracle he had enough strength left to knock Whitehall out. *Praise God! Thank You, Lord.* He pulled the laces from the shoes and then yanked Whitehall's hands behind him.

Jer circled Whitehall's hands with the shoelaces and tied a constrictor knot before he dragged him to the trunk of the tree that had saved Jer from a headlong hurtle to the valley below. He slid out Whitehall's belt and wrapped it around the tree and one of the bound man's arms. "This should keep you from going anywhere."

Jer stretched himself over the edge of the cliff as far as he dared. The vegetation that grew out of the side of the bluff was too dense to view more than a few feet down. "If you can hear me, Whitehall, I wouldn't wiggle around too much, or you'll wind up hanging off the side of the range by your belt. And I, for one, want to see you locked up for your crimes."

What was this jerk doing up here on the trail anyway? Had he followed Kyleigh here? Something or someone had torn the ferns several feet from them as though it had shuffled through the plants. Jer's stomach tightened into a knot. Or someone had been forced through them. *God, please, not Kyleigh. Or her dad.*

Pain ripped through Jer's head. He grasped both sides and collapsed to the ground. Sparkles danced before his eyes. *Please don't let me pass out.*

Jer eyed a cell phone that protruded halfway out of Whitehall's back pocket. He snatched it, scooted two more feet away from the bound man, and punched in Bryce's number. Thankfully, Whitehall hadn't protected the cell with a password. Probably a new burner phone, from the looks of it. As soon as the call connected, Jer blurted out, "Get a team over here to the dirt bike trail I told you about. Whitehall tried to knock me off the cliff. I think he may have done the same to Major Flanagan...and possibly...Kyleigh. And *hurry*. He's tied to a small tree with his shoelaces. Knocked him out." Jer took a deep breath, surprised Bryce hadn't interrupted. "But I'm woozy...I need help."

"Man, I'm so glad you called in. Got it. You sit back and wait for the paramedics and us to arrive. We're on the way. Whose phone—"

Jer accidentally hit the disconnect button, and the line went dead.

Whitehall stirred, then shook his head. He strained against the laces, but they remained in place. He kicked his leg at Jer but couldn't reach him.

Jer backed away a few more feet. "Knock it off, or I'll give you another nap." He lifted the phone back to his ear and keyed in Bryce's number again. "I lost you. Whitehall's alert now. Someone better show up fast."

"Jer, whose phone are you using?"

"Whitehall's. I left the one you gave me at the loft."

"No wonder we couldn't reach you. We stopped by to find out why you weren't answering and found you gone. Never thought to look for the cell. Did you find any evidence of Kyleigh on the trail? Marisa and I searched every road through the range for the Mustang, but when we got back to the major's apartment, his car was here, but the bike was gone."

"Bryce, you can tell me later." Jer took a quick breath. "I was searching for signs she'd been here. What I found was Major Flanagan's wallet. But I haven't found any trace of Kyleigh."

Whitehall cackled. "You won't find her either." He cackled again.

Although his head ached as though it was a coconut split in two, Jer dropped the cell into the dirt, lunged at Dave, and grabbed him by the neck. "What did you do to her? Where is she?"

Whitehall thrashed. Unable to free himself from Jer's hold, he spat in Jer's face. "You're too late to save your girlfriend. She's at the bottom of the cliff...where you should be."

Jer let go of the perp, wiped his chin with his sleeve, and collapsed back on the ground. He rolled away from his captive. "No. You lie."

Whitehall broke into a fit of sinister laughter.

The creep wasn't in his right mind. Jer glared at the criminal. Could the blow he gave Whitehall's head have scrambled his brain? Had to be something else. As well as selling drugs, according to the rap sheet, this halfwit had been busted for drug possession within the past couple of years. His addiction may have taken its toll.

Jer reached for the cell. "Bryce. You still there?"

"Yeah. What were the muffled shouts about? What's at the bottom of the cliff?"

"Whitehall says Kyleigh is. Have you called for backup yet? Either Whitehall has lost it completely, or he's spilling his guts without realizing it. I'm praying it's only his demented mind."

As he hung onto a young tree trunk, Jer's heart dropped like a stone. *God, please don't let what this degenerate piece of work says be true...please. It can't be.*

Jer's legs buckled, and he dropped to the dirt with a thud. At least, he hadn't blacked out...yet.

Whitehall resumed his cackling. "What's the matter, detective? You feeling a little under the weather? Yeah. Swallowing half the harbor and a lump on the head will do that to a guy. You just wait until I get these ties off my wrists. I'll help ya out."

"Shut up, Whitehall." Jer lifted the phone to his ear. "Bryce...make it fast. I'm getting weak. And I'm not sure how long those shoelaces will hold this guy. *Hurry.*"

"Help's on the way, man. Hang in there. Sorry, I hit the disconnect button the first time you phoned. I contacted dispatch before you called back. Stay with me. And whatever you do, stay away from the cliff. You can't help anyone if you're dead."

Lying on his side, Jer attempted a chuckle. But he knew Bryce was serious. Jer cradled his head in his hands and let the phone drop to the dirt. *Stay alert...stay alert. God, please keep Kyleigh safe.*

He glanced up. Whitehall continued to wriggle and twist. No matter how secure that knot was, if he worked hard enough at those laces, he might loosen them.

And if he manages to slip a hand out, I— Glittery flashes of light filled Jer's vision.

Chapter Twenty-Three

Kyleigh followed the muddy path. Several yards into the dense foliage, she came upon human footprints a little smaller than her own. Odd. Were they there at the beginning of the trail? She peered up at the heavy green canopy. The light was fading. A wisp of insecurity churned through her chest. No sounds. Not even from a cricket or bird. But...Dad always said Oʻahu felt like another world when he rode through the mountain. Good thing there weren't any animal noises. Her jaw clenched. Being in this strange place all alone was enough to turn her into a whimpering child. And it would soon be night.

Her father had told her the native Hawaiians believed the hills were haunted by hundreds of warriors who died in the eighteenth century. She'd never believed in ghosts. Not really. Through a break in the trees, Kyleigh gazed up to the cliff from where she'd fallen. Besides, these weren't the same cliffs Dad said the warriors were herded over. What horrendous things people had done to their fellow man. Her skin crawled, and she shuddered.

Kyleigh continued to trudge through the jungle of trees, roots, and strange plants she'd never seen before. Images of jungle movies crept into her mind this time. She wouldn't have to imagine them anymore. She was living in one. As long as some modern-day dinosaur didn't stick its head around the next bend, she'd be okay. Her goosebumps grew goosebumps.

A lower canopy of leaves engulfed her. The thicket grew darker as Kyleigh followed the dirt path further into the forest. Darkness had never scared her before. Not even as a child. So why now? An added chill came over her.

Something moved several feet ahead of her. *What was that?* She stood still and listened. Nothing. *You're letting your imagination get the better of you.*

Kyleigh cautiously advanced a few more feet until a crudely built structure came into view. "Now, this is what you call camouflage." The trees intertwined all around the sides of the structure and stretched their branches over the top so close to each other it was hard to tell if there were walls and a roof at all, except for the front and its rough-hewn wooden door. Was the shack something left over from years gone by, reclaimed by nature? Had the original inhabitants who came to the island built it? This couldn't be a hallucination. She hadn't struck her head when she'd fallen. She'd not been knocked unconscious. But it sure seemed like she'd walked into a dream...or nightmare.

She stepped closer and touched the structure. This was real, not a figment of her imagination. This could be shelter for the night. Her pulse hammered in her ears. All alone...in the dark...through the night. The hairs on her arm and neck bristled. Nothing else to do but wait until morning to start out again. This *was* another world for sure.

As Kyleigh reached out and touched the rough wooden door with vines growing up the sides of it into the branches above, a rustle behind her made her jump. She sucked in a breath and spun, expecting an apparition to float by through the wooded area or some prehistoric creature.

When a petite native with a weathered face stepped into the clearing, Kyleigh released the breath she'd held. The woman stared, eyes wide. Her expression one of confusion and fear. This was no ghost. Kyleigh swallowed the lump in her throat and smiled at the old woman.

The woman's arms carried a huge palm leaf laden with a small stalk of bananas, pineapple, and what appeared to be other fruits Kyleigh didn't recognize.

The two stood frozen to their spots. Where had she come from? *What should I do, Lord?* Tears filled Kyleigh's eyes. She must be going into shock. *Think, Kyleigh. This woman might know what happened to Dad.*

The old woman spoke in words Kyleigh couldn't understand. Sounded like Hawaiian. "I'm sorry. I don't know what you're saying." She wiped a tear that had escaped with the back of her hand and dropped to her knees, lowering her head to her hands. "I-I don't understand. I mean you no harm. I'm lost."

For several minutes, Kyleigh wept into her hands. When she gained control of her sobs, she wiped her eyes with the bottom of her blouse. Had the old woman gone away? Was this her home?

Kyleigh ventured to look up from her hunched-over position. The frail woman had laid the fruit on the ground and walked toward the structure. She stopped in front of Kyleigh and pointed to the scrapes and cuts on Kyleigh's arms and legs. The woman took

Kyleigh by the arm and coaxed her to her feet with a tentative smile.

Kyleigh picked up the fruit in the palm leaf and followed the woman into the shack. Dim light filtered through a large hatch-like hole in one side of the makeshift roof of palm leaves. There had to be an opening between the thick branches over the shack that let the light in. Kyleigh laid the leafful of fruit on a rustic table in the middle of the one square room.

As her eyes adjusted to the dim light, she glanced around the space. No windows, some kind of blanket on the floor in one corner. Her survey stopped at the opposite dark corner. On a small bed made from saplings, another person lay with their back to her. At the sight of his military haircut, her heart leaped for joy. "Dad?"

Kyleigh rushed to the bed and gently pulled him to his back. Placing her hand over his bare chest to check for a heartbeat, she discovered a gummy substance. He stirred when she lifted her hand from the mess smeared across his skin. Thank God he was just unconscious. "Oh, Dad. I'm so grateful you're alive." As she wiped the sticky goo onto her capris, her hands shook. Her pulse pounded. She bent her head, and new tears fell.

Deep red, tacky ointment also covered spots on his arms and neck. Kyleigh turned to the old woman as she sat on a tree stump next to the bed. She spoke in her foreign tongue again. The ointment was no doubt something this woman made.

Kyleigh raised her hands, palms up, and shrugged, hoping the woman would understand she didn't speak Hawaiian. She must've found Dad at the bottom of the cliff and somehow brought him here. She had to be a lot stronger than she looked. Kyleigh gazed at her father's unshaven face. Or maybe Dad found this place the same way she had.

Kyleigh held out her hand to the woman, who took it in hers and nodded.

Kyleigh rested the back of her hand on her father's forehead. He was on fire. She lifted the covering over the bottom half of his body. His pant legs had been torn off, and the skin on one leg was purple and blue from his knee down to the ankle. She covered her mouth and gasped. *I have to find help.* The old woman had taken care of Dad. *But...now what should I do? Lord, help!*

The old woman moved to the other side of Kyleigh and kneeled on the ground next to the cot. She grasped a wooden bowl containing a syrupy liquid. With a wood spoon, she spread the sticky goo over Kyleigh's cuts and scrapes. The burning stopped almost immediately.

The old woman smiled. "Aloalo." She reached for a hibiscus flower which floated in a carved wooden dish and twirled the blossom between her fingertips.

Kyleigh sighed. *Sure wish I understood Hawaiian.* Could mean hibiscus. Was this old woman a native medicine woman here in this strange jungle of the island? That syrup must be what was smeared all over Dad's wounds too. They didn't look infected. Must be safe. Old world remedies, she supposed. At least it had a sweet smell, not like something from the south end of a northbound mongoose.

Her father murmured.

"Everything will be all right, Dad. I found you. And this kind woman has been taking care of you." She laid her hand on the old woman's shoulder and smiled at her. *Thank You for answered prayer, Lord.*

Kyleigh's eyes scanned the interior. This woman had to have lived here for a long time. No modern conveniences. *So much for locating a cellphone.* The only thing she could do was strike out and find help. There had to be other people living nearby.

When Kyleigh opened the door to leave, the woman pulled her back. "I can't stay here. I need to find help for my father. Don't you understand?" Of course not.

The woman shook her head. She pointed to what resembled chicken parts set on a small campfire in another corner of the shack.

"I suppose you're right. I haven't eaten since last night." She only *hoped* it was chicken the woman offered.

Kyleigh lowered herself to her knees next to where her father lay. Waiting until morning would be the wiser thing to do. She didn't want to travel through the middle of a jungle in the dark. But then what? She had no idea where she was or which way to head to find help. Had she and her father slipped into the last century? Who was this woman who didn't speak English and lived in such a place? Did anyone even know she was here? The lack of any noise must mean she was quite a distance from civilization.

Bryce and Marisa jumped out of the Prius. He grabbed her hand. They had to find his partner quick. The last question he'd asked Jer had gone unanswered, and the last sound that came through the phone was a maniacal laugh.

Bryce pulled her along the bike trail until they arrived at the crossing of the three paths Jer had mentioned. They could still make out which way the trails led in the dusk, but just barely. As they came to a halt, he stared at the narrow path filled with muddy tire tracks. "This has to be the way, Marisa. Do you want to wait back in the car?"

"No, I have to find Ky. And I'm not about to stay alone when it's getting dark up here in the mountain. Let's go." She rushed past him and snatched his wrist, almost yanking his arm out of its socket.

"Hey...take it easy." Wow! Marisa was a lot stronger than he thought. "And be careful. Huge roots stick out of the ground all over the place. You don't want to trip over them and sprain your ankle, or worse." He gulped in a breath. "The cliff will be right next to the trail ahead."

Marisa slowed her pace, hopping over the roots and into the mud. "Does it ever stop raining around here?"

Despite the dire circumstances, he couldn't hold his chuckle. "It's usually not this wet in June. Be happy this isn't December when the real rains start. These are only what Jer calls love showers from the clouds, misty rain which drifts over the range. But they can still leave you soaking wet."

As they ran around a bend, he spotted his partner leaning on a rock. "Jer." His head was slumped but rose as Bryce drew near. "Are you okay? What happened?"

"I am now." Jer pointed to the edge of the trail where he'd tied Whitehall to the tree.

The captive twisted and squirmed, spewing a volume of obscenities. He stopped and glared at Bryce, then spat at him. "Wait'll my hands are loose. You'll all meet your fate."

"Shut up." Marisa threw a stick at him. "What's he talking about? What fate?"

"There's my little spitfire." Bryce wrapped one arm around her. Guess he couldn't keep the bad news from her any longer. He turned to Jer. "Search and rescue should be here already. Are you sure Kyleigh's down there?"

Whitehall cackled.

Marisa's eyes grew to saucers. "Down where? At the bottom of the cliff?" She pointed to the far edge of the path.

As streams ran down her cheeks, Bryce put his other arm around her and cradled her head to his chest. "We're not sure. Let's hang on to hope. The perp might be talking crazy for spite."

Whitehall continued his rants and threats, broken by an occasional sinister laugh.

"Right. Hope." Jer sat straighter. "I'm not one-hundred percent, but where haven't we looked? It's all but certain Major Flanagan was shoved over the edge by this lowlife." Jer tilted his head toward Whitehall and showed Bryce the major's wallet. "I found it in a thick clump of ferns right on the edge. He must have lost it when he went over. I can't think of any other way for it to wind up in a clump of ferns at the drop-off. The major struggled with Whitehall, and it came loose from his pocket. Everything's damp inside, so it's been out here for a while. Bryce, I'm scared to death Kyleigh may have gone over too."

Jer collapsed against the rock again. "I don't feel well."

The whir of helicopter blades sounded overhead, followed by fast-approaching footfalls on the trail. A rescue team came around the last bend and rushed to the detectives and Marisa. Jer rolled sideways off the rock and slid to the ground.

Jer's eyes opened as the Honolulu Fire Department paramedics checked his vitals. He began to tell the rescue team his fears about Kyleigh, but words failed him. "Bryce, help, buddy."

"Just rest." Bryce turned to the team and explained about the major's wallet and what Whitehall had said. Before he finished, a yellow and white helicopter appeared over the ravine.

Two HPD officers dashed over the same rise and ran straight to Jer and Bryce. Bryce pointed at Whitehall. "He's all yours, men." The officers cut the captive loose and cuffed him. After reading him his rights, they hauled him back down the dirt path, fighting, kicking, and shouting obscenities all the way.

When the three disappeared on the other side of the rise, Jer turned to Bryce. "Thank God you came when you did. Those laces must have been getting pretty loose. Not sure what would have happened if he had slipped out of them." Jer's head fell into his hands again. "Ohhh...my head."

Bryce laid his hand on Jer's shoulder. "You need some rescuing yourself, man." As the HFD captain arrived and strode past the detectives and Marisa to the edge of the trail, Bryce called to him. "Detective O'Shea needs to go to the hospital, sir. He has a concussion from a blow to the head yesterday. The perp got into it with him up here on the range. Now my partner is completely exhausted and might have further injuries."

"We've got him." The paramedics slid a gurney under Jer. "Detective O'Shea's ready for transport. We'll get him to the hospital in no time."

Before they started up the rise, Jer grabbed Bryce's arm. The paramedics stopped. Jer turned his head to the captain. "Major Flanagan and his daughter may have been pushed over the edge, sir." He pointed toward the cliff.

The captain strode back to Jer. "Don't worry. I'm aware of the situation, O'Shea. Swanson filled me in when he called for assistance. I'll handle things from here." The captain gave Bryce a nod.

"Marisa, we can't do any good here." Bryce took her hand. "Let's go with Jer. They'll keep us informed."

She bit her lip while tears continued to stream down her cheeks.

As Jer pictured Kyleigh smiling at him, his heart ached as though it had split in two. He'd found the love of his life, only to have lost her. His gaze wandered to Marisa. And her best friend was gone.

Chapter Twenty-Four

A s Kyleigh ate the smoky-flavored meat the old woman offered, sounds of something or someone crashing through the forest outside the shack came to her ears. Kyleigh jumped to her feet. "Someone's coming." *Dave.* A chill skittered through her body.

She glanced across the table where the old woman had sat. She was gone. Kyleigh made a quick survey of the room. Behind the bed where her father lay, the trembling woman crouched.

The commotion outside drew nearer. Kyleigh's heartbeat went into overdrive. Dave wanted to make sure she was dead, and he'd brought help with him. *Well, it won't be that easy, buster.* She searched the room for a weapon to defend herself, her father, and the native woman. She couldn't run and let them hurt this kind soul or her father. And her father couldn't even stand, much less run or walk through the jungle.

How had they found this place? She quickly tested the varied lengths of limbs in the woodpile next to the fire pit. One solid, two-foot-long piece had weight to it. It would have to do. Kyleigh pressed her back to the wall next to the door so she'd have a clear shot at whoever opened it.

The old woman's eyes grew wide. She had cowered as far into the corner behind the cot as she possibly could and covered her head with her arms.

The major turned his head toward Kyleigh. He opened his mouth, but his words came out in a slurred whisper. "K-eyelee, wha—" His eyes closed.

Her heart ached to run to him, but it was more important she protect him and his rescuer first. She braced herself to swing the chunk of wood at the first one who entered.

Someone shouted, "Tell the cap we may have found something. I see footprints."

Cap? As in captain? Kyleigh pressed her ear against the flimsy door. She peeked through a crack in the door slats. Men in uniform ran toward the shack along the path. These weren't a bunch of thugs. The piece of firewood dropped to the dirt floor with a thud.

Kyleigh burst out the door and bolted into the woods toward the men. "My father's in there." She pointed to the shack. "He's sick. An old lady too. She tried to help him. He has a high fever."

Two of the rescue team rushed past her while the third led Kyleigh to a log and prompted her to sit. "Are you Kyleigh Flanagan?"

"Yes. My father is Major Charles Flanagan. He's been missing for a couple of weeks. I found him when I followed this dirt path through the—" Her arms and legs throbbed and seemed as if they grew heavier by the minute. She burst into tears.

The rescue worker touched her shoulder. "He'll be taken care of. I'm Lieutenant Jacobs. We'll transport you and your father out of this ravine and to the hospital where he can receive treatment."

When her sobbing stopped, she took a big gulp of water from the bottle he'd handed her. "A tiny old woman in there tried to help my father. She doesn't speak English. When we heard you, she hid behind the cot my dad's lying on. She's shaking. Scared to death."

Kyleigh stared through the trees at the shack. "I thought I'd wandered into some kind of alternate dimension. The place looks like it's been here for hundreds of years—"

The lieutenant laid his hand on her forearm. "Take a deep breath, Miss Flanagan. Not hundreds of years. It was built in the nineteen forties. So you've met Ilima Palakiko. She's been living here in this secluded area for near eighty years. Since the Japanese attacked Pearl Harbor."

Kyleigh whipped her head around and stared at him, jaw slackened. "Eighty years? She doesn't appear to be that old."

"She was a very small child when the attack happened."

Lightheadedness overcame Kyleigh, and she sagged toward the lieutenant. He held on to her arms. "Whoa. I'd better have my men check you too. But from the way you charged out of the shanty, I'd say nothing's broken. I'm surprised. You climbed down from the cliff without a rope, correct?"

Kyleigh closed her eyes and slowed her breathing. She opened them and mentally checked for pain, stretched her back, and let out a sigh. "Yes. I was attacked, lost my balance, and fell backward. Thank God I managed to latch onto the shrubs that stuck out from the rocks. I have some scrapes but no other injuries."

"It's a miracle you weren't killed. The point from which you fell is over two hundred feet."

"That's exactly what it was. A miracle. But how did you know we were down here? How did you find us?"

Lieutenant Jacobs coaxed her to drink more water. "A detective from HPD called in the emergency. His partner apparently had been searching for you on the trail when he ran into the guy who pushed you."

Detective? Jer? Up there? What did he think he was doing? "Are you talking about Detective O'Shea? He should have been resting from a concussion."

"Guess he was more concerned about you than himself. Our captain told us the paramedics have taken him to the hospital. So, don't worry about him."

Jacobs stood. "Excuse me for a second while I advise the captain you're both alive."

The lieutenant stepped into the short clearing in front of Ilima's house, pulled out his cellphone, and contacted the captain. "You'll relay the information to HPD?" Jacobs returned to Kyleigh. "Are you feeling better?"

"Yes, thank you. But how will you get us out of this jungle? How did you get here? Down the side of the cliff?"

"I rappelled from the ridge where we found Detective O'Shea. My buddies inside the hut fast-roped from the helicopter. Now...let me help you up."

She rose on wobbly legs. The rescue worker held her by the arm as they approached the shack.

Kyleigh fought tears. *Was Jer all right?*

As they neared the shack, a woman's scream rang from inside. *My dad. No!* She lurched forward.

Before Kyleigh could reach the door, one of the rescue workers stepped out. "Lieutenant, we have Major Flanagan secured and ready for transport. We tried to ask the old woman if she wanted to come with us, but I'm sure you heard her response. She tore to a corner at the far side of the room as if we were the enemy. She's pretty scared."

Kyleigh took a deep breath and leaned on the doorframe. Thank God that was all it was.

The lieutenant pursed his lips. "No doubt, Tom. We'll leave her. If the police want to question her, they'll have to send someone here to do it. As far as anyone can tell, Ilima has lived in these woods and not ventured out since Pearl Harbor was attacked back in forty-one. From what I've been told, she thinks the Japanese control Oʻahu."

The rescue worker looked shocked but nodded and reentered the shack.

Kyleigh's head dropped back against the structure. She gaped at the lieutenant. "The Japanese...in control of the island?"

"She lives in seclusion." He raised his brows. "Few even know she's back here."

"How is it you do?"

"A childhood friend of mine has known about her for years. Came upon her a long time ago when she ventured off the Manana Trail and into the forest to collect wild fruits. My friend still resides in the easternmost edge of Pearl City closest to the mountain and brings supplies to Ilima on occasion."

After staring at the door for a moment, Kyleigh bit her lip and turned to the lieutenant. "I'd like to try talking her into going with us."

He smiled. "You can give it a shot, but as you said, she doesn't speak English. And her parents apparently taught her everything she needed to live in this old-world setting. But they never taught her to trust."

"I'd still like to see if I can. You're Hawaiian, aren't you?" Kyleigh pushed off the door frame.

He grinned. "I'm hapa. Part. Mom was a native. Dad was from England."

"I've heard the term. But don't you speak Hawaiian?"

"I do. But Ilima doesn't know me any better than Tom. As far as she would be concerned, I'm just an islander living under the thumb of the Japanese government."

Kyleigh entered the shack.

Tom examined the straps on the bed-like basket. He faced his partner from the rescue team. "Check. They're secure for transport of the victim."

Kyleigh wrapped her hand around her father's. His eyes opened, and he smiled at her without a word.

The two rescue workers lifted the stretcher and carried Kyleigh's father outside. Ilima kept her eyes glued to the men in uniforms until they disappeared beyond the door. Her brows pinched, and she chewed her bottom lip.

Approaching the crouching woman, Kyleigh held out her hands in front of her. "Ilima...it's okay. They're helping my father." She placed her hands over her heart and smiled at the woman. Kyleigh reached out a hand to Ilima, who clasped it and rose.

Kyleigh brought her to the cot, and they sat. Ilima's brows rumpled. Kyleigh patted the woman on the shoulder as she called, "Lieutenant."

Jacobs peeked inside through the open doorway. "Yes, miss?"

"Could you translate for me?"

He stepped into the room and lowered himself to the far end of the makeshift cot on the other side of Kyleigh.

"Ilima, these men are here to take my father to the hospital, so he can get well." Kyleigh peered over her shoulder at the lieutenant.

In the lyrical Hawaiian language, he translated her words. Ilima glanced at Kyleigh, who smiled.

"Tell her I have to go with my father, and I'd like her to join us."

Jacobs translated. Fear was written in Ilima's widened eyes. She refocused on Kyleigh and shook her head.

"I don't think you'll persuade her, miss. The friend I mentioned before tried to convince her she was safe now, but she wouldn't budge."

"Has anyone told her the Japanese never took over the island?"

"Yes, but it didn't make any difference. She may have ventured out of the ravine, into the outskirts of civilization, and saw Japanese living here. They lived here before nineteen forty-one. But since she wasn't much more than a baby during the attack, she wouldn't remember that. She exists in a PTSD world of her own. The trauma she must have gone through when the bombing started would have horrified such a little girl. And if her parents never tried to return to civilization or told her to hide here..." He shrugged. "I'm no doctor, but we've all heard the stories of people who experience this in war zones."

Kyleigh pressed her lips together. He was right. This was her safe little world, and she wasn't about to leave it after all these years. The poor dear. Kyleigh touched Ilima's cheek and rose from the cot. Ilima grabbed her arm.

Kyleigh lightly rubbed the woman's back. "Please tell her I'm not in any danger, Lieutenant. Tell her I have to go now to take care of my father. Ask if I can visit her again someday...soon."

The lieutenant once more translated. As she nodded, tears spilled over Ilima's barely wrinkled cheeks.

"I think you made a conquest, miss." He stood and offered his hand to Ilima.

She released Kyleigh's arm and stared at Jacobs' hand. Cautiously, she backed away from him, still wiping tears from her face with her hand. She gazed up at the lieutenant. Jacobs smiled at her and dropped his hand. She turned to Kyleigh. "Mahalo."

Kyleigh glanced at Jacobs. "I don't remember how to say you're welcome. But, I think she realizes we're trying to help my dad."

"Tell her, Aʻole pilikia."

As she wrapped her arms around the tiny woman, Kyleigh whispered, "A'ole pilikia," into Ilima's ear, and then said, "Mahalo."

Kyleigh let Ilima go. She followed the lieutenant out of the shack and into the ravine.

After Dad had recovered, she'd find Ilima and spend time with her before leaving for Houston.

Houston. With her dad's recovery, would she make it back there in time for her tutoring sessions to begin? Marisa could handle all three children instead of just the one she'd planned on.

Oh, no. Marisa and Bryce. Would Marisa want to stay on the island? It was obvious her friend had fallen hard for the handsome Hawaiian detective. *Against my warnings.* She and Bryce hadn't been together long enough to know whether she truly loved him. *Just like Jer and me.*

Jer. Butterflies let loose in Kyleigh's stomach. Right. Marisa couldn't be in love with Bryce any more than...not any more than— the realization struck her with the force of a freight train. *Kyleigh Flanagan, you're in love with Detective O'Shea.*

She had to find out if Jer was okay.

Using flashlights to illuminate the dirt path through the dense trees, it seemed to take forever to reach the clearing near the spot Kyleigh climbed down the cliff. The small area was lit up like the runway of a Hollywood awards show.

She held her breath as the light shined on her father, safely secured and ready for transport. The basket lifted into the air on its ascent to the helicopter.

The sky was almost dark, already speckled with a million glittering stars. The copter blades whipped the air like an overzealous eggbeater in thin cake batter. Kyleigh's pulse raced. "What happens if the winds catch the basket? Will he fall out? Will he be safe?"

The lieutenant rested his assuring hand on her shoulder. "The Stokes litter is as secure as they come. And if the wind were a problem, the helicopter wouldn't be up there with the cliff so nearby. The lifeline will keep it steady. Besides, these men have done hundreds of rescues like this. Hikers who failed to take heed to the warnings of mudslides or simply being careless while they sightsee. Don't worry, the basket will keep him secure."

As she kept her eyes on the contraption rising higher and higher, Kyleigh's fear increased. The chopper and trees swayed without a breeze. She wavered and fell against the lieutenant.

"Are you all right, Miss Flanagan?"

"Guess I got dizzy watching Dad. I've never been fond of heights. It was the reason I took rock climbing classes. To get over it."

He raised his brows.

She chuckled. "It worked to a degree, but this experience has caused a resurgence of acrophobia."

"Understandable. Take a couple of deep breaths."

Kyleigh drew in a long breath of air and exhaled. She repeated the exercise. "Thank you. That helped." If only she could calm her nerves about her father's recovery. And Jer's. Poor Jer. All because he wanted to help her and her father. *You should be ashamed of thinking he wasn't doing his job.* Jer was a good man, a competent detective. He'd done everything he was supposed to do to find her father. Hadn't he? She couldn't wait to see him...as soon as she made sure her father was taken care of.

But what if Jer wasn't doing well? What if he'd seriously injured himself coming out here to find her because she wouldn't listen to him? She'd never forgive herself.

Chapter Twenty-Five

wo weeks after the rescue of Kyleigh and her father, she stirred a pot of Sloppy Joe for dinner and thought back. Time had crawled while she worried over her father's and Jer's health and then wondered why she hadn't heard from Jer at all after he left the hospital. He'd returned to work almost a week ago.

She sighed and added freshly diced onions to the pot. At least her father was well and would return to his duties at the post in a couple of days, cast, cane, and all. "Thank You, Lord," she whispered and went back to stirring.

The snake, Dave Whitehall, would be tried for illegal drug possession, pushing drugs, one count of murder, and attempted murder...three times. If they found anything else to convict him of, she'd be thrilled. The good-for-nothing must have gone crazy.

He'd even admitted to writing the note sent to her, supposedly from her father, after he'd eavesdropped on her dad outside his office. Dave probably thought her father told her his suspicions, so the rat wanted to keep her away from the island and the police. She shouldn't call him a snake. It was an insult to snakes.

She turned the dial on the stove to off and moved the pot to a trivet on the kitchen island.

The front door opened with a squeak. Marisa and Bryce strolled into the room and hopped onto stools next to the island, each wearing a sheepish grin.

"Hey, Ky." Marisa folded her hands on the counter.

"Hey, yourself. What have you two been up to while I've slaved over dinner?"

"Mmm...Sloppy Joe, if I'm not mistaken." Marisa wore a cat-who-swallowed-the-canary expression. "Haven't had sloppies in...at least not since we left Texas."

"Sloppy Joe?" Bryce's brows crumpled as he stared at Marisa. He tilted his head. Question marks flooded his face.

The expression reminded her of her kindergartners on the last day of school, when she'd tried to explain how Labor Day was thought of as the end of summer, but not officially. It was merely symbolic since the Autumnal Equinox was on September twenty-second. *Yeah!* She should have stopped as soon as she'd started and just told them she'd see them back in school after the holiday.

The looks on their faces were the same as Bryce's. She held back a laugh. "You're kidding me. You've never had Sloppy Joe?"

"Not that I know of. Must be some kind of haole food." He snickered.

Marisa squeezed his forearm. "Well. You're in for a treat, my friend. Ky makes the best."

Kyleigh raised her brows. *My friend?* She knew what these two had between them was way more than friendship. And in such a short time. They acted more like an engaged couple every day. Kyleigh pursed her lips. She'd heard of it happening to others. And she could almost hear wedding bells in the future for them. *Again, against my better judgment with the distance that would be between them.* Wish she could have had the kind of relationship they had with—stop it. Her thoughts had run wild with contradiction.

"Smells great." Bryce turned to the living area. "Where's your dad, Ky? Taking a nap?"

She pulled hamburger buns out of the oven and stacked them on a plate. These two were more and more alike each day too. Now he'd picked up on Marisa's nickname for her. But she had to admit. They were so perfect together. Bookends with scenes of happiness between them. A vise clamped onto her heart.

Jer had shown no interest in her after his trauma, catching Whitehall, and being the one who triggered Dad's rescue. He hadn't been around at all since he was released from the hospital. Guess finding out what was going on at Ft. Shafter and what happened to her and her father was the reason he'd paid any attention to her. It was simply his job, and he did it. And that, as they say, was that.

She placed the plateful of buns on the table and turned. Bryce watched her every move. She stared back at him. "Oh. You want an answer to your question. Sorry, my mind has a million things running through it. Dad decided to venture to the store, despite the cast and having to use a cane. His cellphone was never recovered, and he needed a new one. Besides, he was getting cabin fever." She shrugged.

The cell was probably out there, buried under a ton of foliage in the forest somewhere. *Wonder how long it rang before it died.* Could Ilima have found it? They should have checked. "He should be back already."

Bryce nodded. "Will he go to work at the post soon?"

"Yes. Didn't take him long to bounce back. But he'll be wearing his brace for a while yet." She grinned. "Should slow him down. Even though he's already ordered a new bike, he won't be riding on Koʻolau for some time."

Bryce drummed his fingertips on the top of the island. "Has Jer been around?"

Her gaze shot to Bryce. "No. I guess he's been too busy." She turned to hide the tears welling in her eyes. Jer had helped her get over her distrust of law enforcement. And in the process, she'd fallen hard for him, but he didn't care. "Excuse me." She rushed to the restroom.

Marisa hopped off the stool. "What's wrong with your partner, anyway? Doesn't he realize what a great person Ky is? That she's in love with him? And I believe he loves her too."

She opened the refrigerator and returned with two colas, placing them in front of Bryce. She took two glasses from the cabinet and handed them to him. Marisa scooped ice cubes from a container inside the freezer door.

"I've been wondering the same thing." Bryce popped the top of one can and poured the glass half full while Marisa plunked several ice cubes into his drink. When the fizzing stopped, he added the rest of the cola to the glass. "He's been moping around at work. Hasn't wanted to go anywhere with me after we get off...not for dinner or anything. He's not the same old Jer. Quiet and withdrawn now. He won't talk to me about it either. Says he's okay but has personal things on his mind. When I told him I was coming here tonight, and he'd been invited too, he said he was busy. I'm sure he's not with another girl."

Marisa stared at him with her lips pressed tight. "I'm glad to hear it. Still, he's sure acting the role of town idiot."

The major hobbled in with his cane from the front door. "Hi, kids. Glad to see you again, Detective Swanson." The stick thumped on the floor as he limped his way into the living room. "If someone could bring in the bag of groceries from my car, I'd be grateful." He made it to the couch, laid the cane on the floor under the coffee table, and plopped down on the cushions.

Bryce hurried out the door and returned with the bag from the major's car. He set it on the kitchen counter and retook the stool next to Marisa.

She turned to the major. "Sir, what would you like to drink with dinner? Ky has everything ready for the meal."

"A cola's fine with me. Thank you." He grabbed the cane again and attempted to push himself up from the sofa with it and the armrest but lost his balance and fell back to the cushions.

Bryce hurried to give the major a hand. He held the major's arm and pulled the older man to his feet.

"Thanks, Detective. Guess I need a little more practice. And thanks again for not giving up on finding my daughter, which resulted in finding me. I thought your partner would be here tonight for dinner. I'm pleased he recovered so fast from his injuries and is back to work. Don't tell me he's working tonight without you?"

"No, sir. And please call me Bryce. Jer said he...had something to do...that couldn't be put off."

Marisa lowered the can of cola to the table with a clunk and glanced at Ky, who emerged from the restroom and sucked in her lower lip as her eyes grew watery. Marisa hurried toward her friend. "Let's go into the guestroom for a minute. I need to talk to you."

Blinking back tears, Kyleigh lowered herself to the head of the bed and waited for her friend to speak. Dratted tears. She wouldn't cry. She was not...going...to cry. Marissa closed the guestroom door and sat at the foot of the bed.

Bryce had, no doubt, sent Marisa in here to say Jer had gone on with his life. *And I'm not to be part of it.* Not that she'd planned to be. After one fiasco with a long-distance relationship with Paul, she really hadn't wanted to try another anyway. Marisa and Bryce's wouldn't work out either. Too much land and water between this island and Houston. Marisa needed to realize that fact before her heart was broken.

Marisa shifted to face Kyleigh. "Don't let it upset you that Jer was busy tonight. There could be a hundred reasons why he didn't come."

"Why should I let it upset me?" She tightened her jaw.

"Come on, girl. I can tell how you feel about him. These two detectives have gotten under our skin. Almost since the first day we saw them. Go ahead. Tell me I'm wrong." She jutted out her chin toward Kyleigh.

"I'll admit it. I'm attracted to Jer. Who wouldn't be? He's handsome, a gentleman, and he saved Dad's and my lives at the risk of his own. But I'm *not* in love with him." *A lie. Don't you dare cry.*

"Oh. You're not in love with him. Right." Marisa grinned at her. "As much as I'm not in love with Bryce. Ky, this is me you're talking to."

Why did her best friend have to be such a know-it-all? Marisa always could read her. *As if the girl had an x-ray machine pointed at my brain and heart.* Kyleigh played with a loose string from the bedspread and sighed.

"Bryce told me Jer's been moping around for some reason. He's not acting like himself. He won't go anywhere with Bryce except to work or even tell him what's wrong. But Bryce says he's sure Jer's not involved with another woman."

A sense of relief filled Kyleigh's heart. But what claim did she have on Jer? None. It may as well be someone else he was busy with if he didn't care for her the same way she did him. "He can be involved with anyone he desires. We have no relationship outside of rescuer and victim."

"Oh, Ky. Really? I've watched you two together. And you weren't up on the bike trail when he was so scared you were dead. He risked his well-being to find you. Girl, the man is in love with you. There must be something else keeping him away. Something he hasn't told Bryce. Maybe to do with work. Oh, I don't know. But he cares about you, Ky. I'm sure of it."

"If he cares for me, he has a strange way of showing it. Why would he avoid me, not even talk to me?"

Marisa got up and sat down next to Kyleigh on the bed. "I can't answer that one. Nevertheless, I'll bet he has a logical reason for why he didn't come tonight. When did you see him last?"

"The day they released him from the hospital. A week ago. Bryce had arrived to pick him up. I told him I'd drive Jer home, but Jer told me he had something to talk over with Bryce, so he'd go with him. 'Thank you for stopping by,' he said without even looking at me. Then he walked through the corridor to the elevator while I stood in the doorway of his room, stunned. Never said he'd get in touch with me, smiled, or anything. He never looked back." Tears flooded Kyleigh's eyes. She grabbed tissues from the box on the nightstand.

Marisa wrapped her arms around Kyleigh. "I'm so sorry, Ky. Bryce didn't tell me that. I asked him what was wrong with Jer because he didn't come for dinner, but Bryce hasn't a clue."

Kyleigh blew her nose and wiped her eyes. She stood and faced Marisa. "It doesn't matter. Now that Dad's almost mended and will be back to duty, we'll go home to Houston, and Detective O'Shea will be out of my life."

Chapter Twenty-Six

Kyleigh lifted four plates out of the kitchen cabinet as her thoughts drifted to Jer and what he might be doing this evening. Sure, Bryce said Jer wasn't seeing someone else, but he also said Jer wouldn't talk to him outside of work-related issues. He may have met someone at the hospital. An old girlfriend? Perhaps he hadn't told Bryce yet.

Had the time he'd spent on Dad's disappearance and the drug pusher kept Jer so busy he needed a break? Had he been obligated to keep an eye on the major's daughter, the woman who wouldn't follow directions from him? But, according to Marisa, he'd worried about her.

She sighed as she reached the table and placed the plates between two of the four already completed place settings on the tablecloth. Kyleigh's eyes met Marisa's. "Oh. You've done this."

"Ah...yes, I did. Are you sure you're okay, girl? I can serve dinner if you want to lie down and rest for a while."

Kyleigh glanced into the living room, where her father and Bryce were engaged in a discussion. "I'm fine." She walked back to the kitchen and left the extra stack of plates on the counter.

Marisa lifted a tray out of the oven and slid onion rings into a paper towel-lined basket.

As Kyleigh carried a bowl of Sloppy Joe into the dining area, she could feel Marisa's eyes scrutinizing her. Marisa toted the basket and a bowl of macaroni salad right behind her.

Kyleigh sat next to Marisa. "Dad, Bryce, dinner's ready."

"And I'm ready to eat." Her father eased himself to the edge of the seat, grabbed his cane, and stood. "What about you, Bryce?"

"Yes, sir. Can't wait to give this new food my little haole recommended a try." Bryce grinned and winked at Marisa, who turned a beautiful shade of rosy red.

Kyleigh's heart pinched as she recalled when Jer winked at her the day he stayed for dinner after they'd searched Koʻolau for her father. Would she ever see Jer again?

The men took seats at the table. When her dad looked her way and smiled, she forced a smile in return.

Her father reached across the table for her hand and bowed his head. "Our dear Lord, thank You for the meal You've provided this evening and the health to eat it. Thank You for the good company tonight. Please watch over Detective O'Shea, wherever he is. Now bless this food to our bodies. In Jesus Name, we ask. Amen."

Kyleigh fought tears that surged into her eyes at Jer's name. Why wouldn't everyone just stop talking about him? He hadn't given *them* a second thought.

Kyleigh made a small sandwich and took two onion rings from the basket Marisa passed to her.

As they ate, Kyleigh's father asked about the old woman who had taken care of him in the ravine. "I don't recall too much during those days after I lost my grip on the bramble I hung on to and slid the rest of the way to the ground. Landed my leg on a huge rock at the bottom. Pain shot through my body, and everything went black. Sometime later, I opened my eyes to a face peering down at me. She said something in what I believe was Hawaiian, then gave me something warm and bitter to drink. After that, everything was a blank until I opened my eyes and saw Kyleigh standing at the side of the door with a chunk of wood over her shoulder as if she was going to knock a baseball out of the park." He chuckled. "At least I think it's what I saw. Everything else is fuzzy."

"It's exactly what you saw, Dad. I thought the beast who pushed you over the edge of the cliff and attacked me had come to finish us off."

Bryce nodded and swallowed a mouthful of Sloppy Joe. "And if he knew you had survived, he would have come after you if Jer hadn't shown up and taken care of him at the top on the bike trail. From the information we've received on the perp, he left several murders behind him on the mainland. He'll be going away for a long time, if not forever."

Bryce took a long drink of his iced tea. "To answer your question about Ilima, sir. She's been living in the forest since Pearl Harbor was attacked. My mother happened upon her years ago. Mom said she had been curious about the narrow dirt paths not too far from their community. One day, she decided to follow them, looking for wild sweet potatoes. She discovered Ilima instead, fishing at the edge of a stream." He chuckled. "She told Mom she thought an angel had come for her. Normally, she would have run. Hardly anyone's aware she's living in the ravine."

Kyleigh swallowed a lump in her throat along with a bite of onion ring. "When I found her shack, it was *she* who came upon *me*. I suppose it was my crying that kept her from running away. And I'm so glad it did."

"We're all glad she stayed there for you, Ky." Marisa hugged her friend.

"My mother's been bringing supplies to Ilima ever since the day she met her." Bryce popped a small onion ring into his mouth.

Kyleigh rested her elbow on the table and held her fork between her thumb and index finger. She dragged the tines in circles through her food. "Didn't your mom ever try to talk Ilima into coming out of the woods?"

"Yes. She tried. Old Ilima thinks the Japanese are still at war. After she ventured near the edge of the forest and observed Japanese residents, she begged Mom not to turn her in. Now she remains close to the mountain, deep in the trees."

A tear escaped and ran down Kyleigh's cheek. She brushed it away.

Bryce swallowed another mouthful of sandwich and washed it down with his drink. "Ilima told Mom she wasn't more than a baby at the time the Japanese attacked Pearl Harbor. Her parents grabbed her from the front yard of their home and carried her into the mountains."

The major leaned back in his seat. "Poor child. I can't even imagine."

"Where they lived before her father constructed the shack, she never told Mom. But Ilima said he built the structure deep in the woods and planted the surrounding trees to hide them from unfriendly eyes."

In her mind, Kyleigh pictured the old woman's home in the middle of the jungle.

"I've never gone with Mom when she takes the supplies." Bryce wiped ketchup off his lip. "She told me about Ilima when I was around eighteen. Made me swear never to tell anyone about the old woman living in the woods."

Marisa lowered her forkful of macaroni salad. "What a nightmare it must have been for her as a child. For her parents too."

Bryce nodded. "Ilima's father died a few years after the attack on Pearl Harbor. He was a doctor at the base, so he must have had something incurable, and he eventually ran out of medication. Her parents taught her how to live off the land, as our ancestors did. She fishes in the streams, catches wild chickens, and I suppose other things we wouldn't touch to stay alive."

Kyleigh glanced at Marisa, who bared her teeth. "Eeewww...but I've eaten snake."

"Honest? I've heard people eat reptile meat on the mainland, but I didn't believe it. There aren't any snakes here." Bryce turned to Kyleigh. "Marisa is right. This Sloppy Josie is great. My new favorite."

A utensil clinked on the plate, and a loud guffaw came from Kyleigh's father. Marisa slapped a napkin over her mouth, and her body shook with laughter.

"What? What did I say?" Bryce's brows lowered.

Kyleigh suppressed a laugh and smiled at him. It was the first light moment she'd had this evening. *Thank you, Bryce.* "It's Sloppy *Joe*, not Josie. I'm glad you like it."

She laid her napkin over the uneaten half of her sandwich and onion ring. "Tell us more about Ilima. She's such a sweet soul. I plan to go back and visit her before we go home."

"Well, Mom said Ilima feels safe in the mountains, and since she grows her own food, she's survived. Mom may be the only person who's ever seen her...until now."

Kyleigh bit her lip. "Bryce, do you know Lieutenant Jacobs?"

"Yes. He's an old friend of Dad's. Served with him in the Navy."

Kyleigh smiled. "He's the man who kept me calm through our ordeal. He said a friend of his told him about Ilima. Your mom?"

Bryce placed one fist on his hip and narrowed his eyes. "I'll be. Wait'll I talk to her again. And after making me promise not to tell anyone." He shook his head.

"I'm so glad Ilima was in those woods." Kyleigh smiled. "We needed aid. She was there to give it." She glanced at her father. "To both of us."

"I'm glad too." Marisa nodded. "Imagine what would have happened to you and your dad without the woman's assistance. The major might be dead with my best friend lying beside his corpse." Marisa sniffed and brushed a tear from the corner of her eye.

Bryce bobbed his head in agreement. "Mom says the Lord led her to Ilima, so she could help her." His brows pinched together. "I guess the Lord led you to her, so she could help you."

Kyleigh envisioned wheels turning in his head. Jer had mentioned not being sure Bryce was saved, although his mother was. But that he always attended church. Maybe there was more purpose behind this ordeal on Ko'olau than she'd thought. *Was it to reach his heart, Lord?*

Something else crossed Kyleigh's mind. "If your mother takes supplies to Ilima, how is it she didn't report finding my father? Wouldn't she have said something to you?" Had Bryce kept the information to himself?

Kyleigh blew a long stream of air between her lips. *There you go again with those suspicious thoughts about anyone connected with law enforcement.* She should be over that by now.

"Mom must not have taken any supplies to Ilima since the first of the month, her usual time to visit. Too bad she didn't make a trip the week you went missing, sir." He rubbed his chin. "We could have located you much sooner and had Whitehall put away before he got to Kyleigh." One side of his mouth rose. "But I guess God had some reason to delay us."

Kyleigh focused on her plate. So what would the reason be for the way Jer was acting? She'd really like to know. Her stomach tightened. Not hungry. She took her half-full dish to the kitchen and tossed the food in the trash. She turned and studied Bryce as he finished eating in silence.

Marisa got into an animated description of the scene on the top of the cliff that led up to the arrest of Dave Whitehall, but Bryce didn't join the conversation. He tapped his foot nervously, and his usual infectious smile was gone. Was he going over the case to figure out if he and Jer had missed a clue? Or...was he contemplating God having placed Ilima in the right place at the right time?

While the girls cleaned the kitchen after dinner, Bryce and the major relaxed in the living room. Bryce sat on the easy chair and gazed out the sliding glass door to the lanai. The major stretched out his leg on the couch and watched him.

"Bryce, Marisa is like a niece to me. I'm very protective of those girls. Can I ask you a personal question?"

The young man faced his host. "Sure."

"Kyleigh said Jer told her you've attended church ever since your mother got saved a couple of years ago. She's been involved in church activities, but not you. I'd like to hear your testimony. When did you get saved?"

Marisa's head swiveled. She stopped loading the dishwasher and stared into the living room, open-mouthed.

Bryce's tanned complexion turned a vivid shade of rose. He glanced at Marisa and back to the major. "Umm...I..."

Kyleigh laid the dish she was holding in the sink and took Marisa's arm. She hustled her to the guest bedroom and closed the door. "Marisa, it doesn't sound like Bryce is saved."

"No, it doesn't." Marisa burst into tears. "And he asked me to marry him this afternoon. I said yes, Ky. What am I going to do? I can't marry him if he's lost. It wouldn't work." She dropped to the bed and sobbed into a pillow.

Kyleigh put her arm around Marisa's shoulder. Her heart broke for her friend, but she'd warned her she'd be hurt. "Take it easy. Dad's talking to him. It may turn out he's saved after all, but he doesn't realize it." Unlikely. "Or, the gospel wasn't presented to him in a way he understood. Dad will take care of it. Everything will be all right." At least she hoped it would, for Marisa's sake. *God, please deal with Bryce's heart. Show him the only way to heaven is by accepting the price You paid on Calvary for his sins.* She passed her friend a handful of tissues.

After a few minutes, Kyleigh rose from the bed and slipped into the restroom. Bryce had to have sat through hundreds of invitations to accept salvation, not to mention the preaching of the gospel at church. How could he not be saved?

She soaked a washcloth for Marisa. Had he thought being a nice guy and not a criminal was enough to gain heaven? Did he plan to present his credentials as an upstanding citizen to get in? She couldn't believe his mother wouldn't have explained what happened to her. But, would he have listened?

When Kyleigh returned to the guestroom, Marisa was sobbing softly into the pillow. Kyleigh handed her the wet cloth. "Come on, Marisa. You have to have faith that everything will work out according to God's Will."

How would she convince her best friend everything was going to turn out right when her own love life had crash-landed? Did she have enough faith herself? *Lord, we need Your help.*

Several minutes later, Kyleigh and Marisa emerged from the guestroom and stepped into the living room. Kyleigh's dad was alone, sitting on the couch, head bowed.

Kyleigh rested her hand on Marisa's shoulder.

Her father raised his head. "Girls, we need to pray for Bryce. He's as lost as a golf ball in high weeds. But he left with the promise to think about what I said and to read the passages I wrote down from Romans."

"He's lost." Marisa's words were no more than a whisper. She fled back to the guestroom and shut the door.

"Dad. She's heartbroken. Bryce proposed to her this afternoon." A knot formed in Kyleigh's stomach.

Her father patted the couch next to him. "Sugar, we have to pray for them."

Kyleigh lowered herself next to her dad. They needed to pray for more than Bryce and Marisa. Her own heart felt like a cracked egg, but she wanted to be strong for her friend.

Chapter Twenty-Seven

wo days later, Kyleigh glanced up from her bowl of oatmeal and read the sorrow in Marisa's face. Never had she seen her normally jovial friend so miserable.

Marisa looked up from her untouched cereal. "Bryce called yesterday morning and apologized for leaving the night before without saying goodbye. I couldn't bear to bring up his name to tell you." Her eyes glistened. "He said he had some thinking to do, but I haven't heard from him since." A tear slipped over her lower lashes and dropped into the dish.

What was wrong with that Hawaiian Swede? Kyleigh sighed. He was breaking her friend's heart.

Marisa wiped the tears from her eyes with her napkin. "He didn't say one word about...us."

Kyleigh bit her bottom lip. She had to coax Marisa out of this funk. Soon, they'd take the plane home and forget about any romantic attachments in Hawaiʻi. *Oh, Lord, please help my friend. And show Bryce his need for salvation.*

"Marisa, Dad got a lift to the post and left his car for us to use today. What do you say we check out the coffee farm in North Shore?"

"I guess so. Sure. If you want to. I don't care what we do."

Kyleigh picked up her bowl and placed it in the sink. Her friend swirled her cereal with a spoon, staring into it. "Are you going to eat that, Marisa?"

She dropped the utensil into the milk and pushed it away. "Not hungry."

After she ran water into Marisa's bowl, Kyleigh pressed her lips together and peeked at her friend. This was not normal for a gal who couldn't go for more than two hours without a snack. She hadn't eaten anything yesterday. And she hadn't even combed her hair yet.

Marisa slid off the stool and plodded to the couch.

There had to be a way to snap her out of this lethargy. "Come on, girl. Slip on one of those colorful Hawaiian outfits you bought. I'll call Dad and tell him we're going, in case he planned to run home for lunch. We'll find a place to eat nearby the coffee farm where there's traditional island decor."

Marisa didn't say a word. She rose, slogged her way into the guestroom, and closed the door behind her.

Poor Marisa. Kyleigh gazed upward. "I'd truly love to wring Bryce's neck right now, Lord."

Kyleigh rinsed the rest of the dishes and loaded them in the dishwasher. She'd like to wring Jer's neck as well. He'd only pretended to be interested in her. What was it with guys? Wish she and Marisa had a couple of cowboys back home who missed them.

They'd have called every morning and night to tell them so too. No, they had to travel to Hawai'i and fall for—*ugh!* She'd bet Jer had a girlfriend the entire time he'd been babysitting the *major's daughter.*

She flung her mug into the dishwasher. The handle broke off and flew across the room. "*Great!* Now see what you made me do, Mr. Preston Jerard O'Shea?"

Marisa rushed out of the guestroom, dressed in a red hibiscus-patterned blouse and white shorts, dangling her sandals in one hand. "Did I hear you talking to someone?"

"Sorry." Kyleigh shut the dishwasher door and deposited the broken cup and handle in the trash. "I was voicing my opinion about men in general." She smiled at Marisa's choice of outfit. "You look very cheerful. While you strap your sandals on, I'll call Dad."

Marisa shuffled barefoot to the bedroom.

Kyleigh phoned the post, but her dad was in a meeting. "Just tell him we plan to visit the coffee farm at North Shore. We'll be back in time to prepare dinner."

Almost an hour later, Kyleigh pulled the car into the parking lot at the coffee farm. Marisa hadn't said more than two words from Dad's apartment to North Shore. This would be a very quiet day.

Marisa braced her elbow on the door next to the window, chin in her palm, and dropped her head back on the headrest. Glassy eyes stared at the dashboard.

"We're here, Marisa. Let's go in."

"If you say so." She opened the passenger door and swung her feet to the gravel.

Kyleigh hurried around the front of the Mustang and stretched out her arm to help her friend stand. "I know you're hurt, but don't let it ruin your day. That's exactly what the devil wants to do. Fight against it. Fight against *him*. Let God handle things."

Marisa gazed up at Kyleigh, grabbed her forearm, and pulled herself to a standing position. "You're right, Ky. Let's go."

As they approached the building entrance, Kyleigh slipped her arm around her friend's waist. "That's a girl. And we have beautiful weather today to explore all the ins and outs of island-grown coffee. Whatever that means." She chortled. "I'll ask an employee for a recommendation for lunch."

"Ky, I'm sorry for being such a downer. You have every reason to be upset yourself, considering the way Jer's been acting, but you aren't. Thanks for putting up with me."

Coming to a sudden stop, Kyleigh swung her friend around to face her. "Listen. You're like a sister to me. We need to support one another. Things could have turned out a lot worse than they have, but they didn't. And we're still here for a few days, so we can thank God and make the best of the trip."

The first smile Kyleigh had seen since dinner with Bryce formed on Marisa's face. She gave Kyleigh a shaky thumbs-up, and they entered the building.

Inside, the girls took their time wandering around the spacious room full of souvenirs and trinkets. After viewing the displays on Hawaiian culture and history, they moseyed back to the gift area. Marisa examined a handcrafted mug in shades of green and blue with the word aloha emblazoned on them. "I'll buy my parents a couple of these aloha mugs and a set of coasters before we leave."

"Why not one for yourself?" Kyleigh picked up a purple mug with an abstract floral design.

Marisa placed the cup she'd examined back on the shelf. "On second thought, I don't think I want to remember this trip to O'ahu." Her eyes pooled with tears, but she blinked them away.

You said it. Kyleigh sighed. She put the purple cup back on the shelf. No way did she want anything to remind her of this time on the island either. "Let's do the self-guided tour and find out how coffee grows."

The girls went out the shop's back door and spotted a sign over the walkway announcing, "Coffee Garden."

Roosters crowed as they strolled through the wooden entrance. "Farm is right." Marisa searched each aisle of tall, dense plants as they wandered in the grove. She picked up a feather from the ground. "Why are there chickens here?"

Kyleigh pointed to the branch almost above them in the middle of the path. A red and blue rooster studied them, then let out a call. She covered her ears. "To eat bugs? People in Texas say it's why they have chickens...along with the benefit of natural fertilizer." She laughed. "Oh, and for eggs too, I suppose."

Marisa nodded, stopped, and touched a string of green and red coffee beans growing on a stem. "They're like cherries stuck to a twig. I would have never guessed coffee beans grow this way."

"I'm sure the red are the ripe ones."

After touring the garden, the girls meandered back to the building. Marisa perused the menu in front of the entrance to the snack shop. "Ky, they have shaved ice."

Kyleigh pointed to the pile of what resembled creamy rainbow snow the server was handing another guest. "*Shave* ice. Not shaved. A local favorite. Let's order."

They got their icy-cold treat and sat at one of the small tables to enjoy it.

"Mmm. This is fantastic." Marisa wiped her mouth with a napkin.

"Yes, I love the pineapple flavor."

When they had finished, they entered the farm's gift shop once more. "I should take gifts back to Houston for Aunt Maye and some of the teachers." Kyleigh turned the display of keychains and bracelets with wooden Hawaiian designs dangling from them.

"I should too." Marisa fingered the wooden coasters with carved sea turtle designs. "My parents will be disappointed if I don't. Since they grow cacao beans and make chocolates here, I'll choose a selection of those instead of something that will remind me of—"

"Good plan. Besides bags of coffee for Aunt Maye, I'll give her this box of chocolate-covered pineapple chunks. Macadamias and chocolate for everyone else. "

Arms loaded with items, Kyleigh approached a cashier. "Can you recommend a nearby restaurant where we can eat lunch?"

The tanned, dark-eyed young man beamed. "Try the seafood grill up the road about a mile. You won't regret it." He displayed another O'ahu smile that oozed aloha as he handed her a receipt and her bag full of edible treasures.

"Mahalo." Too bad everyone wasn't aloha-minded like him. Jer and Bryce had the grins but not *the aloha* attitude. As she waited for Marisa to pay for her purchases, she shook her head. That wasn't fair. She and Marisa had both been treated better by them than any guy they'd dated previously, until now.

As the girls stepped out of the store and headed toward the major's car, Kyleigh spotted Jer and Bryce on the far side of the parking lot. "No," she whispered and grabbed Marisa's arm.

"There they are." Jer quickened his steps, Bryce right behind him. This would be a difficult but needed conversation. He'd been so wrong in the way he'd acted over the last couple of weeks. Kyleigh deserved better.

She and Marisa turned and hurried back into the gift shop.

"Wait! Kyleigh." Jer broke into a jog to catch them before they disappeared inside. "We need to talk."

He entered the structure and searched for the girls. "Where'd they go?"

Bryce rushed in behind his partner. "They don't want to see us. I shouldn't have waited. Marisa misunderstood my silence and with good reason. How'd I become such an idiot?" He followed his partner through the aisles of merchandise. "She has to hear me out."

"Let's hope they both listen to us." Where could they have gone so fast? Out the back. "Come on, buddy." Jer sprinted out the door leading to the garden.

The men dashed into the grove and searched each row of plants. Finally, they caught sight of the girls.

Bryce called out, "Marisa. Please wait. I have to explain." He raced toward her with Jer on his tail.

Kyleigh halted and turned. She put her arm around her friend's shoulder. Her piercing, deep blue eyes glared at Bryce, then switched to Jer. "You two have had enough fun with us. Go away."

Tears flowed from Marisa's eyes.

"Fun? No. *No.*" Bryce took a step toward Marisa. "I knew I shouldn't have waited. I *knew* it. For two nights, I struggled with what to do, but I never intended to upset *you.* Please listen to me. I wanted to tell you in person, not on the phone." He reached out his hand to her. "I have wonderful news. Everything's going to be fine now."

He withdrew his hand, took a handkerchief from his hip pocket, and handed it to Marisa.

She accepted it and wiped her eyes but wouldn't make eye contact with him.

Jer's brows furrowed. "You carry a handkerchief?"

"At the insistence of my old-fashioned Hawaiian Mom. Old habits are hard to break, but in this case, I'm glad I had it." He smiled at Marisa. "Can we go somewhere to talk...alone?"

She nodded. The couple walked away from Jer and Kyleigh toward the empty rows of picnic benches at the side of the garden.

Kyleigh kept her eyes on them. "He'd better say the right thing to her, or I'll...I'll...break his neck."

After he'd taken in a deep breath, Jer mumbled, "You'd probably like to break mine too. And I can't blame you one bit."

She spun to face him, spitting daggers from her eyes. Each blade made its way into his heart with a piercing blow.

"Kyleigh, we need to talk too. I never meant to—it's my fault. If I had paid more attention to your fears over your father instead of finding the perp, you wouldn't have gotten hurt. I almost lost you. How can I justify that?"

The daggers stopped. Her brows relaxed. "What do you mean?"

He led Kyleigh to a round bench in the middle of the coffee garden, and they sat. "When you first told me your dad was missing, I should have focused on him. I thought Whitehall had something to do with his disappearance because of the information the major gave us. But I'd have been wiser to search for your dad, and with the same effort you put into it. If I had, you wouldn't have had to face the criminal. I was so sure you'd been killed." He closed his eyes and lowered his head.

When he peeked at Kyleigh, her head fell forward. A lock of her long, reddish-streaked hair swung to her cheek. He brushed the strands behind her ear.

"The rescue team on Koʻolau took me to the hospital. We thought you were—" His eyes burned as he gazed at her, not caring if she saw his tears. He deserved her scorn. "No one told me you were alive until the paramedics brought you and your dad to the hospital. When I found out you weren't both dead, I was beside myself with relief. But...I suspected there'd be no way you'd ever forgive me."

Kyleigh shook her head. "How is any of this your fault?" Her hand touched his forearm. "Jer, is that why you wouldn't talk to me?"

He nodded. "Bryce told me I'd been invited to dinner the other night. He kept coaxing me to go with him, but I couldn't face you or your father."

"You were doing your job. It's over now. You can go back to your life...*your friend*."

Jer's head shot up. "My *friend?* What friend? Bryce?" His brows rumpled. "Or as in girlfriend? You thought I had a girlfriend. That I was playing you?"

Tears fell to her cheeks.

Jer wiped them away with his index finger. "Kyleigh, I stayed away because I thought you'd never forgive me for not looking hard enough for your father."

He scratched the stubble on his chin. He should've taken the time to shave before he and Bryce ran out of the house this morning. "Wish *I* had a handkerchief now."

Kyleigh reached into her bag and pulled out a tissue. She wiped her eyes and nose. "I still don't understand why you wouldn't talk to me. While Dad was in the hospital, every time you were there visiting him, you left as soon as I arrived."

"After what happened, I thought you wouldn't want me around."

"But you avoided me."

"I didn't want to put you through the agony of confronting me about my stupidity. You needed to focus on your Dad. But I should have said something to you. Can you ever forgive me?"

"Jer, there's nothing to forgive. Like I told you, you were doing your job. And you sent help to us."

He raised one side of his lips into a crooked smile. "Technically, Bryce and Marisa called for help. I had phoned him and explained what happened."

A half-smile tickled at Kyleigh's lips. Her gaze captured his.

How would he ever live his life without this woman? She still hadn't said she'd forgive him. Maybe deep inside, she couldn't.

"Bryce picked me up at my place this morning, and we left to see you, Marisa, and your dad. When we got to the apartment...oh, wait, you don't know. Bryce got saved last night."

The tentative smile on her face blossomed like a rose opening in the morning sun. "He did?" Her head fell backward, and she breathed out a sigh. "Praise God! Marisa wouldn't marry an unsaved man, although she'd said yes to him." She straightened and pinned Jer with a stare. "He told you he proposed, didn't he?"

"Yes, early this morning. I've never seen the guy so happy over anything except salvation, and as cheerful as Bryce always is, that's saying a lot." A twinge of pain stabbed at Jer's heart. He wanted a *lifetime* with the woman he loved.

"Marisa thought the proposal had been a joke to him. I'm so glad he meant it." She rested her hand on his arm again. "They'll be okay now."

"But we aren't. When Bryce and I arrived at the apartment to surprise everyone with his news and found no one there, we hurried to Ft. Shafter to find the major. He told us everything you and Marisa had gone through. Boy, was he angry. He said we'd better make things right, or he'd skin us alive." Jer shuddered.

Kyleigh's lips pressed together.

"Before we left his office, he told me why you'd acted so strange toward me regarding my job. First warm and then ice-cold. I'm so sorry about your mother, and the Houston police never found her killer."

"Watching you and Bryce work so hard, I realized sometimes there aren't enough clues to solve a mystery."

"It's true. All we can do is our best."

She smiled. "If you hadn't spent your efforts on the drug case and focused on finding Dad instead, I wouldn't have gone up on the range and located Dad's dog tags. He'd have been in the ravine until the beginning of next month when Bryce's mother brought Ilima supplies again." Her voice hitched. "The infection might have killed him."

Jer wanted to take her in his arms and never let go. But she still hadn't forgiven him.

"Don't you see, Jer? God had us in His Hand. Bad things happen, even to Christians. But He took care of both of us as we each made our way down the cliff. Dad did suffer a broken leg, but I didn't. What are the odds of our having survived at all? God also had Ilima waiting for us. I'm positive that whatever the stuff she put on Dad's wounds was, it helped keep him alive. And God's been with Ilima all those years." Her face beamed.

As the corners of her lips turned up, Jer's heart warmed.

Mist from an approaching shower moved in. He snatched her hand. "Let's head for the building. And you haven't said you'll forgive me yet."

"Yes. I forgive you...if you think you need to be forgiven. I had no idea you blamed yourself for everything."

He took a deep breath. "May I risk asking you to dinner this evening, so we can talk without getting soaked?" As they neared the structure, he gazed up at the clouds. The low flying grayness moved through and covered the coffee farm.

Kyleigh broke into a run toward the gift shop without answering him.

Chapter Twenty-Eight

K yleigh stared into the mirror over the guestroom dresser. She chuckled to herself. How mean of her to have teased Jer and not answered earlier at the coffee farm when he asked her to dinner. But he deserved a little punishment for the turmoil he'd put her through for the past two weeks. Didn't he? Regardless, she was glad she accepted his invitation.

She brushed and weaved her hair into one long braid down her back. In front of the full-length mirror on the closet door, she twisted and turned to make sure her black sarong with blue plumerias and purple orchids was tied properly around her neck. There. She was ready for her date with Jer.

Marisa had worn the same sarong in pink and white on deep purple for her date with Bryce tonight. Would they work out this long-distance relationship?

Wow! Kyleigh rubbed her hand across her forehead. So much had happened in such a short time here on Oʻahu. As if they all had parts in one of those dramatic, romantic movies Auntie watched. Boy meets girl, they argue, disaster comes, the hero saves the day, and he and the heroine fall in love. All within two hours.

She and Marisa were leaving next Monday. Her eyes filled with tears, but she willed them away. One more weekend on this gorgeous island, and then it was back to life in the fast lane in Houston. Until they flew back in for Dad's retirement ceremony in November. Would Jer feel the same about her when she was four thousand miles away? November. Almost five months before she'd return.

When she entered the living room, her father hobbled in from the lanai and kissed her cheek. "Beautiful, Sugar. The picture of your mother."

As he turned, she caught his misty eyes. "Thank you, Dad."

He planted himself on the couch and lifted the newspaper off the coffee table. "I'm glad you and Jer, as well as Bryce and Marisa, got everything worked out. Or I'd have to court-martial those two young men."

"Da-a-ad...you know you can't court-martial civilians." She tittered. "And I'm pretty sure that goes double for a native Hawaiian."

"He's not native Hawaiian. Not according to their way of thinking, remember? He's a hapa. Half and half. His dad was Swedish."

"You *still* can't court-martial them." She formed a smug expression, one brow up and one brow down, with a cockeyed smile.

"Humph. I'd find a way. But since they were instrumental in saving our lives, I may have to just shoot them through the hindquarters." He narrowed his eyes.

Kyleigh burst out laughing. It felt so good to laugh again.

The doorbell chimed, and she hurried to answer.

When she opened the door, Jer's eyes rounded. They roved from her head to her feet and back up again. "Wowsers! In that dress, you look like a model for the local glamour magazine. It shows off your...eyes." His cheeks brightened to a rosy glow.

"Thank you." She motioned for him to enter

He followed her into the foyer and stopped. She turned to face him. From behind his back, he swung out a purple and white orchid lei. "May I?"

"Oh, Jer. It's lovely."

He slipped the lei over her head and under her braid in the back and gave her a gentle kiss on the cheek. Warmth spread up her neck and into her face.

"Guess I picked the right color for tonight. Various lei mean different things here. This one says thank you. Although it also means welcome to a new visitor in the Hawaiian tradition."

He was as nervous as she was.

"The *thank you* is for finally agreeing to have dinner with me."

They crossed the room to where her father read the newspaper. He laid the paper on the coffee table and offered his hand to Jer. "Evening, son."

Jer shook his hand. "How do you feel, sir?" He pointed to the major's foot.

"I'm getting around pretty well. Never had a broken leg before this, and I hope I never have another. The worst of it is, I won't be riding the mountain range for some time yet."

"Well, when you're ready, be sure to call me, and I'll join you."

Oh, great! Kyleigh rolled her eyes. Exactly what she needed to think about when she was back in Houston.

"Shouldn't you kids be going?" Her dad winked at her as if he'd read her mind and changed the topic.

She kissed him on the top of his head of thick black hair. Additional silver strands had crept in at his temples since the fall from the Ko'olau trail. But the salt and pepper gave him such a distinguished look.

Jer nodded. "Yes, we should. We have a reservation. Have a restful evening, Major."

"No doubt, without these girls fussing over me for a while." He chuckled. "Will you meet Bryce and Marisa at the restaurant?"

"No. They have different plans." Jer took Kyleigh by the arm and led her to the front door.

"O'Shea. Take care of my little girl. Remember what I told you when you came to my office."

"Not to worry, sir."

As they entered the apartment parking lot, Kyleigh searched for Jer's green Jeep Gladiator. "Where's your truck?"

"Not here. You, my dear lady, will ride in style tonight." He strode toward a sleek white vehicle and opened the passenger door.

Kyleigh's mouth dropped open. The white interior was spotless. "It's beautiful. Did you trade in your Jeep?"

"No. Are you kidding? I couldn't afford this baby...not yet, anyway. This is my Dad's new Tesla. He's going eco-friendly, and this new electric car is the first step. He says he wants to make this world a better place for future generations."

"And he let you borrow it?" Kyleigh lowered herself to the passenger seat, and Jer closed the door.

He sprinted to the driver's side and slipped behind the wheel. "When I stopped by my parents' place to talk to Dad for a few minutes, I told him I was taking you out to dinner. When my mother overheard, she said, 'You can't take a lady out to a fancy restaurant in that rattletrap truck of yours.' Gotta love my mom. My father agreed and tossed me his keys. I didn't argue. This suits you much better."

"I like your old 'rattletrap.' It's loaded with character." She gave him a sideways glance and grinned. "This *is* perfect for tonight, though." She ran her hand across the soft seat. "What did my dad tell you in his office?"

Jer laughed. "I told you. He threatened to skin Bryce and me alive. I guess that includes making sure you have a good time tonight too."

"Where are we going?"

"It's a secret. I hope you enjoy where I'm taking you as much as the ride."

"I'm sure I will."

She gazed out the side window as her smile vanished from her lips. Hmm...she had to tell him before the evening was over.

Jer maneuvered out of the apartment complex, through the streets, and onto the highway. Kyleigh grew quiet as they neared Pearl Harbor. What was she thinking? Second thoughts about him?

When he passed the exit for Honolulu, she turned to him. "We're not going into the city?"

"No. Not this time. I wanted our first *proper* date to be unforgettable. We're headed to Waikiki for dinner on the shores of Kaimana Beach." His heart skipped a beat. He'd make sure Kyleigh knew his feelings tonight. How had they become so strong so fast?

"Kaimana Beach is on the way to Diamond Head, isn't it?"

"Yes. Are you impressed?"

She chortled. "Everything tonight has been impressive so far. Even you." She fingered his collar. "I love this soft cream shirt with plumerias. It's perfect with the tan suit."

When she retracted her hand, he reached across the console and took it in his. "Thanks, this is my favorite aloha shirt. I wear it on special occasions."

Forty minutes later, Jer pulled the Tesla in at the Kaimana Palms Restaurant and parked. The surf roared in the background. He hurried around the front end of the car and opened the door for Kyleigh. Perfume from the tropical garden that surrounded the building filled the air.

"Take a deep breath, Kyleigh. Where else on earth can you experience the combination of saltwater and flowers walking from your car to a restaurant but here in Hawaiʻi?"

"It's wonderful. Gardenia..." She smiled and drew in the fragrances a second time. "...and my favorite Hawaiian flower, plumeria, I believe."

"I'll have to remember that." He opened the entrance door.

Candles flickered on each table while guests spoke in low tones as they ate. Jer approached the podium inside the foyer and gave his name. The maître d' led them to a table on the balcony next to a railing that overlooked the water. He laid menus on the table, then left. Jer pulled out the chair for Kyleigh.

She slid into the cushioned seat and stared at the water as though mesmerized.

Clouds stretched across the sky, changing to colors of gold, orange, and purple as the sun dipped lower, hanging above the edge of the ocean. He smiled at her. "I'll never tire of watching God's brush strokes as he paints a heavenly canvas." He reached for Kyleigh's hand.

She turned to him. "Jer, I have something to tell you."

"Can it wait while we watch the sunset and then order? The view is part of the floorshow here." He grinned.

"Sure." She turned her attention back to the pounding surf.

The golden globe touched the horizon and sent a choppy path of white glow across the waves. After the ball of fire disappeared into the ocean, a million diamonds lit up the sky.

Her expression turned from fascinated to awestruck as her jaw lowered. Kyleigh reached up as though she'd snatch a sparkling gem from the darkness. "Beautiful." She glanced at him, then back to the water.

"Yes, you are. I thought so the very first time I laid eyes on you outside the police station." Even by candlelight, he could see her blush. Surely she'd hear his heart thumping as close as they sat to each other. Did she have any idea how much he'd come to love her?

"I guess we can order now." Jer signaled for the waiter.

After they ordered their food and were served their drinks, Kyleigh sipped on a glass of lemonade. She had to tell him they were leaving. Three days away. Would he care? Sure, he said she was beautiful. Typical line for a handsome man to give his date for the evening. But how she hoped he'd want to keep in touch with her. And that their feelings for each other wouldn't wilt like a plant deprived of water.

Gentle Hawaiian music played in the background, soft and melodic. She closed her eyes and imagined living here on Oʻahu forever. Here she'd found the man she wanted to spend the rest of her life with, even if she had only known him for less than a month. But so far, he hadn't shown her he cared in the same way.

He was interested in her. He'd made it clear many times. If she lived here, maybe after a year, he'd have the same feelings toward her. She shook her head. How would it happen now, with her in Houston and him on Oʻahu? It was hopeless.

Kyleigh found Jer's eyes on her. Had she said any of that aloud? A smile tickled at the corner of his lips. She'd die of embarrassment if she had.

"Kyleigh. You've been quiet so far this evening. I hope it's not because you're sorry you accepted my invitation to dinner." He grinned and took her hand.

His eyes twinkled with light from the flickering candle in the middle of the table. He was being a gentleman, making sure she had a remarkable memory to take back to Texas. *Don't read any more into it.*

"Jer, I need to tell you—"

The waiter stepped up to their table. He lowered Kyleigh's fresh-caught spiny lobster and scallop dish to the table. The artistry of the chef's swirls of sauces and placement of the vegetables on the plate was amazing. Everything about this island was beautiful. Even more so now.

She peeked up at Jer as the server placed his dinner before him. Beef tenderloin. So un-Hawaiian. She smiled. You'd think he was from Texas. Her heart pinched. If he was, there'd be a chance for their relationship to grow. *Oh well.* She had this evening to remember.

Jer said the blessing for the food. After he'd taken his first bite of tenderloin, he washed it down with lemongrass soda. "Bryce took Marisa to pick out an engagement ring tonight before they go to dinner. Your friend sure captured his heart. Funny. And here I thought he was a playboy. It was a shock to find he was terrified of rejection from females. Until he met her. Go figure."

Kyleigh gazed at Jer's downturned eyes. Why was he so sad all of a sudden? Did he begrudge Bryce's happiness? Or anticipate his partner's sadness when Marisa would leave for Texas? She wouldn't see Bryce again until they came back for Dad's retirement celebration in November. How would Marisa and Bryce manage in the meantime? Engaged but separated for months. They'd Skype every day, but it wasn't the same.

"It's going to take some getting used to. My partner, a married man." Jer raised his brows.

He smiled, but the smile didn't reach his eyes. Why? "Yes, I suppose it will. No more bachelor nights out."

"Ha! As if we did anyway. We'd go out to eat on occasion or take in a movie now and then. Never double-dated because...I didn't date much, and I told you Bryce's old fears. I've gone out with a female friend from college once in a while, but nothing serious."

"Jer. I have to tell you. Marisa and I are leaving for Houston this coming Monday. I wanted you to know ahead of time." She hoped Marisa had told Bryce. There wasn't much time left for them to be together. *Or for me to spend with you.*

"I didn't realize you were leaving so soon. I thought you'd be here for most of the summer." His brows furrowed.

Was he disappointed she was leaving? "That would have been fantastic, but we have our tickets. And we have students waiting to be tutored in August."

Had he simply wanted a summer fling?

Chapter Twenty-Nine

Kyleigh gathered the ingredients to prepare shrimp pasta, a dish Jer said he'd never tasted, and began making the sauce. Their date from the night before replayed in her mind. He'd been a gentleman in every way. Not once had he indicated he wanted any more than a pleasant evening out for dinner with her and a ride along the shoreline of Waikiki before returning her to Dad's apartment. He hadn't asked her to come to his place or even tried to kiss her when he'd brought her back to her father's home. Either he decided three days wasn't enough for a summer fling, or she'd drawn the wrong conclusion about his interest in her. She sucked in her bottom lip. She'd been wrong about a lot of things this month.

Kyleigh pulled out a pot from the cabinet, filled it with water, and set it on the stove to boil. She reached for the pasta container in the corner of the counter and unlatched the lid to remove the spaghetti and toss it in when ready.

Last night had been a beautiful evening. The lobster and scallops were as delicious to eat as they were beautifully arranged on the plate. Pretty enough with the fancy cut and roasted vegetables to hang on a wall like a painting. Maybe she should take some culinary classes when she got back to Houston. She needed something to keep her mind off Jer until the memory of him faded away. And her heart stopped aching.

But what if he wanted to stay in contact with her? She closed the lid to the pot a little harder than she meant to. She glanced to the lanai where her father had taken his laptop to catch up on paperwork that had accumulated while he'd been gone from the post. He was still glued to the screen. Good thing Dad was so absorbed in getting back up to speed, and the sound hadn't carried, or he'd have come in here and asked all kinds of questions she didn't want to answer.

She'd better get these little frustrations of hers under control. So what if Jer felt less for her than she did for him? He'd proven himself to be a wonderful man, an able detective, and a...friend. That's all she needed right now. As friends, they'd keep in touch over the miles. If Marisa could stand only talking and hearing from Bryce through Skype, a phone call or two, and emails, she and Jer could, too...if that's what he wanted.

The water came to a boil. Kyleigh added the spaghetti, turned the heat down, and stirred the strands of pasta until they were pliable enough to ease all the way into the pot.

Who was she kidding? *You love the man, and your heart will break into pieces by the time the plane lands in Houston.*

Jer drove his vintage Jeep Gladiator through the somewhat laid-back Saturday Honolulu traffic. A far cry from the evening gridlock coming home from work forty-eight hours earlier. He loved the weekends when he didn't have to deal with criminals. Sure was great that his boss let him and Bryce have a couple of days off to spend with the girls before they left the island. A rock dropped into Jer's stomach.

Last night, he should have told Kyleigh how his feelings for her had grown. The right moment had never come up. After they finished their dinner, she had talked almost non-stop for the rest of the evening. More than she had spoken since the first day he'd met her. While they strolled on the beach, she went on about her tutoring job in August, as well as the plans she'd have to make for her father's retirement celebration. He hadn't had a chance to change the subject to their relationship without interrupting her or being abrupt on the ride back to her dad's either. Almost as if he made her nervous.

Jer parked the Jeep at the Makakilo Kauhale Apartments next to the major's white Mustang and turned off the engine. Jer's lips pressed tightly together. He'd find a time for them to be alone before the evening was over and tell Kyleigh he'd fallen in love with her. He had to know where he stood before she left.

Jer pushed the driver's door open and hopped out. As he strode toward the long, covered sidewalk leading to the apartment, he spotted the bike chain lying half off the pavement. No one had moved it from the support pole where the major's dirt bike used to sit. Kyleigh's worried face on top of the mountain range flashed into Jer's mind. He should have done a better job looking for her father. What details had he missed? When she said it wasn't his fault, did she really mean it?

Tonight, he was determined to find out where they'd go from here. *Lord, I sure need Your help.*

Why was she in such a hurry to fly back to Houston? There might be someone waiting for her to come home. But they could stay friends, couldn't they? If so, he'd resolve himself to be the best guy friend she'd ever had, even if it killed him. But did she want to remain close with him at all?

Jer knocked on the door.

Kyleigh took out lettuce, tomatoes, onions, and carrots from the refrigerator's lower bin to start a salad while Jer conversed with her dad outside on the lanai. She laid the vegetables in the sink. What would her father think of him as a son-in-law? Would Dad mind having a cop in the family after what happened to Mom, or would it be a constant reminder? *Oh, brother!* She needed to get her brain on something other than wedding bells. At least, where she was concerned.

She gave a half-hearted chortle. How could she, when Marisa would no doubt ask her to be her Maid of Honor? Would she make her way through their ceremony without falling apart?

Marisa and Bryce strolled in from the front door. The joyful sound of the couple's laughter sent a dart into Kyleigh's heart. She sighed. She really was happy for them. Envious but happy.

"Hey, Ky. What'cha cooking?" Marisa hopped onto the kitchen stool. "Will there be enough for us too? I'm sorry I forgot to tell you we had no plans for this evening except to sit around and talk over our future. But this is the first I've seen you since the coffee farm. You were gone when I got up this morning. I haven't had a chance to show you the ring Bryce gave me last night." Marisa flashed her solitaire diamond engagement ring in front of her. "He wanted me to pick a bigger stone, but I thought this one was perfect. What do you think?"

Another dart pierced Kyleigh as she forced a smile for her friend's sake.

Marisa wore the telltale expression of a radiant bride as she turned and gazed lovingly at her fiancé, sitting next to her.

His grin couldn't have been any wider. "I suppose a larger stone would have made her fall over since she's so petite." He laughed.

Kyleigh rounded the kitchen island and hugged Marisa. "It's beautiful. Suits you." Kyleigh went back to the stove and focused on the cooking pasta. "I had some errands to do early this morning. Left before you even awoke. Don't worry, there's plenty of shrimp pasta to go around. Would you give me a hand, Marisa? If I can drag you away from Prince Charming here, that is." She faked a laugh.

Bryce slid off the stool and kissed Marisa. "Prince Charming, is it? I like that." He turned to Kyleigh. "I'll join *your* Prince Charming on the lanai." He chuckled all the way out the sliding door.

Kyleigh watched him shake hands with Jer and her father. If her heart got any heavier, she'd drop to the floor.

"Ky. What's the matter?" Marisa's brows sagged.

"Would you like to make the salad for dinner?" Kyleigh turned from her view of the lanai and rinsed off the fixings in the sink.

"Sure, I can. But what's wrong with you, girl? Your jaw is dragging on the counter. Didn't you and Jer have a nice time last night? Did he tell you how he feels about you?"

"No. He just gave me the same old guy compliments any gentleman would give his date."

"You're kidding. Bryce says Jer is head-over-heels for you. I don't understand it. Let me talk to him." She headed for the lanai.

"*Marisa!* No. Leave him alone. Bryce may be mistaken. They're best buds, but they can't read each other's minds. And I don't want anyone to tell Jer he needs to open his heart to me. If he won't do it by himself—" She bit her lower lip.

Marisa shrugged and came back to the kitchen. "I suppose you're right, but I don't understand it, Ky. You didn't see the anguish on his face when Whitehall kept needling Jer that his girlfriend was dead before the officers hauled the reprobate away."

"To be honest with you." Kyleigh lowered the serving bowls from the cabinet to the counter. "I think Jer was simply being a cop. A very caring officer of the law who worried over someone he liked and to whom he had an obligation to keep safe. He told me he felt responsible for everything that happened to my father and me. He blamed himself. Now he's trying to make up for it by being so attentive. But it's not as if the man will ask me to marry him over it."

Marisa gave her a hug. "I think you're wrong, girl. But time will tell."

Kyleigh stirred the rich marinara sauce in the pan. "Time? What time? We leave Monday." She checked the garlic bread in the oven.

"I'm sure Jer plans to keep in touch with you when we're back home." Marisa retrieved the cutting board from the dish drainer, selected a sharp knife, and sliced the vegetables for a salad. "I've heard of romances that started and progressed over the internet. Some of those couples never met until after they'd fallen in love."

As Kyleigh added the colander full of small shrimp to the sauce, she glanced through the glass partition at Jer. She needed time away from him. She'd have lots of time for the next three and a half months until they returned for Dad's retirement. Perhaps it would be better if they didn't stay in touch.

Chapter Thirty

S unday morning, Bryce pulled to the curb outside Jer's apartment. He must be eager to see Kyleigh again to be pacing the sidewalk.

"Thanks, buddy." Jer jumped into Bryce's Prius and attached the seat belt. "I can't believe my battery is dead."

"No problem." Bryce eased the car from the curb. Should he ask Jer if he told Ky how he felt about her or not? Marisa said Ky told her not to meddle.

"Where's your mom? I guess Marisa's riding with Kyleigh and the major, huh?"

"Yeah, Marisa said she didn't see any point in us running all the way to his apartment when we could drive directly to the church, and they'd meet us there. I'm glad the major agreed to come to our service instead of the post chapel this week."

"Me too. Especially since last night, he'd told me the Army chaplain is an interesting preacher and a friend of his. But he didn't mention coming to our church today. So where's your mom? Hope she's not sick."

Bryce turned onto the road that led to their little church at the edge of Pearl City. "She's fine. But you won't believe this. According to my mother, Ilima will be here today."

Jer whipped his head to gape at Bryce. "I thought Ilima never came out of the forest. You said so when you told me about her helping Kyleigh."

As he pulled into the parking lot at Faith Bible Church, Bryce nodded. "Right. But Mom says Kyleigh made an impression on the woman. While Kyleigh's dad was in the hospital, she went back to visit Ilima with my mother. They explained to the poor woman what had happened on the island in the aftermath of the Pearl Harbor attack. A few days later, Mom took supplies to her and asked if she would consider coming to church this Sunday. Ilima agreed. My mother even bought her a new muumuu for the occasion. Despite the short distance from the fringe of her forest to the building, Mom didn't want her to walk after her trek through the brush. It'll be Ilima's first car ride."

"At least that will be something special today."

Bryce turned off the ignition and stared at Jer. "What has you so depressed, man?"

"I never had a chance to talk to Kyleigh alone last night...again." Jer pounded a closed fist down on his thigh. "I wanted to tell her how much I care for her. And now she'll leave tomorrow. I need time to be alone with her today."

Bryce grinned. "Come on, man. Let's go inside. I'm sure you'll find time this afternoon."

As Jer and Bryce entered the vestibule, Mrs. Swanson was talking to a native woman of slight stature in the doorway of the church sanctuary. Their pastor shook her hand. Jer bumped Bryce's arm with his elbow. "There's your mom. And that has to be Ilima next to her. She's tiny." How could *that* little woman have moved the major from the bottom of the cliff to her shack in the woods? *Lord, You have performed a miracle.*

"Mom never mentioned her being so small. Except for the wrinkles and slight hunch of the back, she resembles an average ten-year-old girl. Man, God must have given her the strength to have moved the major from the edge of the range to where she lives. And He's had His hand on her all these years."

Jer stared at Bryce. Boy, he sure had grown fast in his newfound Christianity. *Thank You, Lord.*

"Come on. Mom's waving us over."

Jer followed his partner through the door to the sanctuary and slid into the pew behind Mrs. Swanson and Ilima. Bryce's mother introduced Ilima to her son and Jer. They exchanged greetings in Hawaiian, and the little woman smiled, showing a full set of teeth. She looked remarkably healthy. *You sure took care of this wonderful lady, God.*

He held out his hand to her, and she put her tiny one in his. "I'm sorry, Ilima, but my Hawaiian isn't good enough to say much. I've neglected using it because most people here on the island speak English."

Bryce translated for him.

Ilima nodded and smiled. "Aʻole pilikia."

His partner leaned toward Jer and whispered, "It basically means no problem."

Jer chuckled. "That one I knew." He grinned at Ilima. "Mahalo."

A commotion at the back of the church interrupted them. The pastor had rushed to the back of the sanctuary to welcome the major, Marisa, and Kyleigh. Jer's heart thumped. Would he have a chance to talk to her today? This was killing him. He had to tell her he loved her. But blurting it out in front of a bunch of people was not what he wanted to do.

After they shook the preacher's hand and exchanged names, Kyleigh stepped into the middle aisle with her father and Marisa. Kyleigh's eyes locked with Jer's. He was handsome in his dark blue suit with a light blue aloha shirt. But he'd be impressive in a pair of overalls, as far as she was concerned.

They approached Jer, Bryce, Mrs. Swanson, and Ilima, who stood next to a pew halfway up the aisle. Kyleigh smiled at the old woman. "Ilima. I'm happy you're here."

She motioned for Kyleigh to come closer. When she did, Ilima picked up a lei of white orchids and plumeria from the end of the pew, lifted it over Kyleigh's head, and kissed her on the cheek. Her new friend's face glowed with pleasure.

Kyleigh bit her lip as tears of joy filled her eyes. "Mahalo. How did you—" She shifted her eyes to address Mrs. Swanson. "How did she get this? I thought today was her first time out of the jungle she lives in."

"The first time in many years. Ilima had it in her hands when I picked her up at the edge of the forest. I would say her mother taught her how to make them. Beautiful, isn't it?"

Kyleigh glanced at the flowers around her neck. "This is gorgeous. And orchids have become one of my favorite flowers...along with plumeria, tuberoses, and a few others." She chortled.

As organ music began, people took their places in the auditorium, and Mrs. Swanson motioned for Ilima to move to the center of the pew. Bryce led Marisa into the same row to sit with his mother. The major grasped Kyleigh's hand, and they sidestepped between the seats behind their friends to the other side. Kyleigh slipped in next to Ilima, with her father beside her.

She viewed the room to find Jer, but he was gone. Was he upset that she said nothing to him?

The pastor strode to the podium and greeted the congregation. "Aloha, friends and neighbors."

Everyone echoed, "Aloha."

"Let's start our Sunday school session with a hymn. *Trust and Obey*. Remember, there's no other way to be happy in Jesus but to trust and obey." He nodded to the organist, and she play.

Trust and obey. Kyleigh's heart pinched. She hadn't trusted God with this...whatever it was between her and Jer. No wonder she was miserable.

The congregation's singing was beautiful. She joined in and breathed a silent prayer. *Lord, help me trust You in this situation with Jer.* She had no idea what to think from one minute to the next. If he'd just say something one way or another to her. How he felt or didn't. She needed to know before she left for home.

Sunday school, of course. A smile came to her lips. Jer taught a teen class. That was why he had disappeared. Mrs. Swanson had invited them over after church for dinner. Would he be there? Perhaps they'd talk.

After dinner at Mrs. Swanson's home, Kyleigh and Marisa helped clear the table. Kyleigh peeked at Jer as he went out one of the three open sliding glass doors that led to the wrap-around lanai. He joined her father and Bryce on the wide, covered porch that faced the forest across the street. Jer had been so quiet during the meal. *Lord, I'm trying to trust, but can You help me out a little?*

Jer glanced into the house from a lounge chair, popped up, and strode inside, straight toward her. "Kyleigh, would you take a walk with me? These houses along the wooded area on the edge of Pearl City have beautiful gardens cared for by the residents. I think you'll appreciate them."

Thank You, Lord. "I'd love to take a walk if Marisa and Mrs. Swanson don't mind."

Marisa grinned at her. "Go. Scat. Enjoy the flowers." She winked at Kyleigh.

Jer smiled and led her out the door. "Kyleigh, I've been trying to say something to you ever since Friday night."

They turned onto a path lined on both sides by hibiscus, ginger, anthurium, and orchids. The fragrant ginger flowers reminded her of gardenias, one of her favorite bushes in Aunt Maye's garden. It was a pleasant stroll, yet it failed to calm Kyleigh's pounding heart. As the two approached the woods, Kyleigh gulped down the lump in her throat. He was going to say goodbye. She would not cry.

"What I'm trying to tell you is that I—" His cell rang, and he let out a frustrated breath. "*Hello!*" Jer spun, grabbed Kyleigh's hand, and sped back to Mrs. Swanson's home. "It's Ilima. She collapsed."

Kyleigh rushed into the house with Jer on her heels. "What's wrong with her?" She gazed around the living room where Ilima lay on the couch.

Mrs. Swanson dabbed Ilima's forehead with a wet cloth and shrugged. "I'm not sure. I brought her a glass of tea, but before she took it from my hand, she fainted. Her pulse is strong, from what I can tell."

Bryce held Marisa in his arms. "I've called nine-one-one. Help is on its way."

Kyleigh knelt beside Ilima, slipped her hand under the old woman's, and bowed her head. *Lord, please help her. She's gone through so much. Maybe You want her to come home, but—Thy will be done.*

Jer lowered himself next to Kyleigh and circled his arm around her shoulders. "Hang on. The paramedics should be here in a moment. They'll take her to the hospital, and we'll find out why she passed out."

A few seconds later, the emergency medical team entered the house. As they reached Ilima, she sat up. Her eyes widened as if she didn't recognize anyone. She caught sight of Kyleigh's face and smiled.

"You scared us, Ilima." Kyleigh dropped to the couch. "What happened?"

Mrs. Swanson translated.

The little woman shook her head, then spoke to Bryce's mother.

Mrs. Swanson faced Kyleigh. "A couple of days ago, she did the same thing. She fell to the floor, woke up later, and was fine."

The paramedic told Ilima what he would do and allowed her to hear his heartbeat with the stethoscope before checking hers. He showed her each piece of equipment before he used it. When he finished, he glanced at Mrs. Swanson, then back to Ilima and said, "You'd make a splendid paramedic, just like me."

Mrs. Swanson and the old woman laughed.

"I can't find anything wrong with her. Her vitals are normal, but we should get her to the hospital where they can run tests."

Mrs. Swanson told Ilima, but she moved her head back and forth again, twice as fast.

"She has fear written over her face like the first time I met her." Kyleigh eased onto the couch next to Ilima and put her arm around the woman. "What can we do? We can't let her go into the jungle. What if she faints and hurts herself?"

Kyleigh's father sat next to her. "Let me call one of my friends who's a physician. Since she won't go to the hospital, Lord willing, we can have the hospital come to her, so to speak. I'll ask if he can run over. He lives nearby." He patted Kyleigh's hand, took out his cell, and hobbled out to the lanai.

A couple of minutes later, he reentered the room. "Manu will be here soon."

"Mrs. Swanson," Kyleigh peered up to her, "would you explain to Ilima that a physician friend of my father's may stop by to see if he can help her?"

Bryce's mother spoke to Ilima. She stared back, then nodded.

Kyleigh released the breath she'd held. "Thank you, Dad."

"No problem." He hugged her. "But I hope it's not serious. Convincing this poor woman to receive help will be another story."

"My mom has been trying to lure Ilima out of those woods forever. Do you think this was God's way of getting her to leave? Mom told me last week she wanted Ilima to stay with her." Bryce raised his brows as he studied the old woman listening to his mother. "This might do it."

A knock came on the door. Bryce went into the foyer and answered it. "You must be the major's friend, the doctor."

"Yes. Dr. Kahale."

"Please, come in. Ilima's in here." Bryce swung his arm toward the living room. "She collapsed earlier but seems fine now."

"I have an idea what's wrong. Chuck...I mean Major Flanagan, told me what happened."

Dr. Kahale entered the room and checked Ilima over.

"What's he asking her, Bryce?" Kyleigh observed the old woman. "She doesn't act frightened of him at all."

"Mom told her how concerned everyone was for her health, and I guess when the doctor turned out to be Hawaiian, she relaxed. He's asking her questions about her diet."

After the physician finished his exam and talking to Ilima, he smiled at her. He packed up his instruments and stood. "The dear lady is suffering from a form of hypotension, I believe. I'd prefer to have labs done, although I'm not sure I can convince her. I think her blackout is the result of dehydration. She simply isn't drinking enough. I've explained everything to her, and she understands."

Kyleigh's dad thanked his friend and walked him to the front door while Mrs. Swanson conversed with Ilima.

There had to be some way to help her. Kyleigh chewed her lip. If only she didn't have to leave tomorrow.

Jer glanced at his watch. "Going for a stroll is out of the question now. Evening service starts in thirty minutes."

Kyleigh nodded. "So, what was it you wanted to tell me?" Her stomach lurched.

"Not now." He pulled her into the kitchen. "I'd rather say what I have to in private, and I don't want to be rushed. After church won't work because the pastor has called a Sunday school teachers' meeting I have to attend. Not sure how late the meeting will last. My truck's battery is dead, so I'll get a ride back to my apartment.

But Bryce said he'll bring me with him to pick up Marisa for your flight tomorrow. I figured your dad would want to drive you to the airport." He pressed his lips into a straight line.

"After you're squared away for your flight, I really need to talk to you before you leave. Please?"

I will not cry. Kyleigh nodded.

Chapter Thirty-One

onday afternoon, Bryce drove to the Honolulu International Airport with Marisa and Jer. Bryce peeked at Jer via the rearview mirror. If his partner got any more uptight, he'd burst like a volcano.

Through the heavy traffic on the west side of downtown, the major and Kyleigh followed in the Mustang.

After parking the Prius in the airport garage, Bryce removed Marisa's suitcase and carry-on from the backseat. He slung the bag over his shoulder while she lifted the telescoping handle of the rolling suitcase.

"Oh no, you don't." Bryce laid hold of the handle. "I'll take that."

"You're spoiling me."

"Good."

The major and Kyleigh got out of the Mustang next to them. Jer jumped out of the Prius and took her luggage from the major's hands. "Let me help with these, sir." He hoisted the carry-on over his shoulder and winked at her.

Bryce's brows rose. Would Jer have a chance to talk to her in private before it was too late? *Lord, if You're listening...please work it out for Jer to tell her he loves her.*

The group headed to the terminal.

At the baggage check-in, Bryce checked Marisa's bag against the size limits for carry-ons to see if it still complied. He had watched her stuff souvenirs into the bag at the major's apartment, wondering if she'd have to leave some behind. "You're safe. I won't have to mail most of your cache to you after all." He chuckled.

"Thank You, Lord. I hadn't considered how much space they'd take up in the suitcase. Hope my folks like the cups and coasters. The workmanship is beautiful on every one of them."

She eyed Bryce. "I wish I could bring home my favorite souvenir." She hugged him and giggled.

He lifted her left hand and kissed her ring finger. "Well, you *are* bringing home a *special* souvenir from your vacation. Although I do wish I could join you and meet your parents in person. But I can't take any more time off right now. We'll work something out." He squeezed her.

With a grunt, Bryce loaded her suitcase onto the scale at the ticket counter.

When Marisa finished, Jer hefted Kyleigh's to the scale. "I'm guessing your luggage is a lot lighter than Marisa's. You must've chosen lightweight souvenirs." He grinned at her.

Kyleigh bit her lip.

Bryce's brows rumpled. Was she mad, hurt, or what? He glanced at Marisa. She grimaced and shrugged her shoulders at him.

While the two of them strolled to the security area, Bryce slipped his arm around Marisa's shoulders. He peeked back toward the ticket counter and saw the major and Kyleigh. Where had Jer gone?

He gazed at Marisa's misting eyes. How could he let her go? Four plus months was a long time to wait until he could hold her again. Almost five months. "Are you positive you want to go back to Houston, Marisa?"

She pecked him on the cheek. "No, but I've committed to tutoring a child who struggled in my class last year. And I have a lot of arrangements to take care of since we decided on a winter ceremony. It would break Mom's heart if the wedding weren't in the church we've attended since I was a baby. We'll talk on the phone and email daily. Your job'll keep you busy at the station."

"I'm going to miss you." He kissed her nose.

"I'll miss you too. Preparing for next year's classes should help to keep me occupied. Let's be grateful we have the internet and phones to stay in contact."

"True. I'm glad we picked the weekend before Christmas for the wedding. This way, my extended family and friends can attend. Oh, don't forget to give notice at work."

"First chance I get, so they can find someone to replace me." She spun to see if Kyleigh, Jer, and the major were coming. "What happened to Jer?"

As Kyleigh and her father reached them, they sat near the security line. Bryce made a visual search of the terminal. No sign of his partner. "Ky, where'd Jer go?"

She shrugged. "I've no idea. When I finished checking my ticket at the counter and turned, he was gone. Without a word."

The major put his hand on her shoulder. "Before he sped off, his brows jumped up as if he'd remembered something. Then he ran for the entrance. I'm certain he'll be back."

One side of Kyleigh's lips tugged upward.

Bryce frowned. That expression on Kyleigh's face said otherwise.

She sighed. "Well, Marisa. We need to clear security and find our gate pretty soon. Take heart, Bryce. She'll return to you before you know it." She gave him a weak smile, which faded.

He hugged Marisa. "You're right. I have to be brave. Ky, you won't let my little haole flirt with any of those Texans while she's away from me, will you?"

"I'll keep a tight rein on her."

Marisa pulled on his arm. "Honey, take a walk with me." She turned to Ky and held up her index finger. "For just a minute or two. I promise."

Once they were out of earshot and in a secluded spot near a window, Marisa stopped walking. "Bryce, did you make a mistake about Jer's feelings for Ky? She told me he was a perfect gentleman on their date Thursday night, but that's it. You said he loves her, but Ky doesn't think so. He was polite at dinner yesterday, but not any more than you are toward her. When they went for their walk, I prayed something would happen. But I suppose they didn't have time to say much to each other before Ilima fainted. What's his problem?"

Bryce's brows lowered, and he shook his head. "I thought he was going to tell her he loved her. He said it was his plan when I picked him up today. And you're sure she loves him?"

"I've known Ky since high school. You'd better believe she loves Jer. Her heart may never recover from this. That girl's the boldest, strongest female Texan I've ever met, but where Jer's concerned, she's mush. And now he's disappeared."

"I can't imagine why he walked out. There must be some reason he left. Hopefully, he'll come back before you leave, so we'll have to stall Ky a little." They wandered back to Kyleigh and the major.

"Marisa, we really should move into line before it gets any longer." Kyleigh took the handle of her carry-on from her father and hugged him. "Dad, you be careful with your leg. You may walk better now, but you don't want to mess it up any more than it is."

"I'll behave myself, daughter dear." He kissed her forehead.

"Ky. Don't we have a few more minutes? I haven't said goodbye to Jer yet." Marisa's eyes pleaded.

"He's not coming back, Marisa. Let's go." Kyleigh pulled her bag toward the line of people.

"*Wait!*" Jer sprinted down the hall toward them with two lei made from ilima flowers swinging on his arm. He handed one to Bryce. "Here ya go, buddy. Sorry, I took so long."

He punched Jer's arm. "I forgot. That's where you went. Thanks, man."

"I forgot, too, until we were at the ticket counter. We have to see the girls off in style. I was praying I'd make it back before they went through security, and I lost my chance to—um...is the red one okay with you?"

"Perfect." Bryce turned to Marisa and lifted the lei over her head, bent down, and kissed her cheek. Her eyes glistened. "For my sweet haole. The lei traditionally shows our love and affection toward one another. The red ilima bloom, like this, symbolizes love and is the official flower of the island."

"As in Ilima, your mother's friend?"

"Yes. Her parents named her after this flower."

"That's so sweet." She pulled his face down to whisper into his ear. "What does the orange ilima bloom lei that Jer's holding for Ky say?"

Bryce kissed her other cheek and whispered, "Same as this one." He grinned.

They watched as Jer faced Kyleigh. His face glowed with love for her.

Her jaw dropped as he raised the orange lei above her and gently settled it onto her shoulders. He kissed her on one cheek and then the other. "Aloha."

"Thank you." Puzzlement spread across her face while her brows furrowed and eyes filled with tears. "It's beautiful, Jer."

Marisa grabbed Bryce's arm. "What should we do with them when we're back home in Texas? There has to be some custom concerning them."

His grin grew wider. "When people used to leave the island on ships, they'd throw their lei into the water as they passed Diamond Head and hope to see them float to shore. It meant the person would someday return too. You can't open the window on the plane as you pass Diamond Head, so you'll have to hang on to this until you bring it home to Oʻahu again. Once the flowers are back home here in Hawaiʻi, they need to be buried in the ground, from where they grew. Another tradition. But remember, I expect more than the lei to come back."

"I'll hang it by the picture I took of you and framed until I...return." Marisa burst into tears and threw her arms around him. "Thank you. We'll be back. But I want to treasure this gift forever, so please don't make me bury it."

Bryce wiped Marisa's tears from her face with his handkerchief. "You can let it dry out and hang it somewhere safe."

Kyleigh checked the time on her cellphone. "We'd better get in line." She glanced at Marisa.

"I suppose so." Marisa turned to Bryce. "I don't want to cry, but..."

He held her in his arms. "It's okay." His eyes blurred. "Call me as soon as you land."

The five of them walked to the security check line. Kyleigh's dad hugged and kissed her. "I'll leave you young people alone to say your goodbyes now. I love you, Sugar. Talk to you tomorrow." He strode off.

Bryce kissed Marisa. "I hate to let you go, kuʻuipo."

She returned his kiss for a second but then pulled back. "What did you say? Koo-what?"

"Kuʻuipo. It means, sweetheart. Ipo for short."

She nuzzled under his neck. "Koo-oo-ee-poe. I love it." She let out a rush of air. "God has given us a love for each other that can overcome anything. We have to trust Him. We'll be back together again soon." She raised her eyes to his. "Not as fast as we want...but soon."

"You're exactly what I need. Always so positive." He glanced to the ceiling. "Thank You, Lord."

Bryce directed his attention to Jer, but he and Kyleigh were gone. "The line's moving. Where did they go? Not another disappearing act."

As the line moved closer to the security check machines, Bryce scanned the area for their friends. Had Jer talked Ky into staying? At the end of the line, he finally spotted them in a tight embrace, lips locked.

Bryce spun Marisa to stand in front of him, placed his hands on either side of her head, and aimed her gaze at the couple.

Her jaw dropped. "*Oooo.*"

Jer leaned his head against Kyleigh's silky auburn hair as she melted into his arms. His heart thumped double-time. If only he'd told her right away when he realized he was in love with her. The time he'd wasted. Her lips, so warm and soft. He was a dunce to have waited this long. Now it would be months before he could hold her again. He lifted her chin and covered her mouth with his.

"I'm dying inside, Kyleigh. Over four months until we're together again. I love you."

She leaned back and put her index finger on his lips. "Shhh. And I love you." She sighed. "It happened so quickly. Same as with Bryce and Marisa."

Jer chuckled. "I know. Us and our best friends, at the same time. Who'd've thought?"

When the line moved forward, Bryce and Marisa left their place and fell back behind Jer.

He turned to face Bryce, whose white teeth gleamed in his tanned face. Marisa wore a grin to match. Jer let go of Kyleigh.

Bryce elbowed Jer in the ribs. "About time, man. Guess we'll both be feeling like fish stranded in a tide pool until our haoles come back to us."

Marisa chortled. "You two won't be the only ones. November is looking further away all the time." She winked at Kyleigh, who had turned a shade of dusky rose from her neck to the tops of her cheeks.

As the line progressed again, Jer swallowed the lump in his throat. "Only three more people to check through security." Then Kyleigh'd be gone.

Jer grabbed Kyleigh, wrapped her in his arms, and kissed her again. When he let go, her eyes glistened with tears. He brushed a stray droplet from her cheek. "I'll be counting the days until I can kiss you again."

"Please step up." The security attendant had a sheepish grin on his face as he waved Kyleigh forward.

"I have to leave." She pinched her lips together.

Jer gave her one more kiss. "Will you call me when you land in Houston?"

She moved closer to the checkpoint, still clinging to his hand. "I will."

Bryce and Marisa did a replay of Jer and Kyleigh's scene. Marisa followed Kyleigh through security.

As the girls walked down the hall toward their gate, they turned, waved, and threw kisses until the mob of passengers swallowed them.

Jer glanced at Bryce. "I'm the dumbest detective in the world. Couldn't even detect that she loves me as much as I love her."

Bryce slapped him on the back. "We can't both be geniuses." He laughed. "I'm happy you realized what a doofus you were before she got away."

Jer let out a deep sigh. "Yeah. I'm an idiot, all right. I should've asked her to marry me like you did Marisa. What if Kyleigh gets home and finds one of those Texans is more to her liking? If I had proposed to her, it would have been a genuine commitment."

"Hey, man. Lighten up. Marisa and I know she loves you. Quit worrying. She's been moping around for days because she didn't think you wanted her. I'd say the kiss you two shared made a big enough commitment." His eyes scanned the people milling about the airport. "I'd say fifty or more strangers thought it was real, too, the same as Marisa and I did." His grin stretched across his face from cheek to cheek.

The memory of his lips on hers warmed Jer from his neck to his toes. She was his. "Thanks, buddy. It's gonna be a lo-o-o-ong day."

Chapter Thirty-Two

our months and three weeks later

Jer paced the hall in the Honolulu airport. Three lei hung from his arm, one each of purple and yellow orchids, and the third with pink plumerias. He stopped and glued his eyes to where Kyleigh'd appear from her flight. The knot in his stomach had grown to the size of Texas.

Would she still feel the same about him? Yeah, they had talked every night on the cell or in emails, but he couldn't judge the expressions on her face or tones in her voice. And with the five-hour difference between them, when she'd finish teaching, it was three in the afternoon for her and ten in the morning for him, right in the middle of his morning shift. By the time he called after work, she was dead tired. Although, everything appeared normal on the weekends when they could talk earlier in the day.

With Skype, at least they saw each other's faces. She'd been on the reserved side ever since the day he'd first laid eye on her, except for when she displayed her Irish temper. He chuckled. That was all it was, right? Her being reticent. And now he was being foolish again, wasn't he, Lord?

Bryce stood next to the wall with three lei for Marisa. Two of white and purple orchids, and one of red carnations. He combed the mass of passengers coming toward them, anxiety written across his face.

Jer pursed his lips. He hadn't been alone in his misery, but at least Bryce had made a solid commitment to Marisa before she left the island. How they survived apart through these months was a mystery to him.

If Kyleigh and Marisa didn't hurry up and disembark from the plane, he'd go mad. If he didn't jump out of his skin.

Jer resumed his search of the faces that flooded toward him. Thanksgiving week had taken forever to arrive. He had so many things to talk to Kyleigh about that he couldn't over the phone, in a letter, or online. Men have proposed marriage without a face-to-face in the past, he supposed, but it wasn't the way he wanted to remember such a day.

There she was. He grinned so wide his lips stretched. The strawberry streaks in her dark auburn hair hanging down from her shoulders lightened as she passed under an overhead light. Could a man fall in love with the same woman a second time?

Kyleigh's gaze met his. She smiled and quickened her steps.

Uh-oh. Where was Marisa? Bryce would be devastated if she didn't come.

Kyleigh kept waving as she disappeared behind a group of travelers.

Jer glanced at Bryce. He must have stretched his body another two inches to peer over the heads. A second later, a grin burst onto his face. He'd spotted Marisa.

Kyleigh broke through the crowd and was in Jer's embrace in the next moment. He kissed her mouth. Oh, yeah. She still felt the same about him. He backed away and feasted his eyes on her from head to toe. "I don't believe it."

A pink glow covered her face. "Yes. It's true. We're finally here."

"No. That's not what I meant."

She lowered her brows. "What do you mean then?"

"You're even more beautiful than you were when you left."

The glow on her face deepened.

While they clung to each other, Marisa and Bryce joined them.

Kyleigh raised her hand to cover a yawn. "Sorry. I need rest. Couldn't on the plane. Too many noisy children." She sighed.

Marisa grimaced. "Noisy is right, and a hollering baby. Poor Ky. Too bad she doesn't sleep as soundly as I do."

Jer looked at the three lei adorning Marisa. "Oh, I was so excited, I forgot." He lifted his armful over Kyleigh's head and adjusted them onto her shoulders. "Aloha." After he'd kissed her cheeks, he leaned in closer to her ear. "That was a super-loving aloha." He straightened. "I didn't remember to ask what color you planned to wear on the flight, so I improvised."

"I love the variety." Marisa fingered her flowers.

Kyleigh yawned again. "They're all lovely, Jer. Mahalo."

As the foursome sauntered to baggage claim, Jer slipped his arm around Kyleigh. "While you catch up on your rest today, I have plans to make for this week. Okay with you?"

"That's fine, but nothing too strenuous, if you don't mind. No dirt biking on Ko'olau for the time being. I've a lot to do before Dad's party." She chortled and searched the terminal. "Where is my dad?"

"When we told him we wanted to pick you girls up, he said he'd go to work and catch up with you at lunchtime. Very discreet man." Should he tell her he'd spoken to her father? No. It could wait. The timing had to be perfect. She'd be tied up with the major's retirement party, so better not add any more stress to her mind. And he'd have more time to plan the ideal setting.

Later that day, Kyleigh awoke from a long nap to voices in the other room. She focused on the clock on the bedside table. Afternoon. *Oh, no!* She hopped to her feet and changed out of her wrinkled clothes.

As she checked her hair in the mirror above the dresser, the three lei draped over the mirror's edge caught her eye. Jer was so thoughtful. More than anything, she wanted this relationship to work. But how? Almost five months of emails and Skype was one thing, but a romance needed more. What could they do? He had a job here in Hawaiʻi. She had her teaching career in Houston.

Kyleigh washed her face and freshened her makeup. She'd better concentrate on her father's retirement celebration instead of what might be. *Fantasize about your future later.*

She stepped out into the living room and joined her dad, Jer, Bryce, and Marisa, who were discussing grilling for dinner.

"Hi, Sugar. I was wondering if you'd sleep the day away."

Kyleigh hugged her father and sat on the couch next to him. "It sure was refreshing after being awake for the entire flight."

Jer slipped in beside her. Her pulse quickened. The cologne he wore reminded her of the cedar grove she loved to ride to outside Houston. Strange. She had no homesickness when she came to the island. She gazed into his cinnamon brown eyes. Being here was like coming home after a long trip.

Marisa brought her a glass of cola. "Ky, the fellas and your dad say they'll cook dinner tonight. They won't let me. I guess that goes for you too."

Bryce pulled Marisa onto the arm of the chair he occupied. "Absolutely. What we do need is a list of what to pick up from the store. Whatever you girls want to eat. Right, Jer?"

"You betcha. Remember, I'm a pro at the grill." He winked at Kyleigh.

She tittered. "Yes, I remember."

"And your dad's not doing anything except to ask the Lord's blessing on the food."

Her father chuckled. "I guess I know when I'm not needed." He strode to the fridge, grabbed a cola, and carried his newspaper to the lanai. The major peeked back in. "They'll grill the meat, but I'll bet they pick up sides on the way back." He guffawed and settled into the lounge.

Kyleigh shook her head. "Okay. We'll write up the shopping list for you. While you gather the vittles, I'll drive to Mrs. Swanson's street in Pearl City and then hike out to visit Ilima. I brought her a denim apron from Texas and a few odds and ends I hope she likes."

"She lives with my mom now, Ky." Bryce pinched Marisa on the forearm.

"Ow. What was that for?"

"Still can't believe you're here...with me." He gave her a sheepish grin.

"You nut. You're supposed to pinch yourself." Marisa pinched him in return.

"Yeowch!" Bryce rubbed his arm and snickered. "After you haoles flew to Texas last summer, my mother was able to talk Ilima into leaving the shack. Let me make a call to see if they're at the house. Ilima still treks out to the forest to gather wild fruits and vegetables. Sometimes Mom accompanies her."

He left the armchair, took out his cell, and punched in a number. As he strolled out to the lanai, he talked to his mother.

"Ky, would you mind if I joined you?" Marisa watched Bryce enter the lanai. "I'd love to pick my future mother-in-law's brain about Bryce with him not around." She giggled.

"Your company is always welcome." Kyleigh hurried onto the lanai. "Dad, guess we're going to leave you on your own."

"Not a problem. I've been alone for so much of my life, but I can spare you for a little while." He rose from the chair and gave her a peck on the cheek.

As Kyleigh parked the Mustang in the driveway of Mrs. Swanson's house, she and Ilima came out to greet them. Bryce's mother wrapped her arms around Marisa, and Ilima did the same to Kyleigh. "Ilima, I'm glad you decided to move in here." Now she'd be safe and would receive the help she needed pronto if she ever fainted again.

Mrs. Swanson translated Kyleigh's words as she led the way inside the house and to the kitchen. "I've made coffee and malasadas to go with the fresh fruit Ilima has gathered today. Please have a seat." She poured coffee for everyone and took the chair next to Marisa.

Marisa chose one of the fried confections and took a bite. "Oh, wow! This is wonderful. What is it?"

"It's called a malasada, dear. Very popular here on the island. It's similar to your donuts on the mainland, or maybe what I've heard people refer to as a Bismark donut. Bryce loves these."

Marisa gave her a thumbs up. "You'll have to teach me how to make them."

After they'd each finished with their doughy treats, Marisa pulled a picture of her wedding gown out of her purse and laid it in front of her future mother-in-law. "It's Mom's. She's had it packed away for me. I love it."

Ilima oohed and aahed, then left the room.

"Mrs. Swanson, Marisa and I have a plan for when you come to Houston next month. Since I'm her Maid of Honor, I'll stay with her at her parents' home when you and Bryce arrive. Mr. Romano has arranged accommodations for Bryce and Jer at one of his rental condos on Galveston Beach. That leaves my apartment free for you and Ilima to use...if you can talk her into coming." Kyleigh surveyed the room. "Where did Ilima go?"

Ilima walked into the kitchen holding a cloth drawn up like a hobo's sack in her hands. She scooted the plate of fruit to one side, set the bundle on the table, and said something in Hawaiian. When she opened it, a stunning selection of white, purple, pink, and yellow tropical flowers spilled out. "So that's where you went. To decorate the table." Kyleigh breathed in the exquisite fragrance.

Mrs. Swanson had an undecipherable expression on her face. "Ilima said she wants you to pick the flowers for your wedding, and she'll make the haku...the lei worn as a crown...for you."

"But I'm not getting married. Marisa is."

Mrs. Swanson smiled. "Um. I guess Ilima is confused. I'll straighten her out."

Kyleigh nodded. Had Jer asked her to marry him, she'd love to have the wonderful lady put together her wedding flowers.

Marisa's future mother-in-law turned to her. "Ilima says she wants to make haku for both brides. And anything else you need. Dear, you didn't plan on a Hawaiian theme, did you? I'll talk to Ilima. Perhaps you can accept an aloha lei from her as you leave on your honeymoon."

"No, not exactly. But having seen the gorgeous lei she made for Kyleigh when we visited the church the first time, I think it's a great idea. Mom and I were going to order flowers when I return to Houston. I've only picked the colors purple and white." She fingered a white orchid on the cloth. "These are elegant." She spun to Ilima. "I'd be honored if you'd make a haku for me."

Marisa shifted her gaze to Kyleigh. "But how would we get flowers from Hawaiʻi to Texas for the wedding?"

Kyleigh squeezed Marisa's shoulder. "We'll figure out the details later. Don't worry. I've been to a couple of weddings where the bride wore a fresh lei." Her eyes popped open, and she jerked her head to face Mrs. Swanson. "That means Ilima is coming to the wedding?"

"It does. She's not frightened anymore since she moved from the forest."

As Mrs. Swanson spoke to Ilima again, she picked up the white orchid and placed it in Kyleigh's hair.

"Mahalo." Her heart ached. Why hadn't Jer asked her—

Jer and Bryce strode into the kitchen. Jer lowered himself to the seat beside Kyleigh and scooted it as close to her as he could.

Bryce kissed his mother, then Marisa. "Didn't want to spend any more time away from you, ipo." He spotted the plate on the table. "All right, Mom! You made malasadas." He bit into the largest one remaining.

Kyleigh's brows rumpled. "Ipo? What's ipo?"

Jer laughed. "We'll have to work on your Hawaiian, girl. Ipo's short for kuʻuipo, or sweetheart."

Kyleigh narrowed her eyes at him. "When did your Hawaiian improve, Mr. O'Shea?"

"I've been brushing up while checking on Ilima."

As he wiped the sugar off his mouth, Bryce stared at the blooms on the table. "What kind of flowery arrangement is your roommate making now?" He sat in the chair next to Marisa.

She laid her hand on his bicep. "Honey, Ilima wants to make a haku for me for our wedding."

The older woman spoke a few sentences as she gazed at Kyleigh. When she stopped, her teeth clamped together in a wide grin.

Bryce's brows rose. "She's planning on more than just a haku for *you*, ipo. She intends to do *all* the flowers for you...*and* for—"

"Bryce!" Jer jumped up from the chair and grabbed his partner's arm. "We need to get these ladies back to the major's...so I can start the grill."

Chapter Thirty-Three

The day after Thanksgiving, Kyleigh hurried to slip into her deep blue sarong dress with a pattern of light-yellow hibiscuses trailing down from her waist and around the hem. She swung a pale blue crocheted shawl loosely around her shoulders. She couldn't wait to see her father's face when he came to the luncheon after his retirement ceremony at the post.

Upon arrival at the hall, Kyleigh gazed around the room where the event would take place in less than half an hour. How proud she was of Dad. She always had been. He'd served his country well for twenty-seven years, come what may. He'd tell her, "*From the Dakotas to the southern states, from Maine to Hawaiʻi, I am keeping this nation safe...for you.*" Tears welled in her eyes.

Across the room, Aunt Maye glided through the entrance with Colonel Stevens. They certainly looked as though they were enjoying each other's company this past week since Auntie had arrived. And why not, they'd both been alone for far too long. He'd given her a hand in preparing the pictures she'd brought for the celebration.

Her aunt stopped at Kyleigh's side while her father's commanding officer continued to the raised platform.

"Auntie, I'm so happy you were able to retrieve the album from my apartment. I still can't believe I forgot them. And Dad's thrilled you're here."

"There's no way I'd miss my baby brother's retirement ceremony. Colonel Stevens had a wonderful idea to present your dad's career in a slide show. You know, he contributed pictures he had from Charlie's service here on Oʻahu. We've picked out a good selection from all the photos, and they'll run throughout the program behind the platform." She pointed to a screen that covered most of the wall.

"It was kind of him to help us. The impression I've gotten from him is that he and Dad became close over the last couple of years. And thank you for taking over the organization of the slides for the program. After this afternoon, I can relax." Kyleigh chortled.

As Jer took a seat in the first row, Kyleigh watched him. He was ever so handsome, dressed in a light blue and green aloha shirt and gray slacks. She was proud of him. He'd told her of his commendation and promotion. Honors he shared with Bryce for solving the illegal drug case and her father's disappearance, though they didn't physically find her dad. Sending help to her resulted in his rescue. She blew a long stream of relief through her lips.

Kyleigh caught sight of Bryce and Marisa at the door. Marisa's excitement increased every day as her wedding grew nearer, only three weeks from tomorrow. Another chance to be with Jer since he'd be Bryce's best man. But how often would their paths cross after that? Maybe he'd tire of the long-distance relationship.

When the music began, the guests milling around the room found their seats. She joined Jer, and Aunt Maye sat on her other side. Bryce, Marisa, Mrs. Swanson, and Ilima slipped into the row behind them.

Colonel Stevens started the ceremony with an awards presentation for the major's distinguished service. "...This man went to places few have dared because he saw the need. I'm reluctant to see him go. Tried everything in my power to convince him his country still needs him, but he said his family needs him more now. I can understand that."

As her dad's CO spoke, Kyleigh's heart swelled with love for her dad. At long last, he'd come home to Texas and not have to leave in a week or two.

The colonel's brief speech ended. And after a rousing version of the official Army Song, played by the Army Band, the commanding officer published her father's retirement orders.

Kyleigh leaned over and whispered to Jer. "Now for Dad to express his gratitude. He's been working on this for days."

The major stepped forward and gave an impassioned speech. "...and I want to encourage you younger officers in attendance to give your all for the service. I don't regret any of it. Thank you for taking the time to share this moment with me. The time I've spent with each of you has given me another page in my memories of Ft. Shafter."

When the program ended, Colonel Stevens returned to the podium. "Miss Flanagan has an announcement to make."

Kyleigh approached the microphone and smiled at him. "Thank you, Colonel. We'd like to invite everyone who can join us to a luncheon in honor of my father, Major Flanagan. The invitations with directions are on a table at the rear of the room." The smiling faces of the guests told Kyleigh her dad would never forget this party.

She grabbed Jer's arm. "Let's beat the crowd back to the apartment and make sure everything is ready. I want this to be perfect for Dad."

They approached the major, who was shaking hands with a younger officer. "Dad, we're leaving for the apartment. You take your time."

"Thank you, Sugar. Your aunt and I shouldn't be too long now." He kissed her on the cheek and shook Jer's hand. "Thank you, son." He gave Jer a sheepish grin.

As they left the hall and walked through the parking lot, Kyleigh glanced at Jer. "What was the funny smile for? You didn't tell Dad what my plans were, did you?"

"Are you kidding? Me? Go against your wishes? Your dad told Bryce and me about the log you were going to use to clobber whoever came through Ilima's door in the jungle, remember?" Jer slipped his arm around her waist. "Your surprise is safe. The major was probably feeling happy and had a silly smile in him that needed to come out." He snickered.

Kyleigh narrowed her eyes at him. Hmm...they were up to something. Her birthday in spring was too far off to be the reason. Besides, she and Dad would be back in Houston. *There you go again, Kyleigh.* Suspicious as always. *Stop it!* Jer had proven himself to be trustworthy and true to his word.

Jer waited at the entrance of the major's apartment for him. What Kyleigh had pulled off in so little time after she'd returned to

Oʻahu was unbelievable. A full-blown luau, thanks to the assistance of Bryce, his mother, and a few of their relatives and friends. Major Flanagan would be so surprised. Not to mention thrilled over the phenomenal gift she'd bought him. It was a good thing he'd already canceled the bike he initially ordered and decided to wait until his leg was fully healed. Kyleigh sure was sneaky the way she weaseled the information out of her dad about the dirt bike he wanted.

The major strode up the sidewalk to the entrance with a puzzled expression on his face. "Where is everyone, Jer?"

"Change of venue. Kyleigh sent me to escort you to the party, sir. Follow me."

They strolled around the apartment complex and down to the picnic area to reach the luau pit, where the rest of the guests were waiting. Cheers rang out for the major. Kyleigh threw her arms around him. "Are you ready for a luau, Dad?"

His jaw dropped. "This is wonderful, but how on earth did you manage?"

Kyleigh grinned at him. "I have ways of getting things done." She winked at Bryce and Marisa, who stood behind the major.

Bryce offered a thumbs up. "And connections."

After her father spun, he guffawed. "Pig, poi, and everything?"

"Two pigs, sir." Bryce wore a cockeyed grin

Her father scanned the pit and hugged Kyleigh. "This looks great!"

Jer sidled up to Kyleigh. "This place has a nice setup. The pit was large enough to accommodate two pigs, which is fortunate, considering the number of people who wanted to help you celebrate."

Steam rose from the palm leaves layered on top of the hole where a couple of Bryce's native friends attended to the cooking of the meat for the feast. Dressed in traditional sarongs of long yellow fabric with a palm leaf pattern, wrapped around their waists down to the knees, they provided an authentic atmosphere. Platters of food and refreshments lined a table nearby.

Kyleigh pointed to the buffet. "Mrs. Swanson made your favorite, macaroni salad...Hawaiian style."

The smile on the major's face was well worth the effort Kyleigh had gone through. Jer gave her a nod.

She looked back at her dad. "Guess I'll have to get Mrs. Swanson's recipe for this Hawaiian version. I have to admit, it beats any mac salad I've had in Texas."

Bryce shook the major's hand. "Your daughter has arranged one fantastic luau, sir. Very traditional. Right down to the kalua pig in the pit, thanks to my 'ohana. I'm impressed. Best luau I've seen in a long time."

"Okay, wait a minute, Bryce." Kyleigh held the palm of her hand out toward him. "I thought these were buddies of yours and Jer's, not family members. If I understand the word 'ohana correctly. Just how big is your family, Bryce?"

Jer laughed. "I told you we needed to work on your Hawaiian. 'Ohana can be relations or friends. Anyone close to you."

Kyleigh's mouth formed a circle. She tittered. "Like back home when we call the old buddies of our parents' *auntie* or *uncle*?"

"Well, sort of, Ky." Marisa giggled. "But here, 'ohana is even used for children of your friends...who aren't really blood-related. Jer's right, it can be *anyone*. We'll have to work on your language skills if—"

Jer stifled a laugh at Bryce when he swung Marisa around and hurried her away from everyone. "Major, Bryce's mother made sure the luau was a traditional affair."

In the distance, Marisa's voice traveled to the group. "I'm starved. Let's check out the appetizers." She and Bryce headed for a table full of food.

Jer shook his head. "How does that little slip of a woman eat so much and not gain any weight? Bryce'll be as round as he is tall after a year married to Marisa if he eats like she does." Jer chuckled to himself. "No. I take it back. With all her energy, she'll keep him hopping."

He refocused his gaze on Kyleigh. She'd thrown her arms around Ilima, who had been presenting all her new ʻohana with a lei and kissing each one of them. Kyleigh laughed as though she'd never had a care in the world. He'd make sure she never did again. *Soon.*

Chapter Thirty-Four

The next evening, Jer drove Kyleigh back to Waikiki in his father's Tesla. A smile still lingered on her lips. Nice. Probably thinking about how happy and surprised her father had been when she wheeled out his brand new Husqvarna FC450 dirt bike with the suspension and battery improvements. Whoa, buddy. He needed one of those. But for now, his old bike would do to give him a relaxing ride up Koʻolau. He was glad she was happy.

Jer glanced at the sky. A waxing crescent moon glowed like a smile from heaven. Palm branches swayed in a light breeze. What a perfect setting for tonight.

His eyes gravitated toward the love of his life as she stared out the side window. Gorgeous in her deep green dress with tiny cream-colored flowers scattered from neck to waist. The fragrant white tuberose and carnation lei he'd given her suited her well for this evening.

"Your dad sure was stunned when you brought his retirement present to him. The new bike's awesome, by the way." He reached for her soft hand.

"It gave me such a thrill to surprise him, Jer. It was the least I could do since Dad paid for my entire college education, and I don't have a loan hanging over my head. But who would've guessed I'd win that much money just by paying close attention to instructions? When I read the ad in the magazine, I thought someone was running a hoax or gimmick. 'If you can follow the directions below, you could earn fifteen thousand dollars. Call this number.' Dad taught me to always read the fine print on any paper, especially before signing anything. And believe me, it was *fine* print."

"Fifteen thousand is a lot of money for a business to give away. I wonder why? Did they require something in return?"

She shrugged. "Not from me. Apparently, the president of the company had made a bet with his financial officer that the offer would go unnoticed."

"High-stakes gamblers." Jer grimaced.

"I guess so. When I phoned, I almost fell off the chair. They said I was the first person to respond, and I'd won. They'd run the offer for five days, and that day at five p.m. was the deadline. If no one called by that evening, the money would be donated to a charity. I could hardly believe it."

"So the foundation was out of luck, huh?"

"No." Her smile grew from cheek to cheek. "Here's the best part. The secretary who sent me the check added a note to tell me the company president contributed the same amount to the charity anyway."

"He didn't count on eagle-eye Kyleigh."

She chortled. "And thank you for the suggestion on the gift for Dad. Even though he'd given me the basic information about the bike he'd planned to reorder, I was stumped on which to get. Also, thanks for picking up the bike yesterday morning and bringing it to the luau without his being any the wiser. I loved the oversized red bow you attached." She laughed.

"I'm glad he was pleased too. The apartment manager was a big help. He hid it for us and gave me the key to his storage shed, so I didn't have to track him down when we returned from the ceremony."

"Thanks for telling me." Kyleigh pulled her cell from her sparkling green evening bag and tapped in a message. "There. I'll pick up a thank you gift for him before I leave for home."

Hmm. "Right. You're leaving again. But at least I'll be with you the week of Bryce and Marisa's wedding."

Her smile faded. Maybe she didn't want to go back to Houston?

"Your dad surprised me when he told us he had decided to retire on the island." He peeked at her. "Did his decision surprise you too?"

Kyleigh sighed. "It sure did. I thought he'd be coming home to stay this time. Still, I'm happy if he's happy."

As he slowed for traffic, Jer snatched a glimpse of her. "Does that mean you'll move to Oʻahu...right away?"

She peered at him from under her long black lashes. "Was that a request, Mr. O'Shea?" She tittered. "I have my job in Houston, and I'm not sure Dad needs his daughter for a roommate."

"We've arrived." He raised his brows, pursed his lips as he parked the car, and jumped out. After he'd opened the passenger door and helped her to her feet, he slipped her arm through the crook of his elbow, and they strolled to the Kaimana Palms Restaurant.

Kyleigh bit her lip. "Oh, I was hoping we were coming here. The view from our table on the balcony last June was so lovely, and look at all those stars."

Hope she has brighter stars in her eyes before the evening is over.

After enjoying the same meals they'd eaten at the end of June, the waiter came to the table to take their dessert order. Kyleigh leaned back in her chair. How could she possibly eat any more? "I think I'm too full after that excellent dinner."

Jer pointed at a choice on the menu. "Oh, but you have to have the chef's special. It's...how do you girls put it...'it's to die for.' Don't disappoint me now." He grinned at the server, who nodded in return.

"Okay, what did you order? Something chocolate, I'm sure." She shook her head. "Men!"

"You'll see." His grin grew wider.

She narrowed her eyes at him. "What are you up to? This won't be some kind of food where once I find out what it's made of, I'll gag, will it? You wouldn't do that to me, would you?"

Jer lifted her hand to his lips and kissed the palm. "Be patient."

A few minutes later, the waiter placed a large slice of cake in front of each of them.

Kyleigh laughed. "Pineapple upside-down cake."

"Yup. And the best you've ever tasted, I'll bet." He kept his eyes glued to hers.

She picked up her fork and held it over the edge of the dessert. Was that a piece of glass in the middle? She tapped the hard, translucent object with the edge of the utensil. *It's not glass. It sparkles like a—* She slid the tip of the tines under the shining object and lifted it to eye level, where it reflected candlelight from the center of the table. A ring? A marquise *diamond?* Kyleigh's free hand flew to her chest. Breathless, her eyes met Jer's as her heart beat wildly.

"Perhaps I should take that from you before you drop it and the ring rolls off the balcony." He snickered, then removed the gooey ring from her fork. "Planting it in the cake may not have been a smart idea after all." He swished the solitaire diamond mounted in yellow gold in his water glass and wiped it dry with his napkin.

Jer dropped to one knee next to her chair.

"Jer, what are you doing? Everyone's looking at us."

"Let 'em look. O'ahu's full of tradition." He took her left hand in his and slipped the ring on her third finger. "Kyleigh Flanagan, would you make me the happiest man on this island by becoming my wife?" He kissed the tip of her finger.

Kyleigh opened her mouth, but her words stuck. The only thing she could utter was, "Ah-h-h." *Isn't this what you've hoped for, and all you can say is ah? Snap out of it.* "Yes!"

"Whew! That's better. I thought your dad, Bryce, and Marisa were wrong about your feelings."

"What do you mean?"

Jer rose from the balcony floor and pulled her into his arms. "Bryce and Marisa kept telling me you love me...and they kept egging me on to stop dragging my heels. Of course, I had to ask your dad for his permission...which he gave...with a few words of wisdom. But after all that had happened since you've met me, I wasn't sure how he felt toward me as a son-in-law. And—"

Kyleigh closed the distance between their lips, hushing Jer. Cheers and whistles rose from the other diners. She backed away for a moment and whispered, "You talk too much, Mr. O'Shea." A giggle escaped her at the irony.

She wrapped her arms around Jer's neck. Their lips found each other, and they resumed the kiss to applause.

When they parted, the owner and chef stood near them. The chef presented a small chocolate frosted cake decorated with a white hibiscus in the center. The owner added and lit sparklers on either side of the flower. "Congratulations, my friend. He wahine nani kēia."

Jer's grin couldn't be any wider. She'd dreamed of this day for most of her life.

As the chef placed the cake on the table in front of them and left with the restaurant owner, Kyleigh leaned into Jer's side. "What did he say?"

"He said, 'This is a beautiful woman.' But he's wrong. You're the most gorgeous woman I've ever seen."

He pulled her close and kissed her again until she was breathless.

Chapter Thirty-Five

Seven Months Later

*G*entle Polynesian tunes played on flute, cello, and harp filled the air. Kyleigh glided past trees, hibiscus, and ferns in a white-lace, ankle-length sundress. She carried a bouquet of white and purple orchids with ti leaves trailing to the hem of her gown. How peaceful the ravine was now as she followed the forest path to Ilima Palakiko's old hidden shack. Peaceful and enchanting.

Her father, handsome in his dress uniform, escorted Kyleigh toward the flower-covered tree arch Marisa and Bryce had formed, under which their friends would speak their vows. Behind the boughs waited the pastor from Jer's church, the Kahu, as Bryce referred to him, or holy man.

As she stepped out of the dense woods into the glen, Kyleigh caught sight of Ilima, the old native woman she'd come to think of as a grandmother in the past year...or tutu, as Bryce and Marisa had begun to call her. Ilima stood next to Mrs. Swanson on the right of the trail in a multicolor muumuu.

Kyleigh reached up her hand and touched the traditional haku lei that matched her bouquet. Such a caring soul, Ilima had kept her promise to do the wedding flowers, as she had for Marisa's ceremony in Houston.

The day in Mrs. Swanson's kitchen when the dear woman said she wanted to do both brides' flowers played in Kyleigh's mind. *Ilima knew Jer and I would get married.* He'd confided in her and everyone else before he finally proposed. The interrupted comments from Bryce and Marisa, the secretive looks from all of them...they made sense now. Kyleigh chortled inside. *The stinker.*

Aunt Maye, on the other side of Ilima, smiled her approval.

As Kyleigh approached the arch, her breath and heartbeat quickened. Her bridegroom, in his white suit and pale purple shirt, couldn't be more handsome. He was the kindest, most loving...

Several haku-adorned children from Mrs. Swanson's village lined the path. They threw flower petals in front of Kyleigh as she stepped forward.

Standing beside Jer, Bryce cast a striking figure in his cream-colored suit and royal purple shirt with his usual wide, contagious grin spread across his well-tanned face. Jer's expression reminded her of Marisa's four-year-old nephew at her Christmas wedding as he had stared wide-eyed at the decorated tree in one corner of the church.

When Kyleigh and the major reached Jer, the music ended.

The pastor began. "Dear friends and loved ones, we have come together in the presence of God to witness and bless the bond between this man and this woman in holy matrimony. The covenant of marriage was established by God..."

Kyleigh's heart fluttered as the minister spoke the traditional words of the ceremony.

He looked to her father and asked, "Who gives this woman to be married to this man?"

Her father hesitated, narrowed his eyes, and stared at Jer. Had Dad changed his mind about her fiancé? Now? She sucked in a deep breath.

The major shifted his vision to his daughter and smiled. "I do." He kissed her cheek and winked. "Just teasing, Sugar." He turned and joined Aunt Maye.

Kyleigh let out the breath she held and glanced at Jer.

His eyes relaxed from a rounded state. "Whoa! He scared me for a minute."

The pastor chuckled.

Her father guffawed loud enough for everyone in the glen to hear. Kyleigh had to bit her lip to keep from laughing. She whispered to Jer, "You weren't the only one."

Jer pulled her to his side and squeezed her arm to his ribs.

She handed her bouquet to Marisa, whose deep purple floor-length sarong revealed a slight baby bump in her trim figure.

The minister faced Jer. "Do you, Preston Jerard O'Shea, take Kyleigh Ann Flanagan to be your wife..."

As Kyleigh listened, Ilima's toothy grin glowed like a grandmother watching her only granddaughter. *Surely you'd approve, Mother.* Ilima, the wonderful old woman who the Koʻolau mountain range had kept secret for so many years, just like its other secrets throughout history, had been watched over by God in order to help Dad when he needed aid.

When Jer slipped the ring on her finger, Kyleigh gazed to the heavens. Through openings in the green canopy, the sky presented a display of puffy, sunlit clouds scooting by. Shafts of light beamed through the lush foliage that surrounded them in the glen. *Are you smiling down on us, Mom? I'm sure the Lord is.*

Through a break in the trees, she peered up at the mountain range. *Koʻolau, thank you for revealing your secret to us.*

The End

He that dwelleth in the secret place of the most High shall abide under the shadow of the Almighty. I will say of the LORD, He is my refuge and my fortress: my God; in him will I trust. Psalm 91:1, 2

Just for fun

Interesting facts about O'ahu and Hawai'i I came across in my research for Ko'olau's Secret

~ Hawai'i consists of 137 islands, of which 8 are main islands. Only 6 of those are open to visitors: O'ahu, Kauai, Maui, Hawai'i island (or otherwise known as the Big Island), Lanai, and Molokai. Two, Kahoolawe and Niihau, are off-limits to all except the residents and invited guests.

~ Aloha is one of the most well-known Hawaiian words around the world. But there is so much more to the word than a greeting, farewell, or goodbye.

Aloha comes from Proto-Polynesia and dates back to the early 1800s. The literal translation of is Alo meaning 'presence' and Hā meaning 'breath.' This translates to 'The presence of breath' or 'breath of life.'

Legend says the spirit behind aloha was taught to the Hawaiian children long ago as a way of life embodied in the following acronym:

A: "Akahai," meaning kindness, to be expressed with tenderness
L: "Lokahi," meaning unity, to be expressed with harmony
O: "Oluolu," meaning agreeable, to be expressed with pleasantness
H: "Haahaa," meaning humility, to be expressed with modesty
A: "Ahonui," meaning patience, to be expressed with perseverance

The late Queen Lil'uokalani said, "Aloha is to learn what is not said, to see what cannot be seen, and to know the unknowable."

~ There are three languages spoken in Hawaiʻi; two official and one informal. English and Hawaiian are both the official languages of Hawaiʻi. Pidgin is an informal language spoken on the islands, a mix of Hawaiian, Japanese, Chinese, Filipino, and Portuguese words.

~ Hawaiʻi is the only US state to have an official royal residence, ʻIolani Palace in Honolulu on Oʻahu. ʻIolani was the royal residence of the rulers of the Kingdom of Hawaiʻi, beginning with Kamehameha III and ending with Queen Liliʻuokalani in the overthrow of Hawaiʻi's monarchy in 1893. A group of businessmen and sugar planters forced Queen Liliʻuokalani to abdicate. The coup led to the dissolving of the Kingdom of Hawaiʻi two years later, its annexation as a US territory, and eventual admission to the union as the fiftieth state.

~ If you ever visit the islands, one important Hawaiʻi fact to remember is this. Touching endangered animals is a sign of disrespect in the Hawaiian culture, not just against the law. Keep your distance.

~ The Hawaiian Islands have their own time zone called Hawaiian Standard Time or Hawaii–Aleutian Time. They share this time zone with Alaska's westernmost Aleutian Islands and St. Lawrence Island. Daylight savings time is not observed in Hawaiʻi. Hawaiian Standard Time runs 2 hours behind Pacific Standard Time.

~ Hawaiʻi is the only US state to commercially grow coffee. Seedlings were imported from Brazil and planted in an orchard on Oahʻu in 1825.

~ Hawaiʻi is also the only US state where cacao beans are commercially grown. It started with a cacao plant that was imported from Guatemala.

~ Hawaiians live longer than other US nationals. Life expectancy in Hawaiʻi is at 81.3 years, which is higher than in any other US state. This might have something to do with Hawai'i having smoke-free beaches. It's illegal to smoke at a Hawaiian beach or a state park. And the legal smoking age statewide is 21.

~ Not all lei are made of flowers. The garlands locals wear during celebrations and give to visitors as a welcome token are mostly made of orchids or plumeria. But they can also be made with shells, nuts, or feathers. Hawaiian men usually wear lei made of kukui nuts and, on special occasions, open-ended lei made of maile leaves. Not all lei are worn around the neck. Haku are shorter lei worn around the head, and luau dancers usually wear ankle and wrist lei.

~ The lei symbolize aloha and is a gift of friendship, welcome, and appreciation. It's considered impolite to refuse or remove one in front of the giver. One should wear the lei at least as long as you're in the presence of the giver, with one exception. Pregnant women can politely refuse a lei. In Hawaiian culture, it is believed the lei would symbolize wrapping the umbilical cord around the unborn's neck. A traditional lei is considered bad luck for a pregnant woman. She would wear an open lei.

The traditional lei is not worn like a necklace hanging from the neck. It is to be worn draped over the shoulders and hanging from either side.

~ A woman wearing a flower above the right ear means she's available. Above the left ear means she's taken.

About The Author

Sharon K Connell writes stories about people who discover God will allow things in their lives to bring them to a saving knowledge of Jesus Christ and/or increase their faith. Her genre is Christian romance suspense, always with a dose of humor and very often a mystery. She also writes short stories in other genres.

Although born in Wisconsin, Sharon was raised in Illinois and went to school through college in Chicago. She has also lived in Missouri, California, Florida, and Ohio. Her travels have taken her to all but six states in the United States, and she has visited Canada and Mexico. She is now a resident of Texas.

Sharon is a member of the American Christian Fiction Writers organization, Houston Writers Guild, CyFair Writers, and the Christian Womens Writers Club (CWW). She runs the Facebook group forum called Christian Writers & Readers and puts out Novel Thoughts, a monthly newsletter for writers as well as readers. Sharon also contributes inspirational articles for the online magazine Faith on Every Corner.

She is a graduate of the Pensacola Bible Institute in Florida and holds a certificate in fiction writing from the International Writing Program through the University of Iowa.

Let the words of my mouth, and the meditation of my heart, be

acceptable in thy sight, O LORD, my strength, and my redeemer.

Psalm 19:14

Links

Website: www.authorsharonkconnell.com

Amazon Author Page:
http://www.amazon.com/author/sharonkconnell

Author's book page on Facebook:
https://www.facebook.com/averypresenthelpbook1

Author's Page on Facebook:
https://www.facebook.com/ChristianRomanceSuspense/

Group Forum on Facebook:
https://www.facebook.com/groups/ChristianWritersAndReadersGroupForum/

Twitter: https://twitter.com/SharonKConnell

Goodreads: https://www.goodreads.com/SharonKConnell

LinkedIn: https://www.linkedin.com/in/sharonkconnell

Pinterest: https://www.pinterest.com/rosecastle1/

Other Works

Novels
A Very Present Help
Paths of Righteousness
There Abideth Hope
His Perfect Love
Treasure in a Field

Novella
Icicles to Moonbeams

Short Story Collection
Sharon's Shorts ~ A Multi-Genre Collection of Short Stories

Short Stories in Anthologies
"Ding-A-Ling Holiday Blues"
In *Tales of Texas, Vol. 2*

"Spirit Lake"
In *Dark Visions*

Mahalo for Reading.

Sharon K Connell

Koʻolau's Secret

Sharon K Connell

.